CROWDED

Eleanor Green

CROWDED

Eleanor Green

For you

I do not wish to be light nor do I wish to be dark.
I wish to bloom mercilessly in between.
~Rune Lazuli

Acknowledgements:

I'm a writer of fiction, so real life words are hard for me. I owe a debt of gratitude to those who were so generous with their time and expertise, and a page of thanks never seems enough.

First, a massive thank you to my beta readers! Bless you for always shooting straight with me and helping me see what I needed to see.

My editor, Megan Hand with Story Girl Editing. You kick my ass in such a sweet way, thus helping me put my best work out there.

FTO Colin Lane, because of your expertise I didn't have to pull a Clarice and do my research with Hannibal Lecter's buddies. Instead, with shaky hands after an ass-kicking in the gym, I was able to jot down the real stuff that you experience every day on the job.

For my author friends who took time away from telling their own stories to promote, email, participate in giveaways, join my pity parties, and throw confetti across the states when it was time to celebrate. Your friendship is invaluable.

To the readers, friends, and family that have shared their excitement in this journey, from the bottom of my heart, thank you.

My husband, Kiley, for his undying support, and this gorgeous cover.

Finally, I would like to express my humble gratitude to my creative son, Hunter, for coming up with the ending of this book!

Chapter 1

Bree

The world is an orb of craziness, and I have every intention of spinning it in the wrong direction, stirring up as much shit as possible while I'm riding the insanity.

Someone was watching me, following my every move, and I couldn't shake them. After checking behind every door, I closed the blinds on the windows and went on with my business. Nothing would keep me from going out tonight. Pulling an outfit from the closet, I laid it on the bed and began to dress.

Lace stockings sliding against skin. I loved the feeling. Like a man's rough hand sliding up smooth flesh, eager for the prize. As I slowly raised the elastic band, I savored the delicate fabric against my skin and imagined the hot, young guy from the elevator earlier taking liberty to let himself into my apartment. He wasn't much taller than me, had a stocky build, and buzz cut. I assumed he worked construction or something that involved hard labor.

He would've been a waste of my time, probably made minimum wage at best, and he was also probably too young to manipulate my body the way I needed. But the way he stopped chewing his gum when he gave me a full body check with his eyes, sporting a cocky grin like he could read my dirty thoughts, made the image of him stick in my mind. No doubt I would pull it out and use it later tonight.

Most women would've rolled their eyes or given him the finger. Not me. I loved every glance, whistle, and degrading comment. It fueled each fantasy of my addiction.

Sex addiction, or hypersexual disorder was compulsive participation in sexual activities, including intercourse with multiple partners, compulsive masturbation, seeing a person as something to be used only for pleasure, and sexual thoughts consuming every minute of your life.

I was the textbook case, and I loved it. Who in their right mind would want to seek help for something they loved?

Everyone I talked to on the phone, watched on television, or glanced in passing was a sexual object. Just this evening on the subway, I summed up every passenger in my view. Across from me, a sweet older couple held hands.

How do they get along in the bedroom? Are they still spicing it up and trying new things?

The girl to the right of them, five seats down: *how old was she when she lost her virginity? Fifteen, sixteen? Was she in love or was it a dare?*

Finally, I assessed the tall blond to my right: *Dictionary definition of geek. His skin's never seen the sun, liver's never processed a drop of alcohol, and his lips . . . good*

God, his lips are so smooth. It's obvious he's addicted to Chapstick. Yet, he's an amazing lover. He's definitely researched it, but he's insecure so he makes sure his girl is satisfied before he takes anything for himself. I'd definitely fuck him.

I told you—all-consuming.

I needed to know the favorite sexual position of every single man I passed on the street. Were they loud? Did they know how to please a woman? Were they selfish lovers? Even if I thought they were selfish, I knew I could teach them, train them, help them. Sometimes, if I really tried, I could focus on something else—sunspots on an older man's hands—and take my mind off of sex for a refreshing moment. My mind would take another path and question what he did for a living to get those brown spots, were they cancerous or just permanent memories of his active childhood in the sunshine? Of course, thinking of him running down a dock and jumping into a refreshing pool of water would lead me to wonder if he were alone or with someone. Were they clothed or skinny dipping? It always came back to my sickness. My mind always insisted on anything and everything sexual. Healing seemed as much a fairytale as any of the happily-ever-after princess fables.

***

A full length mirror allowed me to watch the transformation from a regular woman to party girl. If the way I looked was any indication, tonight was going to be a good night.

I fastened the straps on my heels before slipping on the tight black dress that rested mid-thigh, showing a hint of the garter belt holding the lace stockings in place. Winged black eyeliner topped off the smoky eye shadow, bringing my grey-blue eyes to life. One more pass with the straightener and my long dark hair fell down my back like satin. After flashing a wink at the image in the mirror, I grabbed my clutch and headed out for the night.

The warm summer night air caressed my shoulders as I waited for an available taxi. The streets of Manhattan were alive this Friday night. Couples strolling, arm in arm, a bachelorette party, already drunk and swaying on the sidewalk, and of course the men. Men in every direction. Tonight was reserved for only the best, no time for appetizers. Whoever I went home with needed to be loaded. Going home with broke—albeit gorgeous and skilled lovers—didn't pay my bills. Poor dudes had no idea what they were getting into with me. Call girls asked for money up front, but I wasn't a hooker. Hell no. I didn't get paid for sex, I loved being with men, experiencing every shape and size, enjoying the different techniques of each one. Where hookers got paid for their services, I enjoyed myself and then took what I wanted.

Throwing my hand up, I hailed a cab and waited for him to pull up to the curb. After sliding into the backseat, I told the driver where I wanted to go. "Lavish, please." I hoped he knew the address since I had neglected to look it up.

He nodded and wove through traffic while I checked my phone.

I'm here. Where are you?

I imagined Hailey tapping her thumbs across her phone, wondering where I was. If the tables were turned, I would've enjoyed the alone time. Hell, I'd probably already have a couple of drinks in me and a few prospects.

I typed in my reply, struggling to keep myself upright while the driver tried his best to sling me across the back seat.

Almost there.

Friday night held the promise of an exciting evening as I entered the club. A strong bass permeated my flesh, bringing my pulse to beat along with it. When my eyes adjusted to the darkness, outlined with electric blue highlights, I found Hailey, alone at the bar and guarding the empty stool next to her like it was a fine piece of art. I flashed a smile, internally called her a dork, and made my way over.

"Hey," I took the seat next to her and set my clutch on the bar. "Where are the guys you were supposed to collect before I arrived?" I teased.

"Not here," she whined. We both panned the room, looking for anyone desirable.

"I'll handle it." Resting my elbows on the bar, I leaned in, trying to get the attention of one of the bartenders. "Always do," I mumbled to myself.

She heard me. I could tell by her expression she was a little pissed. *Really attractive, Hailey. Let your shoulders slump a little more, that'll line the guys up.*

"Look around." She shifted on her barstool and smoothed her dress, looking bored.

"You're right. Maybe they'll get better looking after a few drinks." I chuckled, but didn't get a response from Miss

Pissy Attitude. "Don't worry, there's a crowd outside waiting to get in. It's bound to bring in something we like."

If the problem wasn't fixed soon, we'd leave and find another club. Although Lavish was the hottest club in town and increased my chances of scoring. It'd only been open a few months, and the place was popular enough to have a line outside. Hopefully our luck would change and we'd stay. I was dressed to kill and ready to play. My dress wasn't tight enough to imply hooker, but it was tight enough to get the message across that I didn't want to sleep alone tonight.

There were five young, hot male bartenders and one female that I checked out and deemed worthy competition. With bad luck on our side, she happened to be the one who took our order.

"What'll it be, ladies?" Her smile pulled at her full, bubble gum pink lips, but she failed to hide the glint in her eyes that told me to fuck off. Jealousy—I understood it, but rarely experienced it.

"Pear martini," I said, trying not to let the beast in me come out to play. I had a habit of giving dirty looks and saying things I shouldn't. What was the point in trying to be anything but a bitch when I was already labeled one? But getting kicked out was not on my list tonight, so I kept my eyes in my lap and studied a chipped red fingernail.

"I'll have . . . let's see . . ." Hailey paused, her eyes scanning the fourth page of the leather bound drink menu. Poor girl would order something off the frozen margarita list if I didn't step in.

After a few more 'hmm's', I couldn't take it. "She'll have the same." I scooted in my seat to face her. "You'll love it. While we're waiting for our drinks, you can look over that menu and decide what you'd like next."

Hailey was a pretty girl, but not on my radar as competition. We were too different and liked different kinds of men. Her dirty blond hair danced along her shoulders as she talked, and I watched her hazel eyes widen as she recapped a story she'd heard in the break room at work yesterday. She worked for a small attorney's office on fifty-second.

When our drinks arrived, I took a long sip, feeling the pear-flavored liquor warm my insides and loosen my nerves some.

"Mmm, you were right. This is good." Hailey smiled, but her eyebrows were scrunched. "It's strong, though."

"Good. You need to loosen up." I sat my drink down on the bar, gave her knee a squeeze, and smiled. "Let's have some fun tonight." Hailey was fun, but she always seemed to need that extra push. We hadn't known each other long—a few months maybe—but I'd learned really quickly that too much alcohol and I was a babysitter, but just enough to loosen her up and we had a good time together. I browsed the room again, envying the ones on the dance floor, moving their bodies to the beat. After a minute, my gaze landed on a guy at the end of the bar. He looked confident, relaxed, maybe a little cocky. Since he was with another guy, I presumed he was either on the hunt like me, or not into women. Hopefully it wasn't the latter.

I nudged Hailey with my elbow. "Check it out. Two o'clock. Dark hair, charcoal shirt."

She gave him a quick onceover and shrugged a shoulder. "He's cute . . . for you." Of course she wouldn't like him. She only liked the hipster type.

"He's hot," I disagreed. "I'm going to bring him and his friend over. Unless they're *together*."

Hailey laughed. "Bring them over anyway. I bet they'd be fun."

"Hell, no." I scowled. "I don't need the competition." I took an encouraging sip of my martini. "If they don't offer to buy us drinks, they're together. I've been wrong before, but I don't think they are. Watch and learn, friend." I winked and offered a confident nod. "The two-second gaze."

Manipulating men was a strength I took pride in. I loved to play the game, and I was good at it. If I could catch his gaze and keep it two full seconds longer than was comfortable, he'd buy me a drink. Any longer than that and he'd assume I was too eager.

"You're not serious." She frowned at me. "There's actually a formula to your madness?"

"Of course." One corner of my mouth tipped into a smile.

I turned slightly in my seat and caught his gaze almost immediately. He flashed a flirty grin, and I allowed my lips to curl into a shy but inviting smile, never unlocking my eyes from his. *One-one thousand, two-one thousand,* I counted and then dropped my gaze and turned to face Hailey. "Now we wait and see if it worked."

When a whole minute passed and they still hadn't come over, I drained the last of my martini and felt my pride plummet. Finally, one of the bartenders—the tall, slender one with the trend-of-the-year beard—walked toward us and slid two orange concoctions in front of us.

"The gentleman at the end of the bar sent these over."

I followed his nod to find my two-one thousand man. A thrill raced up my spine as we made contact, and I shot him a wink of thanks.

"I'm in awe, Bree." Her eyes were wide like a kid experiencing a magic trick. "I can't believe that worked."

"I go after what I want, Hailey." I took a sip of the spicy and sweet mango concoction, not taking my eyes off Mr. Two Seconds and his buddy as they made their way to us. "And I usually get it."

"Mind if we join you, ladies?" His voice was deep, solid. He added the inflection of a question at the end of his sentence, but there was no mistaking it for that. The way he looked at me when he spoke implied he'd already undressed me, devoured every inch of my body, and, if I was lucky, I'd be waking up to a phone number, but not his warm body wrapped around me. Obviously I'd met my match.

Let the games begin.

"Thank you for the drink. Spicy and sweet—nice combination." A smile played on my lips. "I'm Bree. This is Hailey." Instinctively, I drew my shoulders back, concentrating on my posture, knowing it did wonders for my ample cleavage.

"Nice to meet you." He addressed us both but kept his eyes on mine. "This is Fitch. I'm Cal."

Formalities were ridiculous, if you asked me. At that moment, the way our eyes were locked on each other, we both knew we'd end up in bed together. Did it really matter if he knew my name or where I was from? The only thing of substance was the fact that he was single—or pretending to be. I looked down at his ring finger. Unoccupied.

I sipped my drink, waiting for him to make conversation. I wondered if he'd be good at the game, or if he'd cut through the bullshit and go for what he wanted like I did. Hailey and Fitch seemed to be checking off all the proper questions—*where are you from? What do you do?*—while my guy was eye fucking me. Although he was hot and I enjoyed studying his features, if he didn't entertain me soon, I'd have to ditch him.

"I'm sorry, I've been staring," he finally said. "You're very beautiful." He finished his drink and set it on the bar. Our female bartender poured another shot of scotch over ice and slid it to him almost instantly. "Tell me, Bree, do you have a boyfriend?"

"No. Do you?" I tilted my head and raised an eyebrow. I loved gay men, they were a blast to be around, but I didn't have time for friendly. Not tonight.

He laughed, revealing a dimple in his left cheek. It nearly tamed his sexiness, but not quite. When he stilled, he leaned in, placing his hands on the countertop behind me, caging me in. The bass was thrumming through my body, my pulse quickening due to his proximity. Now that he was closer, I could see flecks of gold and green in his blue eyes.

"Let me be clear," his tone was serious, but sultry. "I like women. *Only* women." The room became airless, my breath halting to listen to every word he spoke.

As I inhaled a shaky breath I realized I was losing the game, losing control. I needed to gain composure. "Good. Do you like to dance, Cal?"

"Yes. After I've loosened up a bit more." He raised two fingers and our female bartender dashed over, practically panting with lust. "Two shots of Patron with lime, please."

"That's one way." I winked. "Do you live in the city?"

"No. I work here but live off island. You?"

"Yes, both." I wasn't ready to look him in the eyes yet, so I traced a swirl of granite on the bar.

Cal leaned his back against the bar, his elbows resting on the granite behind him. "I'm not going to ask you what you do."

Dude was cool as ice and that rattled me. *I* made men nervous, not the other way around. "Good. I'm not giving interviews." Thank God he wasn't asking since I didn't have an answer ready. Usually I was a fantastic storyteller—liar— but like I said, I had met my match with Cal. I licked my lips, steadied my heartbeat, and turned to look at him. "It's Friday night, I came out to play."

The smile that danced in his eyes let me know I had control again. Our drinks arrived, ball still in my court. We took our salt-rimmed glasses in one hand and a lime wedge in the other.

"Lick it, suck it, slam it? Or is it lick it, slam it, suck it?" I asked, feigning ignorance. Patron and lime was my drink of choice.

Cal's eyes darkened as he smirked. "Are we talking about Tequila or sex?"

Apparently he knew how to play the game, and so far, he was playing it well. I wondered if we'd make it out of the club or find a back room. My mind went there, thinking about his statement, and I squeezed my thighs together to stifle the need.

His eyes traveled from my thighs, slowly back up to my face, a knowing grin on his lips. He knew the effect he was having. "Lick . . . slam . . . suck."

I swallowed hard, playing the scene in my head. My heart raced in anticipation of what he could offer. "Ready?"

We kept our eyes on each other as our tongues seductively licked some of the salt off the rim, slammed the shot of Tequila, and sucked the juice from our lime wedge. Patron was my favorite. It went down smoothly without the after bite some of the other brands. I loved the way alcohol numbed, but also intensified my needs.

Before I could react, my hand was in his and we were headed to the dance floor. His hands were strong and calloused, leading me to believe his job required physical work. Construction, maybe? The thought left my mind when we started to move. The liquor swam through my veins, making me feel free to move my body along with the beat.

Cal had rhythm and I watched him for a while before closing my eyes, feeling the bass rock through me. My arms were overhead when I felt his hands on my waist. His body pressed into mine from behind, moving fluidly with me as I slowed and enjoyed the feel of him.

I dropped my arms, letting my hands slide around to the back of his neck. When the song changed to something slower, he spun me around and pulled me in. His hands rested on my hips and I instinctively placed a palm over his knuckles while draping my other arm around his shoulder. My fingers tangled in his dark hair. I wasn't sure how much longer I could wait to feel his lips on mine.

Standing on tiptoes, I whispered in his ear, "I need the ladies room." Hopefully he would get my meaning. This guy was doing things to me that I couldn't allow. Getting inside my head was a firm negative, and the only way I knew how to end it was sleeping with him. We needed a place like a bathroom stall—something raw and fast and far from intimate—and I needed it now.

"I'll wait for you at the bar." He pulled back, his expression blank. "Care for another drink?"

Another strike. Was he really that clueless? Fool should've offered to go with me. "Yes." I could tell he was about to ask what I liked, and that would've turned me off. I preferred a man who took control. Not able to afford him another strike, I beat him to it. "Surprise me."

Chapter 2

Bree

Why they'd put the bathroom in the basement was beyond me. Was it an evil plot so they could watch women in high heels try to manage the steep descent? I concentrated on every single one of the twenty-six steps, treating each one as an individual conquest while my heels threatened to betray me and send me to the bottom in a heap.

An arm, dressed in a black suit, hooked under mine for balance. "Let me help. These steps are steep," he offered with a thick French accent.

Taking my eyes off the steps for a moment, I glanced up at my rescuer. Black eyes. That's all I saw. Black eyes and black hair. The mistake was mine for taking my eyes and concentration off of the steps. My right foot twisted beneath me, and I braced for the fall. Prince Accent-and-Black-Eyes gripped me around the waist, holding on until I could get my footing again.

"Damn." The word tumbled out with a small voice that I didn't recognize. Clearing my throat, I tried again. "Thanks."

"Be careful," he began, a grin creeping up his beautiful mouth. "These steps are intense." He kept his grip on my waist with his right arm and held my hand with his left.

It took forever to reach the bottom step, and in that time I learned his name. Marcos, pronounced Marc-ohs, not Marc-us. "Thanks, Marcos." My words were starting to slur after two martinis and a shot of Patron. It usually took more than that to take me down, but my stomach was empty. I'd have to remember to grab some peanuts or share an appetizer with Hailey when I got back upstairs.

"Right in here." He pulled me into a dark room. Having him assist me in the ladies' room was a bit odd, but I'd been in enough clubs with coed bathrooms, so whatever, I followed.

The restroom was dark, so I searched for the light switch, patting my hand along the wall just inside the door. In one swift motion, Marcos turned me and pinned my back to the wall. His lips crashed into mine as he held my waist. Startled, I tried to pull away, but he gripped my arms, holding them by my side, and pressed his body to mine. I was trapped against the wall of the dark room.

It only took a second for me to relax into him. His mouth was delicious as his tongue captured mine, playing with it like we'd been intimate before. I couldn't help melting into his kiss, craving more. The way he smelled—a mixture of soap and woodsy cologne—and the way his mouth expertly kissed me into an intoxicating dizziness was thrilling.

The man waiting for me upstairs never crossed my mind when I felt Marcos' hand slip under my dress. This dude meant business as he slid the delicate triangle of lace aside and stroked my most intimate spot. Was I so easy to read these days? How was he so sure I wouldn't scream or try to fight him off?

"Fuck," I breathed, arching my back off the wall to get closer to the pleasure he was inflicting, urging him to take what he had planned on taking anyway.

My left hand snaked around to the back of his head, while my right hand found his hardening dick. That was the ticket that got things moving faster. After tensing at my first touch, he slipped the tip of his finger inside. A cruel teasing gesture that made me want to grip his wrist and force him to satiate the ache that was building. He dragged his lips along my jaw line to my ear, nibbling on the lobe as he pushed his finger in and out, bringing me close to release. I needed him inside of me.

Condom.

Working his zipper down, I released him and began stroking his thickness.

"Condom?" I panted, wishing he'd already had it on.

He shook his head against my neck. "No."

"The fuck?" I pulled away. No way in hell was I contracting only God knew what this douche-sack had.

"I don't have one on me." He slapped at his pockets, disappointment on his face. Maybe if he slapped one more time, a square foil package would appear. It didn't.

With both hands on his chest, I pushed him away, creating enough space between us to see his face. "I can't believe you don't have a condom. Why did you even bother?"

"I always have one." A flash of helplessness crossed his face before he regained the cockiness that drew me to him initially. "Gave it to a buddy upstairs. I didn't plan on this. You're so fucking sexy . . ." He leaned in, his hand lifting my dress. "I'm clean, I swear."

"Sure, asshole. Your word's the shit. I'm clean, too." I added a smirk to make him doubt me. I was clean, but he needed to learn not to trust a stranger. He was probably the reason why STD's had quadrupled recently. "Sorry. No getting wet without a raincoat." I started to walk out of the room, my body beginning to settle when he grabbed my wrist and yanked me back in.

"We can still play." His eyes, dark with need, disarmed me before his mouth covered mine and promptly recharged the desire. I felt his hand roam over my breasts through the fabric of my dress, squeezing almost too hard and making me moan with a mix of pleasure and pain.

He led me deeper into the dark room, and my eyes began to adjust, making out a large wooden desk. When we reached the piece of furniture, he inched my dress up over my hips to pool around my waist.

"Holy mother of—" He licked his lips as his eyes took in the garter belt and thong. "Fuck me. Of all the days to give away a condom."

In one swift motion, he lifted me onto the desk and leaned me back. I propped up on my elbows, watching him look at me. He lifted one of my legs and set it on his shoulder, repeating the process with the other. What happened next surprised me and had the effect I was sure he'd hoped for. The

17

strings of my thong were snapped easily and thrown aside like meager twist ties. All the heat from my body traveled to my sex. God, this man knew what he was doing.

He took his time, letting his hot breath travel over my inner thigh. His lips replaced the moist heat, placing kisses so light it took everything in me not to grab his hair and make him move faster.

He must've sensed my urgency and smirked before trailing his tongue along the flesh of my leg.
"Patience, beautiful."

Torture. He was torturing me because I wouldn't let him in without protection. Each time I whimpered, he paused. When he finally got close enough to the prize, I bit down on my bottom lip, trying to stifle another sound. I needed this release. I was so close and he hadn't even touched me yet. The excitement alone was enough to push me over the edge with a single touch.

A breathy groan of exasperation elicited a slow grin— a cross between satisfied and evil—before he dipped his head down to where I needed it.

Excruciatingly slow, he swept his tongue from bottom to top. My eyes snapped shut and my head lolled back as I moaned too loud. Anyone from the hallway could surely hear me, but my body was on fire and I didn't care about anything except feeling his tongue again.

His movements were never the same. He brought me to the brink and then let it fall again until I was close to begging him to forget the condom and just fuck me already. His tongue flicked and swirled, a mixture of fast movements and slow, languid ones. I couldn't find anything to grip as he brought me close to the edge, so I dug my fingers into the desk, my joints screaming from the pressure.

He slipped two fingers inside of me just as the most intense orgasm drove through my body.

"Holy fuck…That was . . . fuck!" All intelligence was lost as I lay there, reeling.

Lips and tongue trailed up my leg. I couldn't take another orgasm and almost stopped him when I realized what was happening. But he'd mastered this game, and it felt too good not to let him do it again. The second orgasm was mild, and I lost patience for him. His lips on my legs became annoying. I was ready to push him away and sit up when I realized he was taking care of himself. When he finished, he zipped his pants, leaned against the wall, and lit a joint. *My fucking soul mate.*

I stood and shimmied my dress back down over my hips. Running my fingers through my hair, I tamed the just-been-fucked look and leaned against the wall next to him. Not a word was spoken as he handed me the joint and we smoked it down.

"Give me your phone," he said.

"It's not on me. Give me yours." I typed a fake number in and handed it back to him. "I really do need the restroom now."

***

"Where have you been?" Hailey asked, peeling herself away from her dude for a moment to convey her worry. How had she realized I was gone when the guy was practically dry humping her against the bar?

"Sorry, the line was insane." I looked around for Cal, but he was gone. Fantastic. I wasn't ready for the night to end. Maybe there was still time to find Marcos again, we could stop by a drugstore on the way back to his place.

"Hi, gorgeous." Cal had returned to my side, whispering in my ear, "I tried to find you, where did you disappear to?"

"There was a line." I eyed him suspiciously. If he knew anything, he had an amazing poker face.

Cal glanced across the room, toward the front door. I followed his confused gaze to the sign in the corner. A restroom. No line.

"What the hell? I went to the one downstairs." I let an annoyed tone bleed through my voice— probably a little too much, I had a tendency to overact—and lied about a long line to make up for the time I'd been gone. "A gazillion steps and a really long line." I pointed to the corner bathroom and huffed. "I bet no one knows about that one." Thank goodness he had looked in the wrong place. It couldn't do much for an ego to see the girl you had planned on taking home, moaning beneath another man.

He slid a pear martini toward me. "If it's warm, I'll have her pour a fresh one."

After an exploratory sip, I nodded. "It's fine, thanks."

"Finish it up and let's get out of here." He raised an eyebrow, his expression telling me exactly what he wanted as soon as we got out of there.

"I'd love to," I started, trying to keep the annoyance off my face. "But I haven't eaten a thing today. Want to share an appetizer?" My body was still buzzing from the incident downstairs. I needed a moment to reboot, and I could use something in my stomach. I wasn't the type to get sick or have a hangover the next morning, but I felt shaky and didn't want to take a chance. The night was still young.

After we nibbled on a platter of prosciutto, bruschetta, and cheeses, I said my goodbyes to Hailey and let Cal lead me out of the club. Marcos was nowhere in sight, and I silently thanked the stars. The valet brought Cal's car around—sleek, black, maybe a Porsche or something similar. He held the door while I slid in, then he walked around to the driver's side. Damn, he was sexy as hell. I was more than ready for O number three.

"Which way?" he asked, shifting into first gear.

"Surprise me, lover," I cooed, closing my eyes and resting back in the leather bucket seat.

"Where do you live, Bree?" The words flowed from his mouth like honey, but jolted me like the sting of a thousand bees.

I whipped my head around to face him, my eyes wide in protest. "We can't go to my place." I kept my voice even. I'd given the same excuse a hundred times and pulled it off easily, but I could feel my insides unraveling as the fear of being caught invaded. It was an ugly lie, I knew that, but it worked. "My disabled sister lives with me. My place is not an option."

Something flashed in his eyes. Was he summing me up as a loving caregiver or could he see right through me? I decided he was considering whether or not I was worth his time. Pegging him as an asshole was a lot easier for me than seeing him as a kindhearted man. Those didn't exist in my world. If they did, everything would change and maybe that scared me more than anything else. He let off the clutch and eased off the curb, shifting into second gear when he was in the lane. He maneuvered through the traffic with ease, similar to the way the cabbies drove, but not throwing me around the car. Eventually we pulled up in front of the InterContinental near Times Square, but not before grabbing a bottle of tequila and a pack of cigarillos at a small package store on the way.

"You have a room here?" I asked.

"Not yet." He left the car running and jogged over to my side, opening the door and offering a hand to help me out. A bellman approached, but before he could say anything, Cal slipped him a bill and asked him to park it.

"Last name's Tyler."

The bellman nodded courteously. "Very good, sir. I'll take care of it."

Alright, that was impressive. If I had a soul, I might've felt guilty about my escapade with Marcos. But I didn't, so I wasn't.

I watched Cal's every move, trying to stay focused while hanging onto the last bit of my buzz.

After checking in, we took the elevator to the eleventh floor. As soon as the doors shut, I was in his arms. His lips were soft yet eager against mine. My buzz was rekindled when his tongue found entrance. A current electrified my senses and weakened my knees. I could have stayed in that elevator all night, kissing him. But I wanted more, so when the elevator reached our floor, I stepped out.

Cal slid the card into the door and waited for the light to flash green. He held the door for me to step through and followed me in. Before the door closed, I was against the wall. His hands cupped my face as he brought his mouth to mine. Usually men were rough and eager, but he was tender and thoughtful. He kissed me like I was special and I felt it. Usually I would try to avoid those feelings. I could bring out the animal in him, make him take me from behind so I didn't have to look in his eyes. *Just a little longer.* I couldn't help myself, it felt incredible and surely a few seconds wouldn't change the dynamics. So I let myself go.

One of his hands slid around my waist, finding purchase on my ass. He gave it a squeeze and pulled me in tighter. Our bodies became entwined with each other, his lips softly tracing my jaw, over my ear, and down my neck. He grabbed a handful of my long hair and tugged gently until I tilted my head, giving him the access he desired.

Letting myself enjoy the feeling of being devoured by this fine man, I moaned into his ear. He released my hair, and his hands slid down over my breasts, squeezing them through the fabric of my dress until he yielded another moan. *Nice move.*

"I want you," I whispered. Those three words worked on every man I'd ever met. I had no idea why it was such a powerful sentence. Obviously I wanted him or I wouldn't be in his hotel room letting him strip my clothes off. One day I'd find out why those were the three words that undid a man. I always meant it. I craved sex and most of the time my head was dizzy with desire at this point. Without a word, he gripped my ass and pulled my hips into his bulging erection. Apparently, he wanted me as desperately. With one hand, he reached for the hem of my dress and pulled it up, inch by inch, until it rested around my waist. His fingers trailed over the lace tip of my thigh-high stocking, over the buckle on the garter belt, and traveled up to find my panties. Or lack thereof.

Dammit, Marcos must've pocketed them. Asshole.

"Fuck, yes," he hissed.

In one motion, he lifted me up and I wrapped my legs around his waist. Pinning me against the wall, his mouth crashed into mine as his hands explored my exposed flesh. He backed away from the wall and I slid down his body, my legs quivering as I tried to stand.

His eyes never left mine as he unzipped my dress and let it fall to the floor. Stepping back, he admired my body. I loved being ogled. A body like mine was meant to be appreciated. Full breasts and curves in all the right places, he damn well better take a moment to admire what I was offering. He shook his head in awe before closing the space between us.

Everything was going smashingly at first. I worked on the button of his jeans as he unclasped my bra. The more we hurried, the more we fumbled. I guess it would've been cute if we had been dating, but this was a one-night stand. Cute and fumbling did not suit a one-time fling. We needed to get this moving. Now. Instinctively, I reached for my clasp and he unbuttoned his jeans, removed them, and then gripped the hem of his shirt, pulling it overhead and tossing it aside. *That's more like it.*

I shimmied out of my garter belt and stockings, bending all the way over to remove them. Before I could stand, his hands were on me, stroking my ass and legs. I was so caught up in the moment, I'd forgotten to ask about protection. Surely he had it, but after the incident earlier, I needed to ask.

Turning around to face him, I asked, "You have protection, right?"

He nodded. One of those sharp nods that answered a stupid question. My hands and eyes roamed over his chest and stomach before trailing down to the hem of his black boxer briefs. His impressive erection was imprisoned beneath the fabric, and I couldn't wait to release it and see what prize awaited. Carefully, I moved the fabric over him and lowered them down his legs. As he stepped out of them, I gripped and stroked him.

After reaching for protection, he guided me back onto the bed. His green eyes darkened with desire as he crawled over me and pinned my hands over my head. He pushed into me slowly and deliberately. This was my favorite part, feeling every inch as I stretched around him, what I had missed earlier with Marcos. He pulled all the way out before driving back in, and I arched my back in pleasure. As his pace began to quicken, I wrapped my legs around his back, urging him deeper. I rarely had to fake an orgasm. I always worked myself up so much before penetration that they came easily. The only time I had to fake it is if someone wanted to go all night into the morning hours. I needed enough time for them to fall asleep so I could go through their stuff, take what I needed, and get out.

The frenzy began to build inside of me as he reached under my ass, pulling my hips upward. He was so deep, hitting the spot that made me cry out for more. My body tensed and contracted, milking his release. He was insatiable and he'd met his match. We shared tequila straight out of the bottle between escapades. Tipping the bottle, I pretended to drink, but only let the liquid wet my tongue. Falling into a deep, tequila-induced sleep wasn't an option.

"Will you stay the night?"

Smiling, I cocked my head to the side. "Love to."

When he finally collapsed onto the bed, too tired to pull the sheets over his body, I pretended to be just as drunk, jerking at the covers and slurring my words. "You're too heavy. Move these legs." He didn't. A small part of me felt sorry for the hangover he'd experience in the morning.

As I watched the peacefulness of sleep take away any stress or worry or pain, I envied him. I'd never known a moment where my mind could be free. It was one of the reasons I was alone. Commitment issues? No, it was more than that. I was restless, easily distracted, and unable to be faithful to one man. I needed to be in control and free to do what I pleased. Relationships didn't allow that. Those were the rules, and I couldn't abide by them. So I was alone. Alone with an unsatisfying life.

CROWDED

Gathering my things, I dressed and walked out the door. Before it shut, I caught it with my foot and stepped back inside. Forgot one last thing.

Chapter 3

Anna

Why did it always happen to me? Sure, I would latch onto a man and instantly plan a future with him. But I was ready. Ready to settle down, get married, and start a family.

My fingernails dug into my palms when I saw the photo. There was no mistaking the fact that Stellan's arm was snaked around another woman.

How could you do this to me? Bastard!

In the past, I would've tried to justify the photo—a sister or cousin, possibly—but I'd been burned too many times. If they were related, he wouldn't have had his arm around her waist, touching her skin. Not with the way she looked in a figure hugging dress that didn't leave much to the imagination.

I was unable to see the woman's face. With her head down and angled to the right, the mystery woman's features were shadowed. But there was something familiar about her that made me study the picture longer than I should have. Where had I seen her? What I *could* see was her killer body. That was enough to send a spike of jealousy through me. Like a heartbroken fool, I took a moment to wallow in the misery of imagining them together. The woman was surely a wildcat in bed, hooking the man I thought I loved with her witchery. I couldn't help picturing him panting around her like a horny dog. A chuckle laced with sadness escaped my lips as I thought of him humping her leg. He'd never treated me that way. He'd always showed me respect. But then, sexy didn't work for me. I had tried in the past to be what I thought men wanted, only to fail miserably and look like a desperate idiot. That's what happened when the respectable girl next door tried to be a seductress. Failure and embarrassment. Stellan never laughed at me though. Maybe he thought I would eventually succeed. After all, the woman with him in the picture, looked a lot like an improved version of me.

No matter how many times I was told by men, "You're beautiful" or "Such a classic beauty with regal features" or "Don't you know how stunning you are?" I didn't believe it. Maybe because they always cheated. The same men that raved about my beauty always left me for another woman.

Every single time.

One day, I would stop putting all of my stock in the way I looked and live life for myself, instead of searching for a man to spend my life with. One day, I would find my inner strength, grab the world by the tail, and drag it behind me as I reached every milestone I desired. When I looked in the mirror, I would appreciate the skin I was in, see the physical and inner beauty I possessed, and embrace it with full bravado.

Easier said than done, right?

As I looked at that shy girl in the mirror, I wondered if 'one day would ever come. I blinked my grey eyes that never knew what color they wanted to be. Sometimes they picked up a violet hue, if I wore the right shade of purple, but that was too bold a choice for someone like me. I tried to stick to muted colors—blacks, greys, and creams—to blend in. To hide from the world.

I really thought Stellan was the one for me. I had opened up my heart to him in the six months we dated. He had made me feel beautiful and wanted. Admittedly, I fell for him too quickly—as I always did—and abandoned all of my rules. The most important being not to sleep with a guy before five dates. If you just wanted a fling, fine. But if you wanted a husband, you shouldn't sleep with him before the fifth date. It was fool proof. Yeah, not so much for me. Guess I'd need to up it to ten next time.

No, I wasn't the type of woman to throw in the towel after a dozen heartaches. I was the type to change the game plan. If A plus B didn't work, try B times C, divided by A. There were so many equations, and moving to a new city was supposed to give me a clean pallet, help me start from scratch. Yet here I was, in a new city, with a broken heart. Again.

A tear slipped down my cheek as I thought of Stellan. The jewelry he'd bought, operas we'd seen, and the way he'd made love to me like I was the most treasured being on earth.

How could you? I slammed the laptop closed. *I really loved you.*

***

It was a rash decision, but since no flowers were delivered, no texts or phone calls in the days that followed, I moved. Just packed up and moved. It wasn't like me to do something that wasn't thoroughly planned out, but this felt right. I'd always wanted to live in the city. Manhattan was filled with excitement, if I wanted to experience it. On the other hand, it was a rush of people doing their thing and I could easily get overlooked. Living in my own world for a while, concentrating on what made me happy, doing things like reading in the tub until the water turned cold, sounded perfect.

Finding an apartment in Manhattan wasn't as easy as I'd imagined, but the promise of adventure pushed me until I settled on a small studio apartment on the Upper East Side. It looked more like dorm living, but there were several restaurants I could walk to and a grocery store a few blocks away.

Unpacking boxes was a breeze as I didn't take much with me. Robotically, I stacked the dishes in the kitchen, cleaning products in the bathroom, and my suitcases in the living room/bedroom combo. My mind fixed on the way Stellan and I parted. He hadn't even tried to break up, he just moved on. I had never been treated so badly in my life. I didn't know how to respond or feel. It would have been easy to wallow in hurt and anger, but I decided to keep myself busy and push the feelings behind a wall for a while. I'd deal later. The feelings weren't going anywhere. I had a ton of stuff to do, anyway. My tiny studio could use a fresh coat of paint to cover the Pepto-Bismol color the last tenants had enjoyed, and the bathtub needed a good scrubbing with bleach. Truthfully, the entire apartment needed to be sterilized. My apartment was the perfect symbol of my life. Both needing a good cleaning and covering up of past mistakes.

***

The apartment was dark when I arrived home. Unusual, since I was certain I had left the lamp next to the couch on. Slapping my hand inside the wall before I stepped through the door, I found the switch and the room lit up.

Nothing seemed out of place, so I dropped my bags, shut the door behind me, and locked both bolts. After a long day of shopping for linens, dishes, and paint, I was beat and fell onto the bed without putting anything away or taking my shoes off.

Waking up the next morning in my clothes, my hair stuck to the side of my face where I'd slept on it, I felt rough. No doubt I didn't sleep well like that. Coffee seemed like the most important thing in the world, so I shuffled my feet, rubbing the sleep from my eyes until I reached the tiny kitchen. The coffee pot was nowhere to be found, the filters in the land of the lost, but I had grounds and a cup. Funny the things you contemplate when you're exhausted and in need of caffeine. I thought about boiling water and pouring it over toilet paper filled with my grounds, or a paper towel—if I could find those.

Instead I found the local coffee shop that would hopefully feed my addiction most mornings. Only a few blocks away, I could enjoy a brisk walk each morning, there and back. Nothing compared to the streets of New York City. I hated being crowded, especially by a mass of people, but the flow was smooth. Everyone was in a mad dash to reach their destination, but no one bumped me as we walked, it reminded me of being on a moving sidewalk in an airport. The air probably would've been stale in the concrete world absent of grass and trees, but the constant movement of people mixed with a breeze caught between buildings brought a medley of pleasing aromas. Food trucks preparing their specialties for the day, the clean scent of freshly showered and perfumed bodies, and the steam of already poured coffee from a to-go mug wafted past me. I couldn't help the slight pull of a smile on the right side of my mouth.

As soon as I walked into The Bean, I felt warm and cozy. The walls were painted chocolate and gold, while splashes of turquoise were found in artwork and throw pillows on corner couches. As I stood in line, I mentally chose a two-seater in the corner by the window so I could people watch.

The place was busy, people racing in and out, but no one stayed to occupy the seats. When my turn came to order, the young girl behind the counter was too winded to be friendly. She didn't ask what I wanted, just stared at me and waited for my order.

"Venti nonfat latte, one pump caramel, one pump hazelnut. Hold the whip, please."

First sip to last, it was good. Really good. I almost ordered another one, knowing how full my day would be.

Back at the apartment, I scrubbed the bathtub once again, trying to get rid of the dark stains around the drain and in the grout lines. Nothing was working. Between coats of paint for the walls—the color was Mushroom, but looked like coffee with a ton of creamer to me—I plopped down on the couch and opened up the romance novel I'd picked up a few days ago. When everything was finished, my little space had gone from grungy dorm room to a fresh and tidy studio apartment that any girl in her late twenties would be proud of.

A small porch off the back of my apartment housed my favorite flowers. I filled every inch of the space with the delicate pink blooms of Oleander. They smelled heavenly and I kept the door cracked so the sweet scent would drift in on a breeze.

Once I knew the plants were cared for properly, I was able to relax in the tub with a glass of Malbec and find out what would happen between Cadence and Cade in the book I'd picked up a few days ago. Only a fool would try to get over a breakup by reading a romance novel. My saving grace was that Cadence was the polar opposite of me so I couldn't relate. She was a confident woman with long blond hair who married her childhood sweetheart, Cade. It was a fluffy, too-good-to-be-true story. My favorite kind.

***

At four in the morning, I woke up in the bathtub. The water was cool and it felt like my bone marrow had frozen. A thick robe, fleece socks, and a cup of hot chocolate did little to subdue the shakes. Exhaling a heavy breath, my shoulders slumped. *Not again.*

I'd suffered from blackouts for years. I couldn't tell when they had started, but I hadn't had one in months. I thought I had grown out of them.

"Stress-induced," My doctor had said.

It made sense. The breakup—or blow-off, rather. Plus, I needed to find a job soon. The shitty—but fresh and tidy—apartment I was living in wasn't free, and I hated depending on my small inheritance to get me through. With interest rates at an all-time low, it wouldn't take long to eat through it.

The sun began to creep in through the windows, so there was no use in trying to go back to sleep. Another thing I'd have to dip into my account for, curtains. Since I was wide awake, I opened my computer and began browsing for jobs.

Chapter 4

Bree

Two weeks after Cal, I hooked up with someone at the bar inside of a swanky hotel. He dressed the part and I assumed he was staying at the hotel. Who the hell—other than me—goes to a hotel bar if you weren't staying there? The asshole asleep in the next room. I wasted an hour of my time flirting with this dude, only to go back to his apartment and find out he wasn't as rich as he looked. At least he had paid for my drinks, but a Friday night was completely lost on that loser.

Of course his name was Logan. The name suited him. He was probably the captain of his high school football team, sat the bench in college, but still thought he was all that and a bag of chips.

He wasn't.

I would've loved the opportunity to inform him, but he was out for the count and, measuring the amount of alcohol we'd consumed, he would be out until noon at the earliest. Right before he passed out, I told him I would let myself out. And I would, eventually.

Rummaging through his stuff, I looked for a token of his appreciation. Everyone knew that when you worshipped, you left something in the offering plate.

C'mon, dude, you've got to have something.

I eased the bottom drawer of his bedroom dresser open, watching his body as I did to make sure he didn't stir. In the drawer was a package of unopened boxer shorts, awards and documents of some sort, and finally, beneath a small child's blanket, a small navy box. An engagement ring, most likely.

Ass wipe. I hope she says no.

Or, maybe she had and that's why he still had the ring. I shrugged. Didn't matter to me.

Instead of a ring, the box contained a sapphire necklace. The stone was a nice size. I had no doubt it was real, and I could get a pretty penny for it. It was dazzling with pristine clarity. Looking over at sleeping beauty, I lifted it out and tried it on. It felt good against my skin—smooth, rich—and deserved a quick glance in the mirror.

Stunning! Keep it.

After stuffing the box into my clutch, I made sure everything was in order and pulled a wad of cash from Logan's wallet.

Sometimes I wondered what I would do if I *really* liked a guy, would I keep him for a while before moving on? There was no question with this one. He had been fun for a night—a buff sandy blond who knew how to party—but he was a selfish lover. So I took all he had and didn't feel an ounce of remorse. It was too easy to get away with crime in this town. There were far worse things going on for the police to worry about a petty thief. Still, I erred on the side of caution and always waited to pawn traceable items such as jewelry. Or I'd wear a disguise and keep my head down. It was also smart never to visit the same pawn shop twice in a row, although I could always get more money from Jake in Chinatown.

Insatiable and unfulfilled, I hit up a local biker bar on the edge of town on Cliff Street. I made what I needed financially, now it was time to get what I wanted physically. I hadn't known it was a fantasy to ride a rough biker in leather until I was walking toward the door. Thoughts of men acting and looking like Vikings sent a rush of heat through me.

Stepping inside, the fantasy faded. Women outnumbered men three to one, and none of them fulfilled the vision in my head. I almost turned to walk out, but my buzz was gone and there was a place at the bar calling my name.

"What can I do you for?" The old man behind the bar tried and failed to humor me.

"Whatever you're pouring, straight up." I expected a mug of moonshine, but instead got a short glass of Jim Beam. Probably just as bad, but I swallowed it down and asked for another.

While he poured, I looked around. The bad assess I had expected were nowhere to be found. Jeans and T-shirts scattered the place, most playing pool and darts, some sitting at high top tables, shooting the shit.

After one more pour of Beam, I paid the tab and walked out. Motorcycles lined the front of the building, and I couldn't help wanting to touch them. One in particular that I liked was a cherry red Harley with chrome trim. There wasn't a spot on it that hadn't been shined to perfection. Studying the black leather seat, I thought about riding someone while they drove down a back road. My legs wrapped around the waist of a man who refused to look me in the eyes. Could he keep from crashing while I rocked his world?

"Like my ride?" I heard someone say behind me, followed by the sound of metal on a Zippo lighter.

"A lot." I didn't look at him because I didn't want his physical appearance to ruin it, but instead ran my hand along the soft leather, allowing a few more minutes to enjoy the thrill of my daydream.

"Smoke?" he asked. His voice was rough, the deep throaty effect of a long-time smoker. But he wasn't old. That I could tell by his smooth cockiness. An older man would've gotten to the point. This dude wanted me to come to him. I'd change his ways if he was worth a glance.

A cigarette sounded good, so I turned around. I wasn't disappointed. He was around my age and looked delicious in a black T-shirt and loose jeans. Thick caramel hair was pulled into a messy bun on top of his head, and his matching beard could've used some grooming. A chain swung down from under his shirt and must've looped back up. I wondered if it was decoration or held a leather wallet filled with cash.

Without moving off the wall he was leaning against, he pulled a cigarette from the pack and offered it to me. I walked toward him and took it, not breaking eye contact as I placed it between my lips, still sticky with raspberry tinted gloss. Lifting his Zippo, he flicked the lid back with his thumb and brought a flame to life. I cupped the cigarette with my hands, blocking the breeze, and sucked in a deep breath, sighing as the minty smoke filled my throat and lungs. Alcohol always deepened my craving for sex, cigarettes strengthened the desire, and I couldn't be held accountable for my actions if weed came into the picture.

Which was exactly what happened when we finished our smoke.

"I've got some great shit I've been itching to smoke. Want a hit?"

Of course I did. "Sure." I shrugged a shoulder.

He lit the end of the rolled joint and took the first puff, holding his breath longer than necessary. Eager to get my turn, I studied him. His eyes were closed, so I had no idea what color they were. Not that I cared, I was just bored and couldn't understand why he hadn't passed it to me while he was counting sheep and holding the smoke in.

When he finally exhaled, it came out in a long whoosh and was followed by a satisfied grin. "Fantastic shit." Instead of passing it to me, he placed it between my lips. "Not too much. This shit will fuck you up."

Through the smoke, I caught a whiff of him. He smelled like leather and soap and danger, the perfect blend of aphrodisiac. The weed was amazing, as he had promised, but the sum of all properties had every part of me lit and ready for anything.

"Want a ride?" he asked, not looking at me or giving me the attention I craved.

I'd never been one to pussy foot around, so I gave him a straight answer. "I want to be fucked on this bike."

My motorcycle man didn't flinch, which surprised me. Maybe I wasn't the only one with biker fantasies and he'd fulfilled several women's desires on that bike. Whatever. I was next.

"What's your name, baby?" He glanced up before hiking a leg over the bike and taking a seat on the leather. Clear blue eyes. They contradicted his badass demeanor. Especially at that moment, smirking like a player that had wooed an unsuspecting innocent. What he hadn't known was that *I* wasn't the prey.

"Bree."

He cocked his head to the side, his eyes contemplating something. "Hop on, Bree."

I didn't ask his name. I didn't need it. Pulling my short skirt up to the top of my thighs, I climbed on the back of his bike and wrapped my arms around his waist. Damn, my body was already screaming and he hadn't even started the engine.

He didn't go far, just down the road a few blocks and behind a building. He left the engine running, let the bike rest on the double kickstands, and helped me off.

"Take it off, baby," He hopped on one foot, while pulling a boot off, then repeated the ritual with the other. He was so eager, I almost regretted my decision. He was probably a terrible lay and would be finished before I even got started. The sound of a car whizzing by had me looking around to make sure no one would see us. By the looks of things, the building had been abandoned. Motorcycle man left the headlight on and it provided just enough light to view my surroundings. Leafy green vines crept up the white painted concrete walls of the building and nearly covered the back entrance. I could barely make out a metal door. Every now and then the wind would stall and the stench of old garbage would waft by.

"Whoa," I put up a hand. "Slow down, cowboy." Gripping him by the shirt, I pulled my body to his and tasted his lips. Bourbon and weed. I didn't mind the combination.

Motorcycle Man deepened the kiss as he palmed one of my breasts, squeezing it like a stress ball.

"Careful." I pulled away and started to walk to the bike. Harley's were known for being the loudest bikes on the road, and this bike seemed to top the charts echoing off the concrete walls, but at three in the morning, all surrounding businesses were closed. If I hadn't been so turned on, I might've worried about the fact that, from here, no one could hear me scream if he planned to harm me.

Before I could climb onto the seat, my biker gripped my waist and twirled me around. Surprisingly, he knew what I wanted, lifting me up onto the seat and leaning me back against the gas tank. He could've used a few lessons on oral pleasure, but at least he tried. I gave my best moans and gripped his shoulders as he brought me to the best Oscar-worthy fake orgasm.

Motorcycle sex wasn't what I had expected. Trying not to burn my leg on the muffler while getting the leverage that I needed was near impossible, so I gave up on that fantasy.

"This isn't working," I complained. My left leg shaking from trying to hold it away from the muffler. I'd have to remember to exercise one day, see if I could grow a muscle or two. "Let's move this off the bike."

I ended up against the building and prayed the vine tickling my back wasn't poison ivy. The man hadn't done anything for me on the bike, but suddenly he was a magnificent lover standing. He held me against the wall, my legs wrapped around his waist, panties pulled to the side as he drilled into me, his surprising length hitting the spot every time. I didn't come, but didn't bother faking it either. Too high and a little pissed that my fantasy was a bust, I concentrated on the noises he made. There was something remarkable about a man losing control because of what your body was doing to him.

Another joint was shared while we straightened our clothes and he found the one boot he'd managed to take off. I learned his name was Travis. I also learned that the thrum of a Harley's motor, mixed with the relaxing effect of sex and weed, made it too easy to lift a wallet.

Feeling victorious, I pocketed a wad of cash before inching the leather back into his jacket. During the cab ride home, I counted seventy-five dollars. Not a bad night at all.

Chapter 5

Anna

As soon as The Bean opened, I was in line, giving the barista my order. She was in a foul mood again, but so was I and totally exhausted on top of that, so I didn't even wait for her to greet—or not greet—me. "Venti nonfat latte, one pump caramel, one pump hazelnut. Hold the whip."

I heard a man chuckle behind me. Glancing over my shoulder, I saw his suit and assumed he was talking to someone through his Bluetooth ear bud. Too many times I'd answered someone only to realize they were talking on the phone and not to me.

"So indecisive." The same man made a tsk-tsk sound, causing me to glance over my shoulder again. His arms were crossed over his chest, a smirk playing on his lips. He *was* talking to me.

"Sorry?" I asked, unable to make eye contact, so I focused on the light blue design in his tie.

"You make coffee sound like chemical engineering." His full lips pulled into a smile. I followed it as it took over his face, and dared a glance into his eyes. Kindness. I didn't know him, but he radiated trustworthiness and had kind, gentle eyes.

I felt warm and comfortable in his presence, which was odd in this city. Manhattan had taught me to be on guard at all times. Trust no one. But he demanded trust, pulling it from me like it was natural.

Stop staring. I couldn't look away. The more I studied his features, the more I was drawn to him. *For chrissakes, look away.*

"I know what I like." My voice sounded small and unsure. Not what I was going for. "In my coffee," I added. That time, my voice was stronger—*score*. The fact that I couldn't quit rambling, though, was a huge fail. "I don't like it too sweet, so . . ." God, I was flailing around like a fish out of water trying to talk to this guy. A stranger. In a coffee shop.

Thankfully, the barista was back with my coffee and total.

Slapping my yoga pants, I realized there were no pockets and no chance for a magical bill to be hidden there.

It was that initial panic that struck, threatening to catapult your heart right out of its chest cavity onto the floor. You might as well be standing there without pants than in line, people waiting behind you, realizing you couldn't pay for what you'd asked for.

After the initial alarm, came the silent cursing and personal defamation of character. *Shit! What the hell was I thinking?* And then the real question came, feeling the weighted stare from the too handsome stranger behind me.

Why am I wearing these damn yoga pants, paint splattered all over me, in public?

The time had come to announce my dilemma. Instead of reaching for my nonfat, one pump caramel, one pump hazelnut, hold the whip latte, I had to apologize for the wasted concoction. I'd seen it play out before, but it was usually a scam artist trying to get a free coffee. They would turn and dump it in the sink without missing a beat. This young girl already had a bad attitude, no way in hell was she going to girl code this one for me so I wouldn't look like a fool in front of the hot guy behind me.

I was screwed.

My head began moving left to right repeatedly before the apology left my lips. "I'm really sorry about this, but I left my wallet . . ." I patted my sides, still hoping pockets with money would appear and save me.

As suspected, there was no sympathy, only a perturbed expression for the time and ingredients wasted.

"I've got it." The man behind me leaned around me, getting the barista's attention before she was fully turned around. "And add a dark roast. Black."

"No, no." I raised a hand, unable to face him, knowing my face was crimson. "Thank you, but—"

"Someone covered me last week. Pay it forward, right?" His voice was kind, his words sweet.

The heat in my cheeks hadn't subsided in the least, but I had no other choice than to look at him. He was a terrible liar, but I needed to see how the attempt played out in his eyes. Dark eyes, so dark I had to search for his pupils. In the short four or five minutes since I first glanced at him, he'd become even more attractive. Maybe it was the boyish grin? Or the full, pink lips accentuated by a sharp jawline. No, I was certain it was the dimples that sank deep into his cheeks when he smiled.

Stunning. Married?

My eyes automatically traveled down to his hands, searching his left ring finger.

No ring. *Gay? Probably.*

"Thank you . . . very much." I glanced down at my outfit after looking over his tailored suit. I had hoped I could sneak in unseen before the morning crowd. Patting my sides for show, I again complained about not having pockets. "This is so embarrassing."

"Nonsense." He swiped the air with his free hand. "It happens."

Not to me. "I insist on paying you back."

"Okay." He flashed that grin that made me forget we were strangers. "Thursday, same time?"

I blinked in surprise. That wasn't the answer I had expected. In fact, he took me completely off guard, and I could feel the heat creeping into my cheeks again. I thought he'd give me his business card or something. The last thing I needed was to dive blindly into another relationship. Not that he wanted that. It was presumptuous to think he could be into me, or straight for that matter. Either way, I needed to make it clear right away that I wasn't interested in anything outside of coffee. I mean, I needed time to heal from Stellan, right? Stellan who? I couldn't even remember what color his eyes were.

I cleared my throat. "Do you have a business card? I can send the money to you."

"It's not a problem." His smile faded into a respectful nod. "No worries." He picked up the steaming cup of coffee, pocketed his change, and tipped his head. "Pay it forward for someone."

He's being nice. Why was I being so bitchy?

"Wait." The word rushed out. "Thursday might work. We'll call it a pay it backward." I felt clever when his grin returned . . . then I had to add a dumbass comment that was meant to stay in my head, but came out loud and clear. "Not a date." I winced. Was it a statement or a question?

A broad, cocky smile spread across his face. "Good. That would've been a lot of pressure for a man who hasn't had his morning coffee." He lifted the cardboard cup in a toast. "Here's to paying it backward."

Chapter 6

Jane

He would be dead soon. Jane had just enough time to get everything in order before watching him take his last breaths. To her it was as important as watching the kickoff to a big soccer game. Missing it didn't affect the outcome, but it set the tone and raised the bar of excitement.

She had only missed one death, back in the early days when her craft hadn't been as perfected as it was now. It had spoiled everything, and she'd vowed to never miss that precious last exhale of air again.

There was something morbidly exhilarating about watching someone exit this world, especially knowing you'd caused it. Balancing a soul in your hand, deciding which way to tip their fate.

Holding her palm up, Jane took one last look at Craig Coltman and let her palm fall to the right. *Death.*

Jane clucked her tongue and shook her head. "Too bad," she said, her British accent richly proper with a hint of sarcasm. "Shameful waste of a good Brit."

***

It was said that the Latrodectus hasseltii—or redback spider—kills the male after coupling. But in fact, sometimes they killed them beforehand. After all, the act of intercourse put the female in a vulnerable position, exposing her to predators.

Rolling Craig's large frame to the left, Jane crammed as much of the white sheet beneath him as physically possible and let him fall onto his back again. She padded to the other side of the bed and lifted him enough to pull the sheet through until it was released from the bed. Craig's lips were a beautiful shade of teaberry, swiftly racing to the anticipated shade of Persian blue that would alert her to his final moment.

After removing the sheets, Jane wiped down everything in the room with a white wash cloth and the strong commercial bleach she'd lifted from the maid's cart. With the back of a gloved hand, she swiped at a chunk of dark brown hair that was starting to stick to the sweat on her forehead. The strong aroma of chlorine made her feel alive, burning the tiny receptors in her nose and throat, reminding her of the past.

Bleach and childhood.

Her childhood had been erased in the same way the bleach was erasing evidence of her presence in that hotel room. As she moved to the bathroom and wiped the counter, faucet, and light switch, she remembered the strong stench of the same chemical on her clothing. Her mother had used it in abundance on Jane's clothing and anything else she considered dirty.

Just now, she felt the sting of the concentrated chemical in one of her cuticles. A small slit in her right glove, just above the knuckle on her index finger. Sliding her eyes closed, she embraced the pain, welcomed it. It was a feeling she knew well. Childhood pain used to keep her awake at night. A demon that had robbed her of security and filled her with unimaginable fear. With time, Jane had learned to ease the fear, block it, and eventually control and use it.

The sting spread from her cuticle to her hand, veining up her arm. She pictured her mother's image, as clear as it was eighteen years ago, molesting her mind. *"It's not clean enough."* Down on her hands and knees, Jane remembered scrubbing linoleum in the kitchen. *"It'll never be clean enough."*

That's why her father had left them. He couldn't take it any longer. No promises were made, but Jane knew he would come back for her. As soon as he found a place for them to live, he would collect her and free her from the hell her mother had created.

Late at night, when the house was quiet, Jane imagined what kind of house her father had found for them. A small white farmhouse on green rolling hills seemed perfect. They would raise chickens and rabbits, and have two giant country dogs named Banjo and King. On those days when life was so intolerable she couldn't breathe, Jane imagined her father traveling overseas to find their perfect home. He found the bluest oceans, the whitest sands, and built a small cottage overlooking the water.

But her father never returned. He'd been in an accident, and was healing in a hospital. He'd call soon. He was lost at sea, but he'd find his way back to her somehow. He was a selfish bastard. He didn't care for anyone but himself.

He would die by her hand one day.

When Jane was sure she'd wiped everything down, she looked at the man's body. His chest rose with each slow, shallow breath. It wouldn't be long now, one, maybe two exhales left in him.

She'd wanted to carry his body to the tub and leave him soaking in a pool of bleach, cleansing him of all filth before he slipped away. But he was too heavy.

His bare chest, clean-shaven and broad, would've been the perfect canvas for Jane's artwork. But she couldn't leave a mark—not this time. She was much too smart to leave clues. One sloppy move and evidence would be gathered. As tempting as it was to carve into his smooth flesh, like the first knife-dip into a new jar of peanut butter, she wouldn't leave her mark. But she did linger, tracing her finger along his flesh and imagining what it would look like, how the blade would feel penetrating his skin.

His death was exquisite. An almost silent puff of air left his lips as Jane held her finger over his mouth. She clasped her fingers around the ghost of his last breath-whisper and held onto it as she sang in a musical British accent,

"Ring-a ring o' roses,
A pocket full of posies,
A-tishoo! A-tishoo!
We all fall down."

Dropping the bleach-soaked rag to the floor, she used her foot to slide it along the path behind her as she walked to the door. One last step—wiping the doorknob—and her task was complete. She dropped the sheets and washrag into the large bin at the end of the maid's cart, knowing the wash would be done before they'd be able to investigate.

She took the stairs instead of the elevator, keeping her dark sunglasses in place, and her head lowered for the curious cameras in each corner.

Outside, the streets were empty on the upper east side of New York. The air was still and crisp from the break of dawn. Jane filled her lungs with that fresh air, a feeling of accomplishment penetrating her. Walking down the sidewalk, she dodged trash left by careless tourists and weekend drunks, then she rolled one of the pearls of her mother's necklace between her forefinger and thumb.

She began humming,

> *"Ring-a ring o' roses,*
> *A pocket full of posies,*
> *A-tishoo! A-tishoo!*
> *We all fall down."*

Chapter 7

Anna

A corner table gave me an advantage, having the door and front window in view so I could see Mr. Pay It Forward coming. I'd already paid the barista for both of our drinks but asked her not to pour his until he arrived. It was also the perfect spot to sip coffee and get ready for my interviews. One was a waitressing position at Flyte, and the other would be a phone interview for a customer service line. I could do that one from my apartment, which sounded ideal.

Butterflies skidded against my insides in a game of hide and seek. I was nervous. After rubbing my clammy hands down the sides of my skinny jeans, I fidgeted with a rip on the red leather chair, pulling at the fuzzy fabric beneath.

Although it was just coffee amongst new friends—*is that what we are? I don't even know his name*—it took too long to decide what to wear. I didn't know which thing to worry about more, the fact that I couldn't find the right outfit, or the fact that I was concerned about what I looked like for a man. It was too soon to jump into another relationship. Hell, if I were a smart woman, I would swear off relationships all together since the gods of relationships seemed to find pleasure in knocking me down over and over again. Since I'd made a bad impression last time, penniless and in yoga pants, I'd be damned if I didn't look fantastic for our Thursday meeting. I didn't overdo it. Just a few curls with the iron to add some bounce to my hair and a light touch of daytime makeup.

Seeing him come through the door sent a thrill up my spine. I was able to stare at him for a few beats before he found me. No suit, but I wasn't disappointed. He was wearing loose fitting dark jeans and a plain blue T-shirt that looked like it had been washed too many times. His dark hair flipped in every direction like all he'd done was run his hands through it after showering. Damn, if he wasn't sexy as hell, I might be a little ticked that he didn't have to spend a minute and a half to look perfect. Again, his eyes were mesmerizing. A contradiction of darkness that lit up the room. Before, he had been the picture of professional. Today he was rugged and casual. Not the bulging muscles and tatted arm sleeves rugged, but the kind that rolled out of bed, slipped on a pair of jeans from the night before, and was confident enough to know he was sexy just the way he was.

The butterflies paused for a moment as I watched him look for me, then they continued their game, racing to find purchase between my ribs. *Pull it together, Anna.*

Nodding at the barista to bring his coffee, I greeted him with a smile.

He shoved his hands deep into his pockets. "'Morning. I wasn't sure if you'd show." He seemed nervous—*so am I*—which increased my attraction to him.

Dammit.

"Hi." There was the shyness, filling me up and weighing me down like concrete.

His coffee was brought over promptly and set down on the table. He seemed to be watching my expression, maybe waiting for me to invite him to sit down. After all, I had made it awkwardly clear that I wasn't available for dating.

I lowered my eyes to his chair, a nonverbal invitation. The ball was in his court now. If he wanted to sit—knowing he would remain in the friend zone—he would. Or, he could pick up his coffee, nod a thank you, and leave.

"I didn't catch your name." He sat down, rested his elbows on the table, and took a sip of his coffee. His eyes looked sleepy, as if he'd just gotten out of bed to meet me. I felt the swoon on my inhale and knew I was in trouble.

"I didn't give it." *Sassy. Where did that come from?*

"I'm Pratt." His hand reached across the table. I took it and let the heat travel through my arm and settle in my chest.

"Anna." My head dipped as I watched him through my lashes before concentrating on the steam swirling up and away from my cardboard cup of latte. "Pratt. That's an interesting name." I loved the way it felt rolling off my tongue.

"Mother's maiden name." He smirked. "I believe it was my parent's way of teaching me how to fight."

I gazed up, wondering if I had missed part of the conversation while silently repeating his name. "What do you mean?"

"A name like that's a beacon for bullies." He leaned back, draped one arm over the back of the chair, and grinned. "It was either my head in the toilet every day after gym or learn

56

how to throw a punch." His grin turned smug. "My head's never touched a toilet."

Instinctively, I studied him again. Thick, dark hair—same color as his eyes—a lazy wave with a few curls around his ears that reminded me of a restless sea. He kept it short, and where I had assumed before that he just ran his fingers through it, now I noticed that he'd used gel to tame the front. It was a look made to deceive, as if he didn't care about his looks, but it was obvious he did. His fingernails were clean and manicured, and I imagined his fingers taming each strand of hair until it was exactly where he wanted it. Pratt radiated confidence and had an easy charm that instantly drew me to him.

Racking my brain, I tried to think of something intelligent to say. "Do you live in the city?" *Lame.* But it was the best I could come up with.

"No, I just drive in for the world's best cup of coffee. Totally worth the two-hour commute." He scrunched his nose and shook his head. "It was a lot funnier in my head." After a sip of his brew, he leaned back, crossed an ankle over his knee. "I've lived here about eight years now. You?"

"Just landed," I said, taking a deep breath. If I spun my cup in place a few more times, it was sure to create a permanent indent in the table. Why was I so nervous?

"Really?" Pratt raised an eyebrow in surprise and relaxed back in his seat like he was readying himself for a long story.

"Yeah, that's why I was so scattered last week. I was in painting and cleaning mode."

He flicked his wrist, dismissing the embarrassing memory. "Did you transfer for work? What do you do?"

Swallowing another sip, I answered, "No. Just a change of scenery. I've always wanted to live in the city. I'm currently seeking employment." *Don't give away too much.* "What do you do?"

"Maybe I can help you out." He leaned forward and rested his arms on the table. "What kind of work are you looking for?"

He was bold with the questions, and I gave him a grateful smile. "Thanks, but I've got something lined up in IT. I'm pretty positive I'm in. What do you do?"

"I'm in my last year of residency—"

"Oh no," I interrupted. A wave of wooziness hit me, thinking back to the last time I saw blood and passed out. Head rocking and face turned up in disgust, I looked into my cup. "We can't be friends."

"Why's that?" Disappointment filled his voice. I found the rip in the red leather seat, once more concentrating on the feel of rough cotton inside so I wouldn't get lost in the deep dark pools of his eyes.

"Because at some point, you're going to talk about blood and guts, most likely just before I put something in my mouth, and I'll pass out or get sick." Just the idea made me nauseas.

"You have a weak stomach." He said it matter-of-factly, like he knew my type. "That's a big problem. Really big." He seemed to contemplate something, resting his hands on the table and making a tent with his fingertips. "You're right, we shouldn't be friends . . . especially since I'm a head doctor."

I squirmed in my seat and my gut twisted in preparation for a gory, detailed story. Thinking about the things he did to a brain with a scalpel made me want to run to the bathroom.

But after a moment, he laughed. The kind that lit up his face like before and showed off his prized dimples. "I'm a psychiatrist. No gory stories here." He held up his hands in surrender.

"You're a tease," I argued, relief flooding over me. "Making me think you were a brain surgeon."

An easy smile crept up one side of his mouth and he shrugged a shoulder before bringing his cup to his lips, blowing at the steam, and taking a sip. He really was a good looking man.

We shared easy conversation over two cups of coffee, not a care in the world. My shyness faded and I even pulled a few funny stories out of the old memory bank about a crazed cat I owned. "His official name was Sir Prance-a-lot, because he seriously walked with a sassy prance. But I never called him that. I called him Asshole, Lucifer, and son-of-Satan, because I'm pretty sure he came from hell. Worst cat ever.

"Anna, you make me laugh." Pratt looked at the ceiling for a moment, his grin never fading when he dropped his head and looked me in the eyes. I'd love to do this again next week if you're available?"

I held my breath for what seemed like an eternity, processing what he'd asked. It sounded like a date which made me feel like a sixth grade girl again. Those weren't fun feelings back then, and they were even harder to deal with now, sixteen years later. I couldn't date Pratt, that was firm. But I had made that clear before, and it wasn't like he was asking me to dinner, he was inviting me to repeat this non-date coffee meeting. *As friends.* Pratt waited patiently as I performed the longest Trigonometry equation, aka was-he-asking-me-on-a-date-or-not question. Finally, after debating the pros and cons of coffee with Pratt, I made a decision.

My answer spilled out softly, unsure, and filled with that shyness I loathed, "Sure, I'd like that."

Chapter 8

Bree

My sidekick, Hailey, was out of town on business, and frankly, she was grating on my nerves anyway, so I was out on my own.

"This place is lame, but I keep coming back," said a lanky blonde next to me in line. She was stunning in a silver mini dress, and I struggled with whether to be jealous or make a move.

I decided to feel her out. "What makes it lame?"

"Too crowded."

I cocked my head to the side and gave her a curious look. If she didn't like crowds, what was she doing here, or at any club. It's freaking N-Y-C. "Crowded is good. Means it's a good club." I had never been afraid to flirt or say what was on my mind, so I let my eyes roam her body—lean but curves in all the right places. Her boobs had to have been paid for. God didn't create proportions like that naturally. "You won't have to wait in line long, with a body like that. The bouncer usually picks the sexiest women in line. Sexy women equal more men and more money spent on alcohol."

"Um, thanks." The blonde gave me a funny look and pretended to check her phone. Guess she preferred penis. Too bad. Bitch could've at least returned the compliment.

While I waited for the bouncer to come and pluck hot blonde and myself from the line, I analyzed the crowd. Tall geeky hipster: fantastic lover but a wallet the size of a starving artist. Dark and built like a god: still lived with parents. Suit: probably made good money, average lover, but it would take forever to work out his kinks and get him to relax in bed.

For kicks I lingered on Mr. Suit, thinking about a future with him. I had to bite the insides of my cheeks to keep from laughing when I thought about that kind of life. Dinner on the stove and me in an apron, waiting for him at the door with a glass of scotch. I'd rub out the day's stress before kneeling down and working my magic the way I knew best. All for his approval, worthless fuck. No amount of money was worth what that man was going to put a woman through one day. As bad as I needed a fix, I wouldn't waste my time on that one.

It was then, during that moment of talking myself out of throat punching Mr. Suit for looking like an asshole, that someone gripped a handful of my ass. It took a moment for it to click that someone had the balls to, not only grab, but squeeze my personal property. He pumped his fingers around my flesh once—twice. It wasn't sexy. I doubted it was even meant as a pickup. The only thing I could figure was he . . . or she, was testing for ass implants on a dare.

Hot blonde looked up from her phone to glance at my offenders, but quickly went back to pretending she was doing something important. With a flat expression, I turned around slowly to find three boys. They had to be twenty-one to get into the club, but didn't look a day older than eighteen. Two of them chuckled like middle schoolers. The one that was doing the grabbing stood with eyes too wide and his chest cocked like he was daring me to admonish his deed.

My first inclination was to cuss him down the sidewalk and across the street, but I was bored and decided to play. "I remember you." I inhaled deeply as if savoring an expensive cognac. "Yeah, we had a lot of fun together." I pointed to the guy on his left, the shorter one with a cocky grin. "And you. Damn, you know how to rock a girl's world." He'd never seen me before, but he wasn't about to let the others know. *Too easy.* I waited for him to puff up, feeling proud of his masculinity before running my hand over his chest. "I'll never forget how rough you let my friend get. You took it, though, better than he did." I flashed his friend a beguiling smile laced with evil. "Most people can't handle a cock as big as Antonio's."

The ass-grabber backed off the sidewalk and turned to walk away. "C'mon," he called to his friends. "Whore thinks she's funny."

I could hear the boys ribbing him even after they were around the corner. It was worth every obscene nickname he shouted at me to watch his expression.

"I haven't been that entertained since the Fallon-Timberlake dance off."

Whipping my head around, I faced God's gift to me. Sharp blue eyes. He might have had a great body, but I wouldn't know since I couldn't pull myself from his eyes. The blow of a taxi horn shook me out of the trance long enough to look at his full lips and imagine the way they tasted.

Greeting him with a smirk, I introduced myself. "Bree. Entertaining the line until we're either inside or running away like little pussies." I cocked my head toward the path the fucktards had taken.

"You shortened the line, all right." He smirk-grinned as if torn between wanting to make fun of me or give me a high-five. "Want me to create another opportunity for you?" His arms were folded across his chest, but not in a defensive way, more in a casual, I-don't-know-what-else-to-do-with-my-arms stance.

Now that I had my senses gathered, picked up, and put back in place, I studied him. His head was shaved, slick and shiny, but the Viking amount of hair on his face made up for it. *Damn, when did beards start turning me on?* He was taller than me, even with my favorite stilettos on, and had a broad chest that competed for my attention. I hadn't seen him really smile yet, and I tried to imagine him toothless so my heart rate would slow.

Calm down, Bree. Maintain control.

"Nah, I'm good. But if you have any other ideas on how to get us inside . . ." I watched his lips, waiting for him to tell me his name. I really wanted to know now if he had teeth.

"Blaize Martin." His smile was cocky and lit up the night sky.

Interesting name. I'd bet Blaize could send a fire through me.

I let my gaze trail up from his slacks to the belt around his waist. My fingers twitched at the thought of skimming them over his stomach, watching him tense at my touch. I knew when I met his expression I'd face a knowing, cocky grin. He'd see the heat behind my eyes and realize all he had to do was offer a hand and I would follow him. One night was all I needed to get him out of my system. I didn't need to know if he had siblings or what he did for a living. I only needed him to fill the void for an hour—maybe two if I read him correctly.

The line moved and it looked like we would be in this round. So much for the bouncer idea. If Blaize was going to make a move, he had less than thirty seconds to do it.

"Can I buy you a drink inside?" He shuffled behind me, pulling his ID out.

I flashed mine to the doorman while nodding a yes to Blaize.

The club was divided into two rooms, a long bar in each. To the left was the best drag queen show in town, always standing room only. There was a VIP section, which didn't really mean anything since everyone was on their feet as soon as the first entertainer stepped onto the stage. It never ceased to amaze me the work that went into each entertainer. Hair, makeup, and costume—no expense was spared. And if they were trying to mimic a celebrity, they always did a bang up job of it.

Blaize guided me to the right, his hand on my lower back. Every molecule of the area he touched was on high alert. We headed to the other side of the club and found a seat at the wall length bar. The dance floor was packed with bodies grinding on anything with a body temperature. It was too loud for getting-to-know-you conversation, but we tried.

"We sipped on martinis—mine extra dirty—and covered the bases of age, relationship status, and why the hell we were both here alone.

"Wanted to change things up," I explained, twirling my speared olives through the chilled vodka. "Not a fan of girl's night."

"My boys ditched me for Vegas. Bachelor party." He looked like a kid whose ice cream just rolled off the cone onto the sidewalk. "The timing didn't work out with my job."

"What do you do?" I sipped my martini, hoping the edge would soften soon. This man was doing things to me, making my pulse race and causing goose bumps to break over my skin involuntarily. Plus, I hated the formality of back and forth banter. Couldn't we skip it and go straight to the dance floor, pressing our bodies together? Or even skip that and go straight to his place?

"I'm a—"

Raising my hand, I interrupted. "Don't tell me, let me guess." His hands were rough, so he didn't have a desk job. But he dressed better than the average laborer. My guess was a fitness trainer—it was obvious he'd spent hours a day in the gym—but I liked to play, so I teased, "Lawyer."

He squinted and tipped his head to the side. "Wow, you're good. Prosecution or defense?"

I knew he was lying, the slight pull of his lip on the right side gave him away. I also lied when I answered, "You're one of the good guys, I can tell. Defense."

"Wrong." His eyes darkened, locking on mine in a battle of stare-down that I refused to lose.

Heat traveled through the tiny vessels beneath my cheeks. Without blinking, I raised the speared olives from my glass and sucked one into my mouth. He would not beat me at my own game.

Blaize flicked his eyes toward my cleavage and back up to my face. *I win.*

I didn't mind him looking. That was why we wore these godforsaken outfits that hugged here and plunged there. They weren't comfortable, surely men understood that. No more comfortable than a tie around your neck and freshly polished dress shoes that were so tight they rubbed blisters. We wore these damn outfits to get your attention and keep it. I never understood women who complained about a man whistling or cat-calling. It was when they didn't that I got offended. As hard as I worked for this body, you damn well better appreciate it.

Just to make sure he got more than a teasing glance, I leaned forward and squeezed his knee. "Want to join me?" I purposely didn't specify. Join me on the dance floor, join me in a back room pressed against a stack of boxes, join me for a ménage à trois at the hotel of your choice. Whatever, they all sounded good to me.

He chose the dance floor. Fucking gentleman. I'd fix that.

Blaize had moves. Great moves. He didn't look like a guy who could dance, but I was more than pleasantly surprised. He read my body like we were long time lovers, moving with me to the beat of the music. He blew me away with his stamina and that freaking smile. Had we discussed his smile? It wasn't toothless. It also wasn't the perfect, four-years-of-braces, two-years-of-retainers smile. A few crooked teeth gave him character and a sexiness I wouldn't be able to resist much longer.

The music slowed. Not the arms on his shoulders while he grabs your hips slow, but a song appropriate enough for us to fit our bodies together and move in a rhythm that teetered on a line between sex and dancing.

It was almost too much—the heat of his body against mine. When his knee moved between my legs and rubbed against my inner thigh, I almost fell apart right there. *Fuucckk.* My lids closed and refused to open. My instincts screamed against letting go of the control I loved more than anything. Control I needed. Who was this man, taking everything? We hadn't spoken a word on the dance floor, yet we connected in a way that took me by surprise.

Don't be stupid, Bree. Hang on.

I had to be a hard ass. Protect my heart. I'd let men—and women—do almost anything they wanted to my body, as long as they didn't get too close to my heart.

Sex was fun. Trying new things exciting and risqué. I liked men more because I felt most in control with that gender. Women were like a palette cleanser—a delicate portion of lemon sorbet—to ready me for my next meal. But men encompassed everything nourishing to the body.

Some, sadly, were appetizers, but they served their purpose. Then you had your side dishes. I frequented those most often—the one-night stands that you could have the time of your life with and leave without feeling weighed down. I always took more than I gave. That's just how I worked. They got what they needed, I got what I wanted, and then I *took* what I deserved.

But as a true carnivore, I liked meat the most. You know, the men who filled you, sustained you. They made sure you were fully satiated before they feasted. Those were a rare find, and I'd yet to find one that filled me completely.

This man—now leading me back to the bar—might have a shot. I was certainly in the mood to test him out.

"Another drink?" He was breathless. Beads of sweat speckled his head and his shirt clung to his body that I imagined was slippery with moisture.

Using my best smoky voice, I answered, "Sure, one more before we go."

From the flicker of heat that flashed in his eyes, it was clear he got the message.

Before the bartender could ask what we wanted, Blaize held up two fingers. "Patron."

A shot to move things along faster. I chuckled to myself. *In a rush all of a sudden? Finally ready to taste the poison?*

The Patron went down easily and left a slight buzz, but nothing compared to what I was used to. After looking at the time, I realized we'd been on the dance floor almost two hours. Panic rose in my chest knowing I'd wasted a good part of the evening and hadn't hooked my prey yet. I'd only had a martini plus the shot, so my inhibitions weren't affected at all. By this time I was usually drunk and had bedded at least two people. Sweat trickled down my spine until it found purchase where the fabric of my dress met my waist. *I don't sweat.* Blaize had turned my world upside down, making me lose track of time, go hours without the one thing I came here for, and making me perspire. *Damn it.* Having my inhibitions intact was strange, feeling every sensation and playing out every emotion. Every touch felt amazing, but not being in control scared the shit out of me, and I didn't do scared. I had to get out of here. Now.

Chapter 9

Bree

There still wasn't enough liquor in my system to stifle whatever it was my body and mind were experiencing. This guy had a pull on me that I couldn't wrap my head around. I should've followed my gut earlier when that red flag had waved its ugly flap in my face. Instead, here I was in the back of a taxi, competing with my prey in a duel of tongues and flesh, fueled by the most powerful lust I'd indulged in to date.

Breathless, I pulled away and ordered the cab driver to pull over at the next convenience store. I hustled inside and grabbed a box of condoms, bottle of vodka, and some juice in case Blaize couldn't handle straight up.

Fifteen minutes later, we were in his apartment, tearing at each other as he pulled me toward his bed. I wasn't sure how we got there or what his place looked like. All I could focus on was the lure of desire. Blaize stepped back, hopping on one foot as he slipped off one sock, then repeated the movement for the other. Turning away from his clumsy sock dance, I unscrewed the cap and took another swig from the vodka bottle, trying to stifle the feelings raging through me and gain some control of my head again.

He was behind me in an instant, the unfamiliar feeling of nervousness returning before I could swallow the drink. It went down in a noisy gulp. Blaize lifted the bottle from my hand and I waited for him to take a drink, curious to see if I'd met someone who loved the sauce as much as I did. But he set the bottle down and closed the space between us. "I want you to feel this," he growled, pressing his hard body against mine. "Tomorrow, when you're at work, you'll still feel me."

He had my attention.

Sex. *It's only sex.* I could leave these strange feelings out of it. But if it were only sex, why would he want me to feel it? If it were nothing but sex, he could've cared less if I was sober or wasted, as long as I wasn't passed out. Maybe he thought I was the type of girl you call the next day, a repeater.

Sorry, I wasn't that kind of girl. *Sex,* I told myself once more, *it's only sex.* By the way his boxers were tented, it was going to be *fantastic* sex.

His lips stayed glued to mine as he pushed me back toward the bed. I felt the edge of the mattress meet the back of my knees and was tempted to fall back and pull him with me. He gripped the zipper on the back of my dress and eased it down, his other hand on my skin as soon as it was exposed. Fingers splayed, he followed the length of my spine as he pulled the zipper down the rest of the way. Hooking a finger under the strap, he slid the material off of one shoulder and then the next. The weight of the dress carried itself down to pile at my feet.

The only time our lips separated was when I tried to slip out of my heels, working the strap down my left heel with the toe of my right foot.

But before I could get them off, he barked, "Leave them on." His voice was commanding, a complete change from the man I had met in the club.

I loved it.

He reached around, searching for the clasp of my bra. Since my mouth was occupied, I brought my arm up between us to unhook the front clasp. He gripped my wrist and placed it at my side before coming up between us to free my aching breasts. Both were in his hands like he was testing the weight of them. He was gentle, a thumb grazing across a nipple, causing me to moan.

Forget the foreplay! My body screamed. I needed him to satisfy me already.

Lifting my hands to his shirt, I started working the buttons. Blaize helped and a few popped off into the room somewhere. His body was mesmerizing, and I hoped I'd have a chance to study it more later. His arms, chest, abdomen, and sides were inked in colorful artwork and beautiful script.

Bringing my hands to his boxer briefs, I hooked my thumbs and inched them over his erection and down as far as I could get them without breaking our connection. My fingers wrapped around his smooth, large shaft before sliding down the length of him, measuring, appreciating. His low groan vibrated against my tongue, causing the ache between my thighs to consume me. His fingers dipped down and stroked over my panties. *Ah, a little relief.* I pushed into him, needing more pressure.

He accommodated for a moment and then removed his hand. *Fuck!* The loss pissed me off, and I released him from my grip, pulling away from his kiss. He grabbed me by the hips, his fingers digging into my flesh as he guided me back onto the bed. I scooted back while he crawled over me until I reached a pillow and laid my head back. Without missing a beat, he snapped the thin fabric of my thong and tossed the ruined material aside.

What's with these dudes murdering my panties? I scowled at him. *They're expensive and it'll cost you.*

A large, rough palm started at my calf and traveled up to my knee. He stopped there for a moment, dipping his head between my legs and glancing up to meet my gaze. It was almost embarrassing to be so turned on. I squirmed, eager to feel his fingers on me, in me. Without warning, he drew a languid stroke with his tongue from bottom to top. My back arched as I whimpered in pleasure, clenching his comforter with both fists.

A good lover always took care of the lady first, and he did just that. After finishing me off, he flipped me over like a ragdoll and took what he needed. I pretended not to appreciate the way he was slamming into me like a cheap whore—knowing that was what he needed to get off—but it was what *I* needed, too. Breathing through the building sensations only intensified them, and I had to bite down on the pillow to stay quiet.

Blaize Martin would never know he made me come twice. Wonderful son of a bitch.

***

In the middle of the night, I watched Blaize sleep. The suckers always begged me to stay, promising waffles the next morning. I knew how to play the game, doe-eyed and appreciative for not making me hail a cab in the middle of the night. I mean, I lived off island after all; at least that's what I had them believe. His breathing was slow and even, but just to make sure I ran my hand along the length of his arm. No movement. Thank God he wasn't a cuddler. Heavy arms draped across my body drove me insane and it took forever to escape their grip, moving inch by inch and stuffing a pillow under their arm to replace myself. Instead, Blaize was turned away from me, on his side of the bed, dreaming of marshmallow clouds . . . or whatever it was that tattooed weightlifters dreamed about.

Slinking out of bed, I scavenged for every piece of my clothing and carried the handful, plus Blaize's wallet, to the living room. Once I was dressed, I flipped through his wallet and found two crisp hundred dollar bills, a twenty, and five ones. His living room didn't offer much, but I found an ornate knife on a shelf. It was resting in a red velvet case and looked like it had never been touched. The handle appeared to be solid gold with ornate carvings and gems. I wondered if it was a movie prop or the real deal. For some reason, I didn't lift it. Next to it was what I assumed to be a picture of his grandfather dressed in a military uniform.

At fifteen minutes to five in the morning, I decided to put the money back into Blaize's wallet—a first for me. At ten minutes to five, I broke my most important, vital, number one, unbreakable rule: I found a piece of paper and scribbled a note:

Thanks for a good time. I'll be at Muse next Saturday night. ~Bree

But just before stepping through the front door, I turned around, lifted the note, wadded it into a tight ball, and stuffed it into my purse. The most important thing about one night stands: they were never repeated.

Chapter 10

Anna

The bartending position at Mix was already filled when I arrived Friday afternoon. Saturday I interviewed for an IT position where I would be able to work from home, but it wasn't a good fit for me and the money was lousy. That afternoon, I walked to a local farmer's market to gather fresh fruits and vegetables. The colors and smells lit up my senses and added a skip to my step.

On the way home, I passed by the cutest flower shop and decided to step inside. A bell hanging over the door frame chimed as I entered, and a blonde with bubble gum pink lipstick popped her head up. She was leaning over the counter, reading a magazine and chewing a piece of gum like it was her mission.

"Can I help you?"

"Just passing by and wanted to see what you had," I answered, offering a smile. Immediately, I spotted a section of orchids and strolled over to admire them.

"Are you looking for something in particular?" The blonde closed the space between us and straightened one of the pots.

"No, just admiring. Floral design is a hobby of mine." Dipping my head, I inhaled a pot of gardenias before moving on to the rose section.

"Have any experience arranging?"

"I do."

"They're looking for someone to help out part-time." The blonde blew a bubble and then sucked it back into her mouth.

"Really?" For the first time, I looked up and studied her. She was young, early twenties. Her stick straight hair was cut just above her shoulders and tucked behind her ears.

"I am looking for some work. Is the pay decent?"

The blonde shrugged a shoulder. "Pays my bills." She strolled back to the counter and returned with a business card. "Give Harry a call. He's a sweet old man, but I'll put in a good word for you just in case."

"Thanks." I offered a grateful smile and started to give her my hand but changed my mind last minute. "I'm Anna, by the way."

"Claire." She shoved her hands deep into the pockets of her Bermuda shorts. "I hope you get it," she looked unfazed. "I could use some time off."

"I hope so too, Claire." Pulling a plant with tiny white flowers from the shelf, I carried them to the counter. "And I'll take these."

Chapter 11

Anna

Two weeks ago I got the job at the flower shop and I was enjoying every second. Arranging colorful flowers with berries and greenery in oversized vases. Wrapping ribbon around wedding bouquets stuffed with white roses, gardenias, and bouvardia. All of it was right up my alley. I had always dreamed of opening my own floral shop one day. Having the place to myself most of the time allowed me to pretend and envision that dream.

Harry, the owner, was the cutest old man I'd ever met. He kept his white hair short and combed to one side. His short sleeved button down was always freshly pressed and tucked in, but he wore white sneakers with neon green trim every day. What made me truly love him was his personality. He had that spunky wit to match his shoes. His wife Gertie had passed away ten years ago. "But I'll never marry again," he'd said in the back of the shop just before we opened on one of the busiest Saturdays of the season. The kindness in his eyes faded to a dull sadness that you felt in your bones. "No one can ever take the place of my Gertie."

I couldn't imagine anyone that would take him at his age, but I loved how loyal he was to her. That kind of love didn't come around often, and I loved watching his face light up as he talked about her.

"Not many get to experience a love like ours." He lifted a fully bloomed gardenia to his nose, closed his eyes, and breathed in. Smiling, he said, "She loved hard and deep, and for fifty years she took care of me." He lifted a small frame from a shelf behind him, gazing at the picture for a long moment before shoving it into my hands. "That's her. She was nineteen, waitressing at a diner. I made my buddy go with me every Saturday and eat a piece of pie so I could talk to her."

"She's beautiful." She was. Black hair swept up on top of her head, porcelain skin, and the longest lashes I'd seen on a woman.

"She didn't want to marry me at first." His chest puffed up like he was proud that she had refused him. "I had to work for her. But she was worth it." He took the picture back, shaking his head as he looked at her. "Worth every piece of that damn chocolate pie." Glancing up at me, he wore a wide grin. "It was chunky or lumpy." He waved his hand in the air. "She never could get the lumps out. Cooked it too long or something. But I swallowed it down with a proud smile . . . every Saturday for almost sixty years . . ." His voice trailed off as he traced her face with his finger.

I gulped just watching him. I never wanted to feel that kind of heartache, the loss of the most significant love of your life, but I desperately wanted to feel the depth of that kind of love.

CROWDED

"Thank you for sharing that story with me," I said. "I can only hope to have a love like yours and Gertie's one day."

"I know you will. All you have to do is—" Before he could finish, the bell above the front door chimed and he was lost in another thought, rummaging through a filing cabinet as if he'd forgotten I was there.

Tiptoeing backward, I joined Claire up front and began filling orders. Prom was a demanding season, but I loved what I did and time sailed by when we were busy. I got to know Claire a little better as we worked, finding out that she was in art school, hoping to make it as a painter. I'd have to remember to ask about her work, see if she'd show it to me. She was dating a fellow artist, someone she'd met in night school, who owned a tattoo shop and a motorcycle. I didn't envy her lifestyle, but it made for interesting conversation.

"Do you have any?" I asked, making a pink rose and boronia corsage. "Tattoos."

"Three," she nodded. "One on my back, one on the ribs, and one on my left foot."

"Which one hurt the most?"

She wrapped a single white rose with green floral tape, added a pearl stick pin, and closed it up in a clear box. "Ribs." After sticking a label on top of the box, she pulled up her shirt and showed me the ink scripted across her side. "Motherfucker hurt like hell. I thought I would die before it was over."

I laughed and shook my head. "That was the last one then?"

"No," she pulled her shirt back down and smoothed it with her hand. "It was the first one. Within six months I was desperate for another. It's addicting."

"The pain is addicting?" My brows cinched together. She was a little on the goth side, in an artsy way, but she didn't look like the masochist type at all.

"No, the ink." She shook her head, smirking at me. "It's a way for me to express myself, put my thoughts and shit on my body. I'm an artist, and I've got more than one thought, so . . ."

"Let me see the others," I asked.

The one on her foot was a haiku she wrote, and the one on her back was an entire garden of floral. It mesmerized me and I could've studied it all day.

"How long did this take?" I asked, tracing my finger along an intricate red peony.

"Three weeks." She peeked her head over her shoulder to admire her back. "We had to go in stages. First the outline, then color. It took longer than it should have because Noah did me after hours. Plus, he was a pussy and stopped every time I grimaced."

"How long have you been together?"

Her eyes brightened when she looked up and flashed a grin. "Six months. But we're close, we've—"

The bell above the door rang and we both looked up to see a man walking in. He was dressed like a preppy frat boy in khakis and a plaid shirt, his ball cap pulled around backwards.

"Help you?" Claire asked.

"Yeah, I need a dozen roses." He paused. "Actually, make it two."

"Sure." Claire dropped her head and whispered so only I could hear, "Wonder what he did."

I chuckled softly. "I don't know, but two dozen roses mean it's serious. And if it's that serious, flowers aren't going to undo whatever sin he committed."

We shared a look that replaced the cackle that would've been inappropriate. Claire pulled two dozen roses from the cooler. "Want these in a vase or wrapped?"

He leaned across the counter, a too strong scent of Kouros cologne wafting in the air, and gave Claire a seductive look, then turned the same look on me. "What would you dolls prefer?"

I wanted to make a gagging sound. *I'd prefer to see them shoved up your ass.*

I watched Claire bite her lip, barely holding it together as she got him to throw down as much money as possible. "Honestly, plain roses are so cliché. I'd do a vase of red roses, purple orchids, and white phalaenopsis." She offered the sweetest smile and I wondered if he would catch the venom she hid behind it. "No matter what you've done, she'll forgive you with the arrangement I can put together."

By his response, I was pretty sure all he heard was 'arrangement' and 'together'.

"Can you?" He looked back and forth between me and Claire, his eyes darkening with the hope of getting us in bed together. He sized us both up, dragging his eyes up my body and back down hers. "What do you say we—"

I interrupted before one of us smashed the closest vase over his head. "The gardenias smell divine right now. Let's add a few of those, too. Your girl will be very happy."

Claire and I left the snake at the counter while we collected the stems. I couldn't help but feel sorry for the girl on the receiving end.

"Asshole!" Claire said, plucking sprigs of boronia from their container like splinters. "Can you believe the way he was looking at us, like we would take him in the back and make a porno?"

"I can't take it." I palmed my forehead. My vision of working in a floral shop had been sweet and lovely. Little old men buying anniversary arrangements for their mates, guys picking out something special for that first date. Never did I imagine a tool like the one out front. "I hope his girlfriend knees him in the junk and throws the vase at him." I shook my head in protest and huffed out a laugh. "Actually, knee him in the junk and keep the flowers, girlfriend, they're gorgeous."

Claire was nothing like me, the polar opposite probably, but we were on the same page when it came to assholes, flowers, and coffee—sort of. She loved the brew as much as I did, and we filled up on it every time we worked together. She liked it black, and I liked it loaded with sugar and cream. I giggled to myself when I compared it to our taste in men. I definitely preferred the sweeter brew when it came to dating, but imagined her tatted biker boyfriend was the stronger, rob-the-pot, tar brew. I'd never met him, so it was speculation of course. I hoped Claire and I would become friends, get to know each other more. If we did, I'd probably meet her boyfriend. And who knew, maybe they could hook me up. A double date would be nice.

Chapter 12

Bree

A week passed and all I could think about was fucking Blaize. Thursday night, I looked for him in the eyes of Ryan. Friday, I tried to imagine Hayden's hands were rough and determined the way Blaize's had been. Since I wasn't satisfied, I also hooked up with a girl named Addison in a back room. It was so easy to please a woman, knowing exactly what you liked yourself and performing it on her. No matter how hard she tried, though, she couldn't get me off, so I stormed out and went home with a lumberjack-type named Ian. He reminded me of Blaize, other than the color of his eyes. And if he hadn't talked to me during sex, I would've made it through my fantasy the way I had intended. Instead, he ruined it with his voice, and it wasn't even the kind of dirty talk that flipped my switch. So I took all the cash in his wallet, a mediocre watch, and his platinum edition Star Wars DVD collection. I lifted that last item just to piss him off.

I was off my game.

One more fix with Blaize was all I needed. Hopefully he'd show up at The Dark Room, and I could finally get him out of my head. This time I'd take that damn knife and see what else I could find.

***

Another week passed uneventfully. In fact, I didn't remember much about it, thankfully. Friday night, Infinity was popping but didn't have a line outside. A cool breeze greeted me as I stepped through the door, masking for a moment the stale stench of cigarette smoke and a muddled fusion of cologne.

An older couple laid a few bills on the bar and left two stools for me to choose from. I took the one farthest from the wall and ordered a Kettle One, extra dirty. Scanning the bar, I noticed several targets. An older man, probably in his late fifties, with peppered hair and a dinner jacket that needed to be pressed. This place was out of character for his type, so I was certain he was here for the same reasons I was.

Easy target, if needed.

Across the bar, I spotted three young guys, all dark-headed. The one in the middle possessed enough confidence for all three and showed it in his full right arm tattoo sleeve. He was good looking but knew it, and I could tell just by looking at him that he was terrible in bed. Dude to his right was a tool in his flannel shirt and ball cap turned around backward. It was the one on the other side that intrigued me, and I found myself staring, trying to figure him out.

He was wearing a plain black T-shirt, his concentration on the television. His movements and lack of interest in the conversations going on around him stumped me. At first, I thought he was socially awkward, but when he ordered another round for his buddies—the control in his voice and the way the bartender left two cosmos in the shakers to fetch three beers for them—I knew there was something to him. He was bored, in control, and always got what he wanted. Why? Because he was filthy rich.

Bingo!

It didn't do much for my confidence trying to get his attention. In fact, it was the first time my two-second gaze hadn't worked. I needed this guy. Needed the money. But it wasn't happening so I moved on. The older guy was much easier. One glance and he was buying me a drink. He turned out to be very interesting with a great sense of humor. Before I knew it, I'd finished my drink and my cheeks were hurting from laughing so much.

A light tap on my forearm jerked me out of my good time. I looked up to see the bartender sliding a shot glass toward me. "From the gentleman." He nodded toward the threesome and tapped his finger on the napkin sitting beneath the shot glass.

"What is it?" I asked.

"Goldschläger."

Before making eye contact with my big spender, I read what was penned on the napkin.

Meet me outside.

Three words. Commanding words. I hated them. I loved them. It was refreshing to let someone else have control, but at the same time it pissed me off.

Tapping my fingernails on the bar, I contemplated whether or not to go. The whole reason I had come out was to make some money. I could've been wrong about him. He might've been a twenty-five-year-old still living with his parents. On the other hand, I had also come out to get laid. He *could* meet that need. But was it worth wasting a sure thing with my old guy?

Sex or money, sex or money?

Fuck it.

Picking up the shot glass, I made eye contact with him, brought the glass to my lips, and swallowed the silky liquid down. "Well," I scooted my stool back and stood, patting my bar companion's leg. "Thanks for the company." Before he could say a word, I turned and walked outside.

Mr. Goldschläger was right behind me as I leaned against the brick building and lit a Marlboro Silver. Filling my lungs with the minty nicotine instantly calmed any nerves that tried to rattle me.

He didn't say a word as he joined me on the wall, hiking one foot up behind him and resting back. He would've reminded me of James Dean in that position, but he had a hint of dork in his appearance up close. Instead, he reminded me of Jay Baruchel from *The Sorcerer's Apprentice*. Dark eyes and hair that went in every direction. Had he even taken time to brush it? He had a long face but full lips to balance his features.

He blew out a stream of smoke and exhaled his name, "Constantine. My friends call me Gus." There it was. A hint of darkness swirling through him, just enough to balance the dork.

After another pull of my cigarette, I leaned my head back, exhaling toward the sky. "Bree."

The valet brought his car around, a sleek black Lexus. Just as I suspected, he had money. "Shall we?" he asked, kicking off the wall.

Just before I climbed into the car, I got the distinct feeling someone was watching me. There were people everywhere, but no one in particular stood out. It wasn't the first time the hairs on the back of my neck tingled, the eerie feeling of someone following my every move.

I slid into the passenger seat, the leather cool on my bare legs, and tugged the hem of my white dress before Constantine made his way to the driver's side. Pulling the seatbelt strap around my chest, I clicked it into place. I had no idea where we were going, and the most important question I wanted to ask was, "How did you get Gus out of Constantine?"

"Middle name."

"The name and accent," I toyed with him. "Greek?"

Apparently Gus wasn't into fun. He nodded, keeping his eyes on the road as he weaved in and out of traffic. "Another club or my place?" he asked as if giving me a choice of red wine or white. He was throwing me off my game, and I didn't like it. I needed to regain control and there was only one way to do that—sex.

"Your place."

***

Gus pulled the car up to the curb in front of his apartment on the upper west side and killed the engine. By the looks of the building, his apartment was going to blow my mind. I only hoped he wasn't one of those that kept all of his valuables hidden behind paintings in a wall safe. The last two weeks had been exhausting, so an easy in and out was second on my wish list. Every now and then I let the idea of being an escort make its case. I'd easily make the money I needed and wouldn't have to work as hard with the mind games. Not having to wait for my victim to fall asleep before I collected my earnings was a nice fantasy. But the notion always left before it found root. Knowing I'd have to give up control and share the money I'd worked for was a firm thumbs down. No way would I give some bitch a percentage of my earnings for sitting behind a desk with a little black book. My way was best. Always. Another thing—perhaps the most important reason I did things my way—was my mother. I watched men climb in and out of her bed. She didn't choose which ones came through the door, or what they were allowed to do to her body. The price was the same, no matter the fantasy or fetish, and her pimp got most of it. I had no respect for my mother, but she did teach me one very important thing: never be like her.

"Let me come around and get your door." He tossed his keys into the air and caught them with his right hand before getting out of the car. I loathed his confidence. The way he jogged around the car to my door like he was freeing me from a life of mediocrity and eager to share what he had. I knew he was picturing himself rocking my world like no other. Fucker wasn't worth my time. He didn't have anything I needed, or wanted.

Except that one thing: money.

Before we even stepped inside, I knew his apartment was beautiful. I could tell by the intricate wooden door that had to be hand carved.

"Beautiful," I said, tracing my fingers along the swirled edging.

"France." He slipped the key into the lock, turned it until I heard a click, and pushed the door open. It didn't take as much effort to move the massive door as I imagined.

We stepped through, into the foyer. Two lamps on a black granite table lit the space, and I took a moment to look around the modern space. Dark floors, dark furniture, ornate gold frames that wrapped around oil paintings that didn't make sense to me. *Probably paid a fortune.* The sound of the door closing echoed through the space, and I turned to meet Gus's cocky grin.

"What've you got to drink—" I started to ask, but he was on me before I could finish. He twirled me around to face the wall, gripped my wrists in one of his hands, and pinned my arms overhead.

"You're so damn sexy." His mouth was so close, I could feel his hot breath moisten the delicate flesh of my ear.

He wanted me to feel his strength as he pressed his body into mine, letting me know he was in control. I was fully charged, desperate for more of the excitement pressing into my ass, but I had to regain control. I couldn't do this otherwise.

Something shut down inside of me when a man forced too much control. There was a fine line between rough sex and overpowering someone. One was enjoyable; the other pulled at a thread that was mentally disastrous for me.

Trying to regain some power, I pushed my ass out and ground into him. A deep groan escaped his lips.

"Tell me what you want." Hot breath cascaded over the back of my neck, teeth scraping against my shoulder. I hated this game. He knew what I wanted.

A drink. A bowl of vanilla bean ice cream. A man who knows what I want and doesn't have to ask.

"You." Parts of you, anyway.

With his free hand, he brushed my hair off to the side, exposing my neck. His movements were slow and calculated, heightening my excitement, but at the same time, fear. He pulled at the zipper on the back of my dress, inching it down until he reached the small of my back. Coarse fingertips brushed against my skin as he took his hand off the zipper and released my hands. I remained still, waiting for him to slide the material off, but there was no movement, only the sound of his breathing behind me.

When I dropped my head and looked around, I found him sitting in a chair against the opposite wall, watching me, arms folded across his chest. Did he expect me to dance? Not happening.

Shoulders back, I stalked through the large apartment and found his bar. He followed, but didn't say a word as I poured liquid from a crystal decanter into a glass and swallowed back the contents. Brandy. Peach, if I had to guess. It was delicious, so I poured two more and offered one to Gus.

"Do you have a bedroom?" I asked, ready to get this over with. He had a way of draining the fun from the night with his strange quirks.

With a quick glance, I spotted several items small enough to pocket and definitely worth some major change. Tonight wouldn't be a total loss, either way.

He sipped half of the brandy in his glass, took my hand, and led me down a long, narrow hallway to his bedroom. Black and gold seemed to be his favorite colors as was the theme throughout. But his bedroom was a contrast. The bedding was stark white against silver walls. Three large photographs framed in glossy black, hung on the wall behind the bed frame. When looked at as a whole, it was the backside of a naked woman lying on her side.

Before Gus could make a move, I pushed my palms onto his chest and urged him to sit on the black leather bench at the foot of the bed. Holding his gaze, I slipped the dress off my shoulders, letting my hands trail over my flesh behind the falling fabric. When the dress piled around my feet, I stepped around it and turned away from him. Bending over, my ass in view but out of reach, I unclasped the straps of my heels, taking my time to drive him insane and hopefully ensure that he didn't last long.

Slinging my hair back as I stood, I turned to face Gus. His dark eyes were a demonic black, glazed with lust and boring into me like a predator about to devour his prey. My heart rate kicked up into the warning stage, my fight or flight response begging me to flee. But the excitement was too much, and I made the mistake of letting a whimper slip from my lips.

He was on his feet in an instant, pulling my body into his, and something took over. A force I couldn't have won, so I didn't try fighting it. We came together powerfully, tongues tasting, taking, consuming. Our mouths only parted long enough to pull his shirt over his head while I worked the button and zipper of his slacks, using my foot to push them the rest of the way down so I didn't have to break the kiss.

My arms wrapped around his neck as his hands slid around my waist. He lifted me up, wrapping my legs around his hips as he made his way to the side of the bed and set me down on the raised king-sized bed.

I reached for the waistband of his boxer briefs, but he stopped me and stepped back. "Not yet."

He wedged himself between my legs and unlatched my black lace bra. Moving tortuously slow, he swept his fingers across my shoulders, sliding one strap down and then the other. A surge of energy coursed through me, desperate for him to touch my exposed nipples. It was obviously a game for him, holding back, making me squirm. He traced a finger between my breasts, down my stomach, and over the lace trim of my panties.

I watched the heat behind his eyes build, his chest heaving with each erratic breath, and every ounce of the self-control he was trying to maintain drain from his body. Gus pulled his boxers off and guided me back onto the bed. He raked his gaze over every inch of my body before hooking his fingers into the waistband of my panties and sliding them down my legs. At least he knew how to take them off.

He reached for protection on the bedside table and handed it to me. I carefully put it on him. He crawled on top of me and laid me back, positioning himself at my seam. After pushing in the tip, he paused to move my legs farther apart before filling me completely.

My favorite part of sex was the end. Hearing a man moan, calling out my name, his body tensing and contracting because of what I'd done to him. Yes, that was the best part. Control.

He moved in and out like a piston, his pace increasing as he thrust harder with determination to find his release. He was a selfish lover, like a lot of them were, so I'd have to take control of my own pleasure. Slipping my hands between us, I pushed him up until he got the hint, holding himself over me on his hands rather than elbows. Now I had the room to pleasure myself while he rammed into me. A wicked grin crept over his lips when he saw what was happening.

"That's right, doll." He thrust harder.

It was painful, but as I got closer to release, my endorphins kicked in, making my body believe the pain was pleasurable. Once I was dangerously close to the edge, I arched my back and whimpered each time he filled me like he was the best I'd ever had. It worked every time, egotistical bastard.

"Fuck," he groaned as he thrust into me one last time, gripping one edge of the pillow beneath my head until his body calmed. Then he rolled off and collapsed beside me, a satisfied chuckle whooshing out with his breath.

Eager to get home, I slung my legs over the side of the bed and sat up. It was too early to feel this sore, so I knew I'd need to soak away the pain in a hot bath as soon as I got back to my apartment. I had planned to wait for him to fall asleep, rob him of everything I could stuff in my bag, but the little warning alerts from earlier were now screaming for me to get the hell out of there.

"Where do you think you're going?" Strong arms pulled me back down for another round.

I tried to pull away, but he was already deaf to my protest and blind with desire.

Fuck. It was time for Plan B. Too bad I didn't really have a Plan B. The only thing I could think of was liquor, it knocked most men on their ass trying to keep up with me. They had no idea I wasn't really consuming the liquid. I'd pour, we'd both gulp it down, and when I returned to the bar to pour another, I spit the contents into the sink.

"Just getting us a drink, lover." I let the back of my hand stroke down the length of his arm before rolling out of bed and heading toward the bar.

Chapter 13

Bree

The first blow didn't hurt—a backhand so forceful I found myself folded over the back of a leather couch, gripping at the slippery cushions. I knew the sting would come later, once my nerve endings received the message my brain was sending. All I could think about was making sure he didn't do it again.

"I'm not into that, asshole." The words ground out through my clenched teeth.

He had been out cold after three rounds of the roughest sex I'd ever experienced. I couldn't understand how he was standing here, in the middle of the night. It had to be after two. I'd been rummaging through his stuff for a good forty-five minutes and he hadn't even stirred. Yet there he was, wide-eyed and crazed. *Drugs.* I could see a white residue beneath one of his nostrils. *Cocaine?* When had he gotten out of bed, had the time to snort coke, and how long had he been watching me?

He narrowed his eyes. "No one steals from me, bitch."

There it was, the sting of his hand on my left cheek. It crept up my flesh and took residency in my eye, fingering out to every nerve like fire ants on a mission. My eye was going to explode if I didn't get some pressure on it.

Before I could push myself off the couch and upright, Gus gripped the back of my hair and swung me around to face him. A man of his stature and level of rage was a force to be feared. But I couldn't let him see the uneasiness or give him the upper hand.

How did he know I had emptied his wallet? Did the man sleep with his eyes open? "I didn't steal anything from—"

Red faced and wide eyed, he lunged forward, wrapping his fingers around my neck with his right hand. As the pressure increased, my windpipe began to crush beneath his grip. At first it felt like I was choking on a piece of steak lodged where his fingers pressed inward. In a few seconds that feeling was replaced by an intense burning in my chest, my lungs desperate for oxygen. It didn't take long to feel dizzy, the clutch of death too close.

Think. Fight.

But as hard as I tried, I couldn't pry his fingers away from my throat. In a few moments, I'd lose consciousness and wouldn't have the option to fight.

This was not how I was meant to go out—weak and controlled by a man. This was *my* game and no one had beaten me at it.

Anger over the impending defeat took over. With renewed strength—if only an ounce—I gave him all I had with a knee to the groin. He flinched, but I hadn't hurt him as much as I needed to. The cocaine must've affected his pain tolerance and added to his strength. Another knee to the groin got me knocked across the room. My head came down hard onto the marble fireplace. I felt the pain immediately, but at least I was out of his grip and could gulp in a few agonizing breaths of air.

My hand went up to cover the most painful spot—my forehead—where blood seeped through my fingers too quickly.

The room wouldn't be still and tiny flecks of silver darted before my eyes.

He was going to kill me.

I was about to die on his cold hardwoods. I wondered what he would do with my body. Wrap me in a carpet and let me sink to the bottom of the river? Or maybe he'd toss me in a dumpster with no regard for my body. No one would miss me. I had no family to wonder where I'd gone or why I hadn't checked in. I was going to die alone.

Blackness began to consume me, a taste of my fate. Then I remembered I didn't believe in fate. A person made choices, created their own fate.

Next to me on the floor, I spotted a decorative brass elephant. It looked heavy. I felt another presence in the room—the person who had been following me. *She's back.* Just as I closed my hand around the base, darkness enfolded me.

Chapter 14

Anna

Every Thursday for the past two months, I looked forward to coffee with Pratt. He had to miss last week because of an exam so I was eager to see his smile, feel his presence. There was something about him that brightened my mood and made me feel safe and warm in a world full of frigid strangers.

It was unseasonably cool for June, so I wrapped myself in an oversized cashmere sweater. Dark clouds dimmed the sky and leaked a spray of constant rain that had already lasted two days. Gripping my umbrella, I tried to hold it at an angle, blocking the rain that came in at a slant. It didn't do much to protect my legs, though, and by the time I made it to the coffee shop, I felt like a drowned rat. Opening the door to the shop, the rich aroma of coffee greeted me, instantly mollified me with its promise. Pratt was already at the counter when I arrived, so I stole a glance at his fine backside before he turned to see who was coming through the door. His smile lit up his face, lit up my world. Claiming our corner table, I watched him walk toward me with a coffee in each hand.

"Nonfat latte, one pump caramel, one pump hazelnut for the lady." Pratt slid my coffee onto the table and took the seat across from me. A smile crept across my face and bled into my pores, heating me to the core. He did something to me and I loved it. As long as he was near, I could weather the harsh New York winters with ease.

"You remembered the extra whip, right?" I teased, raising an eyebrow.

The look of shock on his face made me giggle. He'd been so confident about getting my order right. He reached for my cup, but I stopped him. "I'm kidding. I hate whipped cream."

Pratt blew out a breath, relief washing over his face, and smiled. "That's the most un-American thing I've ever heard." He shook his head and leaned back, studying the oddity before him. "What am I going to do with you this winter? I can't share a hot chocolate moment with someone who'll ask for it without mini marshmallows and whipped cream."

An electric charge chased through my veins, knowing that he thought of me in the future. "I didn't mean that I had an aversion to whipped cream," I offered. "It just doesn't go with coffee."

"Good." His lips pulled into a satisfied smirk. "Maybe there's room for you in the cool crowd, after all." He winked and my coffee lodged in my throat, refusing to ease down without threatening a choking scene.

I gulped the liquid down and coughed into my fist. "Wrong tube."

Pratt was easy to talk to since we had no expectations. We had developed a connection, a possibility. These last few weeks, it hadn't taken long for me to stick my toe out and smudge the imaginary line in the sand that kept us in the friend zone.

"Tell me about your day." He leaned back, slung an arm over the back of his chair, and gave me his full attention as I explained the latest drama at the floral shop.

"Mrs. S didn't like the funeral wreath she ordered, so I had to add more calla lilies and take out all of the daisies she originally insisted on." I rolled my eyes. "Your turn. Tell me something exciting. Anything." I tipped back my cup, sucking the last drops of goodness onto my tongue.

"You know I finish up my residency in three years and I'll be able to have my own practice?" I nodded with shared excitement for him. "So, I've been researching something really exciting."

"Tell me," I begged eagerly.

He leaned forward, his expression serious. "It stays between us."

I agreed with a nod, wondering who he thought I would share it with.

"There may be a way to curb the cravings of drug addiction." His eyes lit up as he spoke. "I'm part of a team studying the effects of a new drug on meth addicts. We think it'll work on all drug addictions."

I felt something deflate inside of me. His news wasn't as exciting as I hoped. I'd never known anyone who'd done meth, so my level of understanding was slim. But I watched

Pratt's mouth as he detailed the research process, his lips moving faster and his pitch rising the more excited he got as he told me about the process. His face radiated joy and that was enough for me.

***

Each Thursday, when my cup was empty, I dreaded the next six days without him. We didn't call each other or text between coffee dates. Our lives went on without the company of the other until we met at our corner table the following week.

I wanted more, or at least I wanted to test the water and see if we had what it would take to handle more. But I had so stubbornly put my foot down in the beginning, I couldn't find a classy way to lift it. And Pratt was the kind of guy that respected a woman's wishes. He wouldn't make the first move unless given the go ahead.

Giving the go ahead would be my responsibility, which put the ball right back in my court. I hated sports, so what the hell was I supposed to do with that damn ball now that it was in my court? I'd have to make the move. But take my stubbornness, add a dash of insecurity, and we were at an impasse.

Sitting across from Pratt while he filled me in on his week, I couldn't help the frown, dragging my features downward. I'd always heard the good and bad voices in my head, just like everyone did. My subconscious, rooting me on to move to a new city, all alone. *You can do it!* Or that same voice that was now telling me I was worthless. And if I suggested something deeper with Pratt, he'd spit his coffee out like I'd just told the most hilarious joke.

Forget it.

My knuckles whitened as I gripped the edge of the table, trying to keep my expression flat and hush the battle inside.

"I can't stay. I'm sorry, I forgot about a large flower order I need to start on." I stood and collected my trash.

"Oh, okay." Pratt seemed disappointed, which should have made me feel good, knowing that he wanted to spend time with me. But I hated knowing that I put that crestfallen look on his face. "I'll see you next week?"

I nodded and tried to look cheerful, when all I felt was pain and regret.

Pratt stood and smiled, but it didn't reach his eyes as he watched me walk away.

As I rounded the corner, I stole a glance at him. He was still sitting at our table, finishing his coffee and scrolling through his phone. Why did I always have to make everything difficult?

Because he's too important to screw it up.

There was no flower order to fill of course, so I hailed a cab and asked the driver to take me to St. Mary's, an assisted living center that I had been visiting twice a week. Being an orphan myself, my heart bled for widows living alone. I couldn't do the nursing homes. I'd tried, but they were too much like a hospital. The assisted living center, however, was more like an apartment setting. The only difference was they took their meals in the on-site restaurant rather than having cooking privileges. Mary Elliot and I connected immediately when we'd met five weeks ago. That day she'd been sitting on the front porch, knitting, before I'd walked in to ask the front desk who was in need of some company.

"Who are you here to see, kid?" she asked, glancing up briefly before going back to her yarn and needles.

"I don't know yet."

She stopped rocking, ceased knitting, and looked up with a squinted eye. "What do you mean, you don't know?"

I shrugged a shoulder. "I wanted to see if there was anyone that could use some company."

She glanced up, her expression flat. "Ah, looking to fill your charity duties."

I frowned. The woman confused me. I wouldn't peg her as a mean older lady, but she seemed to speak her mind freely. "No, it's not like that at all. I—"

"Well, sit down if you're going to talk to me, kid." She patted the seat next to her and offered a kind, but impatient smile." My old neck can't take the strain of looking up at you all day."

She was bold and crass and lovely all at the same time. She had to be in her late seventies, maybe early eighties, but she wore a short blond curly wig and her makeup was flawless.

It was then that I gave her everything, for some reason. Maybe because I thought I'd never see her again. Maybe because I didn't even know her name. Or maybe because I was that desperate for a friend.

"You want to know the truth?" I asked.

"Nah, just make something up. But make it good," she dared me. "I don't have much living left to do." She giggled, and then the dam was loosed. I believe I spewed fourteen thousand words in one sentence.

"I just moved here and I only have one friend." I shrugged a shoulder and leaned back in the rocking chair I had taken next to her. "Well, two, if you count the girl I work with. But I don't count that. So I'm lonely, you know. Did I tell you my only friend is a man? So I can't really talk to him. He's really good looking, too, which doesn't help matters. And I came here because I wanted to find someone who needed company, but the truth is I need someone to keep me company." After going on and on about my move and breakup, I heaved out an exhausted sigh and waited for her to smack me around with her old lady wisdom.

Instead, she told me about the devastation of her husband's death and how their only child was too busy with his new wife and baby to visit her. "They moved to Florida. Where it's warm. Why the hell they left me up here to freeze to death is beyond me." She puffed out a sarcastic laugh. "His wife is smart. A bitch, but smart. She manipulated him into leaving me up here. Probably for the best." She shrugged a shoulder. "I would've kicked her tiny, liposuctioned ass and spent my last days in prison."

Laughter took over, the heaviness of all I'd just shared with her melting with each giggle. "I'm Anna." I stuck out my hand and she gripped it hard.

The corners of her eyes wrinkled when she smiled, "We're going to make a good team, Anna. Glad to meet you. I'm Mary."

I tried to visit Mary twice a week, and had only missed once in the five weeks since we met. Today, while Mary was at the salon, I visited with Emma, one of the nurses. She was younger than me, with a cute caramel-colored bob that accentuated her high cheek bones and an over-the-top personality.

"I didn't know you were coming in today." Her hair bounced while she talked. "Mary will be away for a few hours, but I'm glad you're here." Emma wore a wide grin that melted my sour mood immediately. She seemed truly elated to see me and I felt the same.

"Em—"

"I'm so excited to see you, Anna." She was practically bouncing in her navy blue Crocs. "I almost called you last night, but I didn't know how you'd feel about me looking up your number. And now you're here, so . . ." She stepped closer, a skip in her step until she reached me. I braced myself for what I thought would be a hug—we hadn't hugged before, so I wasn't sure why she would do it now—when she flung her hand out toward me. "Look! I'm engaged!" A large round stone sat atop her ring finger. It was brilliant with that brand new sparkle.

For a moment, I was so jealous I hated her. But I snapped out of it and managed a smile. She deserved a great life, a happy life, and I was obliged to celebrate this joy with her.

"Can you believe it?" she gushed. "Ben asked me last night. It was magical. First he took me to the marina and . . ." she went on, and I tried to listen.

My heart knotted with envy, and I had to lift my eyebrows, faking excitement to keep them from pinching together in disappointment. First, one of the baristas in my coffee shop, then the lady in my apartment building with the fake boobs, and now Emma. It didn't help that she was younger than me. Not that twenty-eight was over the hill, but I wanted it more than anyone, and it didn't seem to be written in the stars for me.

I let her voice fade and concentrated on her eyelashes, counting each one as she rambled on and on about how the love of her life had planned an extravagant candlelight dinner on a boat he'd rented for the evening.

I'm happy for her. I am, I chanted so the happiness would stay glued to my face. But I wanted it so much. *When will it be my turn?* Just a dab of happiness. Was that too much to ask?

I cracked my neck to the left, then right. *No more.* It was time to take control of the inner demons and my life. Remove the lead boots, lift my damn stubborn foot, and move forward with Pratt. All I'd ever wanted was to fall in love and start a family. It seemed everyone was living my dream, except me. If Pratt was the one, I needed to know. If he wasn't, I still needed to know.

"I'm so excited for you, Em. So excited." I paused a few beats to make it believable and excused myself. "I hope you took pictures so when I have the time to sit down and chat you can tell me every detail." I had to get out of here before I burst into tears in front of her.

"We have a video," she squealed. "Next time you're in, we'll have coffee and I'll show it to you."

"Perfect." I threw up a hand for a quick good-bye as I headed to the elevator. Thankfully, the doors opened and I was able to step inside and hide. I could hear my keys rattling in my purse as I fished around in the deep abyss. My fingers wrapped around the prize just as I reached my white Ford Focus. As soon as I pulled out of the parking garage and had phone service, I pulled over and texted Pratt.

Dinner tonight? I deleted the text and retyped it. **Dinner tonight. My place.**

I only had to wait a few seconds for his response.

I'll be there. Address?

It was a big step telling him where I lived, showing him my personal space. But I was ready.

***

I didn't have time to make the elegant meal I'd wanted, after scrubbing every surface of my apartment down and making sure the place looked perfect. First impressions were important. Heaven forbid he step into my space and realize I actually lived here. A dirty coffee mug on the coffee table or my shoes by the door would've totally given away the fact that I was human. Normally I'd laugh, but my insides were a mess of nerves and excitement.

I ordered takeout from Margeaux and transferred it to my own dishes. My stomach rolled when I heard him knock on the door. Smoothing down the floral pattern of my cooking apron, I strolled to the door, taking slow, deep breaths to calm my heart rate before I reached the handle.

"Hi, come in." I stepped aside, welcoming Pratt into my small space. I hadn't thought about what his own space looked like until I realized my bedroom and living room were one and the same. Was his place equally as tight? Suddenly, I was embarrassed.

He handed me a bouquet of wildflowers and grinned. "Hi, Mrs. Cleaver, I'm here to see Anna."

His greeting was lost on me.

"The apron." He pointed to my waist. "Mrs. Cleaver . . ."

"Right," I looked down at my apron and laughed. I loved that Pratt always broke the ice quickly and made me feel at ease with him. "These are beautiful, thank you." Lifting the flowers to my nose, I enjoyed the sweet smell of lavender and mock orange. "Let me put these in water and check on dinner."

"Smells amazing. What can I do to help?"

"Open a bottle of wine." I handed the opener to him and pulled out a vase for the flowers. "The glasses are on the table."

I felt like a fraud, pulling the casserole dishes out of the oven and carrying them to the table. But I'd keep that nugget of information to myself.

Pratt handed me a glass of Malbec and lifted his for a toast. "To the cook."

I lowered my head and huffed out a laugh. "I didn't make any of it," I admitted shamefully. "Mrs. Cleaver and I are so far removed from each other that I don't even know how to boil toast."

Instead of the judging eyes I expected, Pratt laughed so hard he had to set his wine down and hold himself up with the back of the chair. "Boiled toast. Anna, you always surprise me."

I couldn't help laughing with him. I had meant to say boiled water. Why toast came out of my mouth was beyond me.

We took our seats and dined on eggplant parmesan, spaghetti carbonara, and buttery garlic bread. Neither of us touched the mixed greens salad. There was no point in trying to add a little healthy to our carb-rich dinner I suppose. When our bellies were full and the bottle of wine empty, we took our plates to the sink.

"I'll take care of these later." I turned, shoved my hands in my pockets, and asked, "Do you have time for a movie?" I searched his eyes, not able to hide the hope in my own. I still hadn't decided if I was going to say anything about moving forward with a relationship, or take the easier road of hinting at it instead.

"I do." His eyes sparkled. "What've you got?" Pratt took the liberty of pulling another bottle of wine from the rack. "Mind?" he asked.

"Not at all. You pour and I'll see what's available."

While Pratt opened the bottle, I scanned the variety of movies and called them out. "*The Grand Budapest Hotel, Straight Outta Compton, Southpaw, Burnt, Paranormal Activity*—"

"Yes!" Pratt took a seat next to me on the couch and handed me a glass of wine. "Let's go with scary."

This was my chance to let him know I wanted more than friendship. But what would I say? *I won't be able to sleep alone.* Too forward. *Will you hold me if I'm scared?*

"Okay, as long as—"

Pratt's phone buzzed. He pulled it out of his pocket, flipped it over, and read the text. "Shit." He palmed the back of his neck and rubbed a spot like he was contemplating a decision. "Anna, I'm sorry, but I have to go." He looked pained as he stood, taking his eyes off the message and looking at me. "A patient," he began, a struggle on his lips. "I don't think I'm breaking patient confidentiality telling you this much, and I feel I owe it to you. I'm the intern on call tonight for Dr. Owen's patients, and we have a suicide attempt to deal with. I'm so sorry."

Jumping up, I walked him to the door. "I understand. Of course you have to go." I couldn't hide the disappointment in my voice, although I really did understand.

"I'll call you if it's not too late." A look passed between us and I couldn't tell if it was an apology or the desire to kiss me, but something was eating at him. I wanted to erase his worry and let him know I really did understand and we'd do it again, but I froze when he moved closer.

He leaned in and my heart skidded to a halt. I died. My heart wasn't beating, my lungs refused to take in air. I was definitely dead.

Pratt inched closer, his lips settling on my cheek in a friendly peck. "Thank you. I really enjoyed tonight."

My lungs finally took in the oxygen they needed and my heart pumped again. Then the pace slowed again when I realized where we stood. The ball was still balanced between my court and his, unable to move.

Our relationship still didn't have a title.

Chapter 15

Anna

My green dress was perfect for the occasion. Pratt had agreed to meet me for a drink at a tiny Mediterranean restaurant we'd stumbled upon once for lunch. The food was top notch and the atmosphere took you out of the present, straight to a tiny Mediterranean town. Since it was halfway for both of us, it seemed like a good choice.

After our evening had been interrupted by his suicidal patient, we'd shared a few texts, short phone conversations, and our weekly coffee meeting. It was more than we'd ever had before, but still wasn't enough to satiate me. I'd always been the girl that jumped in with both feet. Most of the time I sunk to the bottom, but I still jumped. Every time.

Three weeks had passed and had taken my courage with it. So tonight I planned to try again. I had a lot to lose since Pratt's company was all I lived for lately. And if my confession made things awkward between us, I didn't know what I would do. But at twenty-eight I needed to get on the horse or slap it on the ass and move on.

The taxi pulled up to the curb, two blocks shy of the restaurant. I asked him to stop there so I could walk off some of my nerves. I'd worn strappy sandals, comfortable enough for a short walk, and clipped through the crowded sidewalk. It was just what I needed—fresh city air, the combined smells of food carts, exhaust from the constant traffic jams, and several appreciative glances from the opposite sex. With my confidence boosted, I opened the door to the restaurant and was immediately accosted by the delicious, savory aroma of roasted vegetables, fresh herbs, and garlic.

"Hi." Pratt greeted me with a chaste kiss on the cheek. "You look amazing." He glanced around. "Bar or table?"

"Table if you're not in a rush." I could use more than one drink tonight.

The hostess picked up two menus and led us to a table against the wall.

"What's the matter?" Pratt's expression was one of concern. "Bad day?"

"No, no." I waved a hand. "Good day." Nervousness crept back into my muscles, causing my body to tense. I was so stiff after only a few minutes of the self-induced stress, I was sitting as straight as a librarian balancing a book on her head. I tried to relax back into my seat. "I'm sorry I couldn't meet for coffee yesterday morning, but I'm thrilled to have more hours at the flower shop. I really enjoy working there."

He smiled sweetly. It didn't meet his eyes—hadn't in a while now that I thought about it. I missed it and longed for one that revealed his dimples. "I'm happy for—" Our server approached the table and took our drink order. Pratt ordered a beer on tap, and I chose a glass of Sirah. As soon as he stepped away, Pratt rested a forearm on the table and continued. "I'm happy for you, Anna. It's hard for most people to find a job they love."

"Everything okay?" I asked. I hoped he would tell me what it was that had been sucking the life out of him lately. He was tired, rundown, and it showed.

"Fine." He nodded slowly while fingering through the container of sugar packets. "Just fine. You?" I'd never seen him so distracted.

My brows knitted together as I searched his face. "Are you upset with me?" My mind worked overtime trying to remember something I may have said or done.

"What?" His eyes lifted to mine. "No. Of course not."

"You're so far away lately. Please tell me what's going on." I reached across the table and covered his hand with mine.

He flinched before settling and offered a smile. "I'm exhausted. I guess work is finally getting to me."

"Talk to me." I had to get to the bottom of this. My feelings could wait.

Before he could answer, our drinks arrived. Pratt wrapped his fingers around the frosted glass and tipped it up, taking a long drink. "Nothing, really. Just the same old stuff." He huffed out a sigh and leaned back in his chair. "Maybe this study's getting the best of me. It's a lot of work with very little outcome. It wears a man down." He picked at the label on his bottle. "I'm ready for things to change." His eyes locked with mine, his expression flat and unreadable. I had the feeling he was implying a change between us. Although I couldn't be sure, it was the open door I needed.

My head bobbed in agreement as I listened. Of course I had no idea what he was going through or how tough his project was, but I knew something was eating at him. Maybe this wasn't the best time to lay my feelings down in front of him, or maybe it was. Even worst case scenario, his mind would be rerouted to think about something else. "I . . ." *Don't be nervous, you've got this.* "My timing is probably way off." I couldn't look him in the eyes as I started to ramble. "It usually is. I always seem to pick the most inopportune times to say or do something." I ran my finger across the fork to my left, concentrating on the way the design of the handle felt. "But I have to say what I need to say before I lose the nerve. I have to get it—"

Our server suddenly appeared, as if to spite me, knowing how close I was to the finish line.

"Are you ready to order?"

"I'm good." I glanced at Pratt. "Do you want something? An appetizer? Dinner?" *Somebody stop me.* I couldn't quit talking.

Pratt dismissed her without taking his eyes off me. "No, we're just going to enjoy our drinks for now, thank you." He gave a slight nod, urging me to continue. I suppose he was used to dealing with abnormal ramblings.

A deep, cleansing breath centered me. "The reason I wanted to see you tonight . . . I've been under a lot of stress and . . . No." I shook my head, erasing the last statement. *Shit, this is hard!* "Actually, what I'm trying to say is, I like what we have. I do. But I . . ." *Protect your heart. For once in your life, protect yourself!* I guzzled half the glass of wine. It was the liquid courage I needed.

"Pratt," His name spilled from my lips with determination. "I want more. With you." I had done it. No going back now. If he laughed, so be it. If he kept his expression flat and apologized for not feeling the same, fine. I would survive. But if he looked at me with pity—*God, please, anything but that*—I'd crawl under the table and die.

The anticipation was grueling. In the split seconds that followed my ugly confession, it took all I had not to bolt. *Stay strong.* "Say something." I tried to keep the fact that I was falling apart off of my face, but I readied myself to ooze into a puddle on the floor.

Reaching across the table, Pratt took my hand in his and rubbed a thumb over my knuckles. His expression remained stoic as he searched my eyes for something. Was he trying to make me uncomfortable? I was already squirming in my seat and wishing he'd grabbed my right hand instead so I could finish my glass of wine. A lot of lefties were ambidextrous. I wasn't one of them.

"You're serious?" Even in the dim lighting of the restaurant, I could see how somber his expression was. Eyebrows slightly lifted, his gaze firmly planted and igniting the blush zones on my face and neck.

What did he ask? If I was serious? Was he acquainted with women evil enough to joke about something like this? A bubble of laughter rose in my throat as I thought about the timing of a sarcastic answer. "*Nah, I just wanted to see your reaction. Shall we order food now?"* Did people do that? Surely not.

A whisper I could barely hear myself escaped my lips. "I *am* serious." I dropped my head and concentrated on the way the napkin was folded across my lap. Not in half, but a three-quarter fold, the edges lined up so everything was even and centered.

I felt my fingers being squeezed. Another squeeze, this time harder. Lifting my gaze, I was awarded with the prize. His smile finally met his eyes like it did when we'd first met. Nothing was said in that moment. We sat there, holding hands, looking at each other for the first time really, and breathing in the new air that moved between us. It happened instantly—the change in the way he looked at me—like I had a different head, one he liked better.

The layer of friendship was still there, we wouldn't toss that aside. It was what our relationship was built on and carried trust and safety. On top, a layer of possibility was added, and over that a gentle fabric woven from curiosity, desire, and craving.

"You know . . ." He cleared his throat. "Surely you know I've wanted this since the day we first met in the coffee shop."

The tension in my neck eased as I shook my head, the bubble of laughter floating to the surface of my throat, not able to be ignored another second. "Yoga pants and unable to pay for a coffee . . . you always set such high goals?"

We shared a comfortable laugh. "The highest. I liked that you were confident enough to go out in whatever you damn well pleased. And I was hooked when I saw how sweet you were." The luminous glow of happiness in his eyes anchored me. "You don't find that anymore—a woman who's kind and soft."

Hanging on every word, soaking up every ounce of joy in the room, I couldn't remember a time when I was happier. Another round of drinks was delivered to the table and we decided to order food. We ordered light, a sampling of hummus, tabbouleh, and falafel to share. Pratt lifted his bottle of beer to the center of the table. "To us and the exciting adventures ahead."

I lifted my glass, noticing my hands had finally stopped shaking. *Thank God the fear has settled.* "Salute."

Neither of us had been as hungry as we thought. The energy and excitement in the air was overwhelming, eager to be explored and indulged. My mind was warring with wanting to go to bed with him or take things slow. *Enjoy . . . savor,* one side began. *Live in the moment,* the other argued.

After Pratt took care of the bill, we took an evening stroll. Holding hands led to an arm around my waist. His touch felt amazing and I wondered why I had waited so long to tell him how I felt. So many nights wasted that could have been spent together. We talked about everything and nothing, from politics, work, and travel desires, to nonsensical topics like what if there was a zombie apocalypse, and would you rather be stranded on an island all alone or in a city full of people that couldn't communicate?

Early evening bled into nighttime and the streets began to clear. Still, we walked and talked. He told me about his two brothers. "My older brother, Matt, lives in Maine with his wife."

"Do they have kids?"

He shook his head. "Don't want them."

Was that something that ran in the family, not wanting kids? I wanted them. It was high up on my list of must-haves. "They don't want children?" I asked. "Do you?" I hadn't meant for that last part to slip out. It was too soon to talk about kids. Why couldn't someone invent a shocking device that jolted you before you said something stupid?

"I do. Not anytime soon," he chuckled. "But one day."

He went on. "My baby brother is studying architecture at a university in Tennessee. He's still dating his high school sweetheart." Pratt clasped his hand over his heart like a woman swooning.

"That's sweet." I gave him a playful slap on the arm. "Tell me about your parents."

"They're enjoying retirement in Florida." He mumbled under his breath, "Or at least Mom is."

"What does that mean?" I pried.

"My father will never really retire. He may not practice medicine anymore, but he'll sure as hell tell everyone else how to."

I sensed some discourse between him and his father. I didn't want to push him since we were having such a wonderful night, so I changed the subject. "Do you get to see your family often?"

A flash of sadness haunted his eyes as his mouth turned grim. "The only time we're all together under one roof is

Christmas." He smiled then, all sadness gone from his face. "We have a cabin in Tennessee and meet there every year. It's easier for Walker. My parents still think he's too young to travel more than an hour from school."

"Walker's the youngest?" I loved the way our arms swung through the air as we held hands, like young teens in love. "The one in Tennessee?"

"Yeah."

My apartment was close, only a few blocks away now, and my heart began to pick up an unsteady pace as we neared. "Three sons." I shook my head, unable to make intelligent conversation any longer. All I could concentrate on was the way his hand felt in mine and the way the words he spoke rolled off his tongue in a rich, masculine tone that had me wanting to taste them.

Pratt gave my fingers a squeeze and slowed our pace to a stroll. "You've heard my life story and we're almost to your apartment." He anchored his attention on me with a curious gaze. "I don't know anything about your family."

I shrugged a shoulder. "Not much to tell. I'm an only child."

"Where are your parents?"

"My mother died when I was a teenager and I never knew my father."

"I'm so sorry, Anna." Pratt stopped walking and stepped in front of me, placing his hands on my shoulders. One heavy brow slanted in sadness as he searched my face. "What did you do? Who took care of you?"

This conversation was a buzz kill and needed a change before we got any closer to my door. "Family members took me in until I started college." It was a lie, but I wasn't ready to tell him I grew up in foster care. It put us on totally separate playing fields.

I tugged on his hand and started walking again. Trying to diffuse the melancholy mood hanging in the air from the talk of death, I raised the inflection of my voice to a happier note. "Where did you go to college? Were you one of those geeky med students with a pocket protector?" As hard as I tried to picture that scenario, it was impossible. If there was a nerdy gene in his body, it wasn't visible now. He was dark and brooding. Not the image I pictured of a future shrink.

He chuckled, flashing those delicious dimples. "I went to USM—University of Southern Maine. At the time, I wanted to get as far away from Tennessee—and my parents—as possible." He smirked and shrugged a shoulder. "Funny how the thing you hate most is the exact thing you crave when you're old enough to appreciate it."

"I've never been to Tennessee." I pictured rolling hills filled with grazing sheep, people strutting around in cowboy hats and boots.

"We'll go." He tugged at my hand and I wondered if he was excited or nervous. His expression was sweet, but unreadable. "I'd love to show you the trees in fall."

I knew it was just a polite thing to say and we'd probably never go, but I allowed myself a moment to imagine it. Pratt reaching for my hand as he led me up a trail through the mountains, unpacking a blanket and picnic lunch at the top. You could see for miles up there and the air is clean.

We climbed the few steps leading up to my apartment. I glanced down at the potted plant in the corner and made a note to water it in the morning. Pratt dropped my hand and leaned against the brick that framed the door. The porch light cast a buttery glow, spotlighting his handsome features.

"You'd love Tennessee in late October, when it's cool enough for a fire." With his arms crossed against his chest, he glanced up and pulled his lips into a shy half smile.

I was lost in Pratt's dark, unblinking gaze. "Sounds wonderful," I said in a love haze, not sure if the words actually left my mouth, or if they were audible.

Pushing off the wall, he closed the space between us. His hand came up to my face and gently cupped my chin while his thumb caressed my jaw. A thrill swept up my spine, and I had to fight to stand on boneless legs. Of all the kisses I'd experienced, this one was the best and his lips hadn't even touched mine yet.

The sensations pricking my skin made my pulse prance. Pratt leaned in and pressed his lips to the corner of my mouth, lighting a fuse that traveled from the top of my head to my toes. I could've ridden the high of that corner kiss for days, but he was standing in front of me, willing to give me more and I planned on taking it all. Our breath mingled as he pulled back slightly and rested his forehead on mine.

"I'm going to kiss you." He nuzzled his nose in my hair, his breath tickling my ear and causing goose bumps to invade my flesh. "As soon as I catch my breath."

His admission melted my heart and took away the little bit of strength I had to hold myself up. I backed up and leaned against the brick door frame, hoping I wouldn't slide down, my chest heaving as I tried to remember how to breathe.

With a knowing smirk, Pratt leaned in and pressed his lips to mine.

Floating.

Melting.

Sweet prickles of warm, fuzzy electricity.

My eyelids slid closed, while my heartbeat, strong and demanding, rattled my ribcage. His kiss, as tender and gentle as a whisper, made me feel woozy and intoxicated. It also left me hungry and needy.

My left hand, of its own free will, snaked around his neck to the back of his head and pulled him in for a deeper kiss. His tongue traced along the seam of my lips and I opened, allowing him in. Like most first kisses, we explored and tasted and danced together. But the pull was stronger than I'd ever experienced before. I couldn't part from him at this point, even if the building caught fire.

Shallow breaths. Fluttering heartbeats. Exhilarating dizziness.

Finally, Pratt pulled back, placing his hands on my shoulders as he caught his breath. I wanted to invite him in, but the words wouldn't form. I could see the struggle in his eyes. He wouldn't invite himself in, he was waiting for me. I paused too long and the decision was made.

"Goodnight." He leaned in and kissed me once more. "Sweet dreams." He backed up, holding the railing as he took the first step.

"Wait." I sucked in my bottom lip nervously. *Stay.* I couldn't speak it, but surely he could see it in my eyes. Why wasn't my mouth working?

Pratt climbed back up the stairs and kissed me hard, once. "You have no idea how much I want to come inside." His eyes pinched together. It was obvious he was struggling with wanting to stay but needing to leave. "I wanna go slow. You mean too much to me." With a chaste kiss on the forehead, he jogged back down the stairs, backing down the sidewalk with a wide grin. "Goodnight, Anna."

I'd never met anyone like him before and couldn't contain the silly grin permanently etched on my face. "Goodnight, Pratt."

My thumb traced along my bottom lip as I watched him. Pulling out my key, I turned the lock and opened the door. Pratt waited on the sidewalk until I was safely inside. I inched the door shut, gazing at him like a lovesick teenager until finally it closed.

Once inside, I fell to the couch and let the cushions envelop my Gumby limbs. I'd fall asleep here tonight, with a smile on my face and the memory of Pratt's lips.

Chapter 16

Jane

Mutilation was not her thing. Carving an intricate piece of art into someone's chest appealed to her, but bashing someone's head until their brains wouldn't stay in place any longer was a bit much, even for Jane.

But he had it coming. What else could she do? She had killed men for less than what he'd put that poor girl through. No man had a right to put his hands on a woman like she was a rabid animal.

The problem with beating a man to death was the mess. Jane had no idea how much blood a man of his size could expel. Not only would she have to clean the tiny folds of the weapon, but there was blood spatter on the walls, lamps, and couch. Blood everywhere. It would take hours to clean the sticky gore off the floor, walls, and couch, and even then, she wasn't certain she could erase every piece of evidence.

After every surface was wiped down, no evidence of blood—the apartment was checked twice—and sheets washed, five hours had passed. Exhausted, furious, and starving, Jane marched to the kitchen and looked in the man's fridge. *Bingo!* Jane pulled out a box of leftover pizza and ate it cold while she studied the man's body and contemplated what to do with him. She wouldn't be able to lift him onto the bed and leave him like she usually did. Besides, how could she possibly make it look like an accident? She wasn't strong enough to roll him up in something and take him with her. The thought of chopping him into pieces and stuffing him into a cooler crossed her mind, but she'd spent five hours cleaning up blood and wasn't about to make another mess for herself.

Bloody hell, what shall I do with you?

Once she finished the last bite of pizza, Jane bagged up the lampshades, throw pillows, picture frames, and anything else that might have held a trace of blood she missed for the incinerator.

Fire fascinated Jane. The beautifully bright flames licking at anything they touched until all evidence was erased. Fire was Jane's biggest ally. She loved its constant reliability, used it when she needed it, respected it at all times.

Fire was the answer.

Chapter 17

Bree

Four days were spent in and out of consciousness. Most days I didn't know where I was or what had happened. To this day, I didn't know how I got home or what had become of Gus. Was he dead? If so, my fingerprints and blood were all over his apartment. Of all the cop shows I'd seen, they would've come for me by now, so I had to assume he was still alive. I probably knocked him out and escaped just in time. Hopefully I'd never run into him again, knowing how pissed he was. *Motherfucker should be scared of me. He owes me.* Since I didn't come home with the goods I'd tried to lift, not only was I bruised and sore, the entire night was a waste.

The bruises on my cheek and forehead were a nice shade of puke green, but I managed to cover them with an expensive bottle of concealer and untrimmed bangs. Even so, nothing would stop me from going out tonight. It was Saturday, after all.

My bed looked like someone had come in and ransacked the place, clothes strewn all over. I finally chose a red, off-the-shoulder dress that showed off my legs, and a pair of red Manolos with a silver heel. After the final touches of makeup, adding a few red extensions to highlight my long, dark hair, and painting my lips to match candy apples, I was ready to go.

Before heading out, I stuffed four condoms in my clutch. Gus had beaten me and taken more than a week from my life, but I wasn't about to let him wreck me. Tonight was about healing, gaining control back, and living life the only way I knew how.

As expected, the line was long at The Dark Room. Casually I looked around, always hoping Blaize might be in line. Praying he wasn't. Once inside, I found a seat at the bar and ordered an extra dirty martini, extra olives. Without wanting to, I desperately searched the room for Blaize, or anyone that resembled him. I needed a man's hands on me and if I didn't find someone soon, I'd have to resort to desperate measures and find the first willing male to get me off in the bathroom. My needs were growing stronger by the minute.

I tossed my head back, swallowing the last half of the martini to numb the hunger, but it had the opposite effect. "Another," I snapped at the bartender. Typical. Just like a cocaine addict, my world revolved around sex and if I didn't get my fix soon, shit would get serious quick.

Bitch better remember my two olives.

If she hadn't slid my extra-dirty-two-olives martini in front of me at that very moment, I would've taken off to the bathroom for a quick hit with my finger vibrator. My hand trembled as I picked up the glass, plucked an olive off the decorative pick, and sucked the salty treat into my mouth.

131

Panning the room, my eyes stilled on a black man with dreadlocks. He reminded me of Lenny Kravitz—soft lips and a fit, sexy body. He was leaning casually against the bar, one hand tucked away in his tight grey suit pants. *Delicious.* I licked my lips before lifting the glass to my mouth, never taking my eyes off sexy Kravitz. I could tell he didn't have money—and I really needed him to have it—but black men were the best lovers, and I was desperate. He must've felt my stare when he dipped his head in my direction. As if he were looking for a luxury car, he let his gaze cruise the length of my body. He was a presumptuous, arrogant son of a bitch, just how I liked them.

I started my two second count, about to go in for the kill when I smelled something. Someone, actually. They were standing behind me—too close—and the smell was so familiar, like someone I'd known my entire life. He was as familiar as home, but sent a rush through me like a forbidden sin. I hadn't turned around to see who he was. I knew.

"Hey, beautiful." His sultry voice betrayed him. I heard the excitement lacing his words.

My pulse raced as I tried to gather my wits. How was I supposed to answer that line? *Hey, handsome.* I had nothing.

I opened my mouth to speak but felt my breath stutter, so I swallowed hard before trying again. "You can do better than that," I said, sipping my martini and not turning to face him—a crucial moment in keeping the upper hand. Which I felt slipping from my grasp as my body began to crave him.

He was quiet, but I knew he was still there. "You're right." He pushed my hair around to fall over my right shoulder and exhaled, his hot breath tickling the back of my neck and ear.

My eyes slid closed and I thanked fate for keeping him behind me, unaware.

"Good to see you in the flesh instead of invading my dreams every night." I cringed at the cheesy line, but he made up for it by sweeping his fingers over my shoulder and burning a trail behind them. "You've had me so distracted, I dropped a fifty-pound weight on my foot."

I whipped my head around and looked down at his feet. "Where's the cast?" No way had he shoved broken bones into those shoes.

He chuckled, which caused me to look into his blue eyes, which must've been the reason his mother had named him Blaize. "Pinky toe and the one next to it." He shrugged a shoulder and smirked. "Not much you can do about it besides man up."

So I had been right about his career as a fitness trainer. "You must not have many clients to defend, Counselor. Always in the gym . . . breaking toes." I matched his penetrating gaze with my own and held it.

"I'm just that good." He leaned forward and rested his hands on the sides of my bar stool. "I know how to get it done, and I do it right."

One, he was no lawyer. Two, both of us knew we weren't talking about lawyer shit. He was talking about the way he controlled my body like no one had before. Fucker.

I cocked my head to the side. "Prove it." My voice was silky, but my thoughts were anything but. "Bathroom, now."

I didn't have to look to see if he was behind me. I knew his type, using his cock to dominate women. They probably all fell for his charms, panting after him like the golden rod of libation was tucked in his pants. But he'd met his match in me. I had not only controlled his type, but cast spells that left them knowing they would never meet another like me. I'd had marriage proposals from assholes before they could get their pants zipped up. This fucker—as hot as he was—would be wreckage in my wake, and he didn't even know it.

Blaize was behind me before the bathroom door closed, pressing me into the wall next to the paper towel holder. "I'm going to fuck you so hard, the—" He paused as a mortified blonde came out of one of the stalls and exited the bathroom.

"No more talking. Get to the fucking part." Ducking from his arms that tried to cage me against the wall, I walked to the bathroom counter and hoisted myself up.

Blaize unzipped his slacks, freed himself, and slid a condom on his already raging boner. When he stepped between my knees, I wrapped my legs around his waist. Pulling my panties to the side, he eased himself in, slowly but deliberately, letting me get used to his size. Once he was settled, the party began.

I leaned back on my elbows, lifting my hips so he'd hit the magical spot. My head was way too close to the mirror, tapping against it at first. Soon my head would be cracking into the glass and that wasn't going to heighten the experience. Before I could slide toward him, moving away from the glass, Blaize slid his hands under my ass and pulled me toward him.

The angle from having his strong arms under my ass was perfect. Each time he drove into me, he hit a spot that made me cry out. I couldn't help myself, it was excruciating and mind-blowing all at once. It felt like I was going to pee and orgasm at the same time. I couldn't decide if he should stop, change positions, or drive harder.

"Harder," I demanded.

With one last thrust, my body contracted and convulsed with the most intense orgasm. My legs held him to me in a vice, unable to let him go until the strongest waves subsided. His fingers pinched into my hips as he cursed through his release. "Fuck." Another jerk of his body. "Fuck."

I closed the stall of the bathroom and waited for him to leave, but he never did. When I came out, he was waiting for me, leaning against our sex station. "Can I buy you a drink?"

"Only if you're up for another round later." I slapped my hand down onto the bathroom counter.

"No question." He flashed a cocky smile and held the door open.

My body screamed, urging me to forget the drink, grab his wrist, and pull him back into the bathroom. My appetite was usually strong, but for some reason I was insatiable, starved. But something held me back, made me want to be chased a little first.

Blaize nodded to the bartender, a tiny woman with the hottest body and waist-length blond hair. I watched Blaize, wondering if he'd be into a threesome. It was the first time I was torn—wanting them both but not wanting to share him. If he was checking her out, he was too slick to let me see it.

"SoCo and lime, please." Blaize held up two fingers.

"What the hell kind of drink is that?" I scrunched my nose. "Sounds gross."

"It's not."

Blaize had my full attention when he pushed the drink my way. It was served in a short glass instead of the typical shot size. "Ready?"

I lifted a brow. "Always."

The sweet, citrus-infused liquid slid down my throat smoothly. Not what I expected. "That's delicious." I studied the glass, disbelieving. "Another."

After our second shot, I was feeling good. Nice and relaxed, ready to go. The DJ played a remix of "Wicked Games" by The Weeknd, and before I knew it Blaize was pulling me to the dance floor.

Didn't he want me naked?

As soon as he gripped my waist and pulled me to his rock hard body, I was lost. Lost in the music, lost in the pull of everything Blaize—his gunmetal blue eyes, broad shoulders and arms that fought against the constraining fabric of his black shirt, and a scruffy beard that had my skin begging to feel the burn it left behind. I was suddenly lost to who I was and needed to be to survive.

Blaize leaned down, nuzzled his nose in my hair, and traced a path from my throat to my ear. I inhaled his scent before his lips met mine. I couldn't say how long we stood there, how many songs played, or how we ended up in the back of a cab. All I knew was how it felt to straddle him, feeling his excitement beneath me as we made out like lovers who'd been separated for months and had finally been able to come together.

We didn't mess around with the sexiness of undressing each other when we stepped through the door of his apartment. Instead, he made sure I was slammed against every wall from the back of the door, down the hall, to his bedroom. Between moments of uncontrollable hunger, our lips and tongues exploring and devouring, we stripped off whichever article of clothing we could. Blaize had gotten his pants and boxers down around his ankles, but forgot to step out of them before trying to get me through the door of his bedroom. He caught himself, but not before smashing me against the door frame.

"Fuck," I grunted.

"Sorry, baby. You okay?"

All I heard was *baby*. He was too close. *Too close.*

My mind was in full panic mode, begging me to flee, but my body demanded to be satisfied. To appease them both, I slid my panties down around my ankles, handed him a condom, and turned, splaying my palms up over my head against the wall.

"I can't wait," I breathed. "I need you inside of me." An added whimper so he couldn't resist. "Now."

Pulling his shoes off, he freed his legs from the jeans and kicked them out of the way. His right hand covered mine, his left pulling my hip until I was bent over. "Is this what you need?" he asked, stroking me with his tip.

I hated rhetorical questions and refused to answer with words. I moaned instead, hoping he'd stop playing the games and give me what I wanted. As long as we didn't make eye contact, it was casual, meaningless sex.

Sorry, baby still played in my head.

There was no foreplay, no testing to see if I was ready for him. He entered me in one painful, rapturous movement. We both gasped and he gave me a moment to accept him, feel him. Then something happened. A moment of regret not being able to see him, and a craving so strong chills invaded my body like I was feverish.

Sorry, baby.

The feelings swirling through me were so strong I wanted to cry and laugh at the same time.

Baby . . .

I felt hysterical and out of control.

He moved again, pulling almost all the way out before filling me. He moved slowly, as if something wasn't right. As if he wasn't into it any more. He ran his hands up over the curve of my waist and back down, holding himself inside me.

Nothing like this had ever happened to me before so I didn't know what to do or think. It wrecked my confidence for a moment and threatened to destroy me.

I need to get out of here!

"Turn around," Blaize commanded. He pulled out and took me by the shoulders, turning me to face him. I couldn't look him in the eyes. He lifted me in one swift motion and carried me further into his bedroom. Not what I had imagined playing out.

Neither of us said a word as he laid me on the bed and hovered over me. The heat behind his eyes dissolved me and it felt like I would liquefy and soak into the depths of the mattress. Our bodies came together again, and Blaize moved like he'd studied the art of lovemaking and had received a master's and doctorate degree in the craft. He was magnificent, beautiful. I got lost in watching him, forgetting that I was letting go of the control I so desperately needed in order to survive. But the way he looked into my eyes like I was a prize made me feel something. It felt good and comfortable. Ninety percent of me still needed to be in control and begged to make a run for it. But that ten percent was a strong motherfucker and persuaded me to bask in the feelings a little longer. I knew it wouldn't last and my flight response would take over, but for a moment, even if it was a brief one, I wanted to hang onto it, live in it.

Skin sliding against skin, lips pressed together, fingers gripping flesh, we rode out the aftershocks together. There was no doubt in my mind that something was happening between us. Something so strong and powerful, I'd have no chance in gaining control over it.

So I ran.

"I have to go." I threw my legs over the side of the bed and hopped down. "I'm sorry, but I totally forgot about . . ." *Think!* "I was supposed to meet my father." I wasn't sure why those words left my mouth. I never knew my father and didn't pretend to grieve the fact that I didn't have one.

"It's midnight." Blaize was out of bed, following me around while he hopped on one foot, trying to get his boxers on.

"Yeah, he's going to be so worried." I didn't bother putting my bra on, I just slipped my dress over my head and carried my shoes and bra with me toward the door.

Blaize wrapped a hand around my wrist and stopped me. His eyebrows knit together with a worried expression that made me feel for him. "Can't you call or text him?" He handed me my clutch.

"Listen, Blaize." I shifted my weight and bit the inside of my cheek. This was going to be tough. "I'm not that kind of girl." I was the kind of girl that bounced from one bed to the next. I took pride in not turning out like my mother. She took whatever came her way. I didn't. I gave it.

"The kind that texts her dad when she's late?" The corner of his mouth began to curl into a smile but stopped short. He rubbed the back of his neck. "Listen, I don't care what kind of girl you're not. I know what kind you *are,* and I don't want her to leave just yet." He folded his arms across his broad, bare chest. It was the first occasion I took the time to study his ink. He had stars and colorful designs, a bold script that read *thicker than water*, an intricate eye with flames instead of eyelashes. Several skulls, flowers, and a beautifully scripted name, Leylah. I wondered how long their relationship had lasted.

I huffed out a breath and cocked my head, eyeing the Leylah tat. "You're a romantic. You probably believe in fate and happily ever after. In fact, where's your coat closet? I'd bet money your armor's hanging in there," I spat. Maybe a harsher tone would get my point across and he'd take the hint. "I don't do romance." Blaize was a statue, unmoved by what I

140

had to say. With my hand on my chest, I stated my case. "I'm in charge of my fate. And I definitely balk at happily ever after." My hands were in the air, flailing as I spoke. "Doesn't exist." I could feel my lungs constricting as my heart rate went from a trot to a full gallop. Panic attacks were not fun, nor pretty to watch. "I need." Breath. "To." Gulp. "Go." Gasp.

I reached for the door, but Blaize pulled me to him. "Breathe. Slow. In through your nose, out through your mouth."

I tried to pull away.

"Trust me, my sister used to have attacks all the time. Feel me, listen to the rhythm of my breathing and follow along." His voice was calm as he whispered in my ear, his hot breath moving a strand of hair to tickle my shoulder. "I promise it'll pass." He continued to breathe in through his nose and out through his mouth. Eventually mine slowed and matched his, our chests rising and falling in sync. I'd completely forgotten how important it was for me to get out of here.

"How old is your sister?" I asked, the side of my head still pressed against his chest.

"She would've been twenty this year. She died six years ago." I could hear the grief in his voice. He and his sister must've been close.

"I'm sorry." I wanted to ask how she died, but it wasn't my business and I was eager to get him out of the sadness and back to being the badass I'd met two weeks ago. I couldn't handle emotions. Not my own, not anyone else's. "Ley and I were really close. I miss her every day. But she was so sick,

I'm glad she doesn't have to endure the pain and shit this world offered her anymore."

Leylah. I let the name sit on my mind for a moment, wondering if she looked like her brother. I couldn't imagine a female resembling Blaize, there wasn't a single feminine feature about him. So the tattoo was in honor of his sister, not the longtime love of his life. Actually, she probably was, which somehow made me admire him.

Blaize walked me over to the couch and we sat down. He pulled me into his chest and covered us with a soft, brick red blanket, and then he flipped on the television. "Movie?" he asked.

I nodded into his chest. It was no use fighting the feelings of comfort and warmth and safety he brought. Not only was I exhausted from the panic attack, it had been years since I allowed myself the freedom to feel. I'd never trust Blaize, I'd built strong, fortified walls. But feeling something—even if it was pain—was better than not feeling anything at all. "Something funny."

We landed on one of Melissa McCarthy's movies, sure to make me laugh and toss aside the fuzzy feelings swirling through me. But before she even stole the first identity in the opening scenes, Blaize let his hands roam where they pleased, which led to more sex. I'd lost count of how many times, but each time seemed better than the last. I had never run a marathon, or even a half marathon for that matter, but I was certain my body was experiencing the same fatigue as someone who had just crossed the finish line.

However, after that last time, we couldn't stop kissing. I think we fell asleep on the couch with our tongues tangled. I woke up at some point—still dark outside—and tiptoed to the kitchen for a glass of water. Blaize was sitting up when I returned, scrubbing his hands over his face, fucking sexy as hell. He spotted me staring at him and flashed a sleepy grin.

"You need some sleep," I offered, nodding my head toward his bedroom door. It surprised me that I cared whether he slept or not, but I did, and knew that if I didn't get in bed with him, we'd be up all night arguing about it. And I was too tired to argue.

Blaize stood, walked over to me, and took a drink from my glass. He took my hand and pulled me to his room, climbing under the covers after I was in and wrapping an arm around me. It was the first time I didn't tense up and consider how I'd get out from beneath his hold on me. I let myself indulge in his warmth and the safety of his arms. Right before I fell asleep, or maybe it was that first dream phase, my father wrapped his arms around my mother and she rested her head on his chest.

When I woke the next morning, the sun was bright and high up on the walls. Blaize was propped up on an elbow, wide awake, scrolling through his phone.

"What time is it?" I asked.

"'Morning, sunshine." He grinned. "Eleven-thirty."

"Holy shit." I sat up too quickly, the blood rushing to my head and making the room spin. "I've never . . . I have to go."

"Let me pour you some coffee first." He rested a palm on my thigh before climbing out of bed.

"I really don't have time, but thanks anyway." I had no idea where my clothes were. Not that I was modest, but if we were both naked in the same space, there would be another marathon, and I really needed to get home.

"It's Sunday. Where've you gotta be?"

"Nowhere, I just . . ." Traipsing through his living room, I gathered my bra, dress, and one of my shoes. "Where's my other shoe?"

"Give me your phone," Blaize demanded, his palm upright and stretched out.

"Why?" I asked, pulling my dress over my head and searching for my panties.

He huffed and rolled his eyes. "I'm putting my number in."

No way in hell I was giving him my phone. I wasn't sure why, but it didn't seem logical.

He held my other shoe out. "Trade ya."

Shit. I gulped, eyeing the shoe in his hand. I liked those shoes, but I could do without them. Rolling my eyes, I thought about a walk of shame with only one shoe. "Fine." I swiped the screen, entered my password, and went to contacts. "What's your last name?"

"Martin."

I let him enter his number and took the phone back, shoving it in my clutch. I'd probably delete it later, or maybe I would keep it. Just in case I needed another hook up. This business was getting old, but I had no choice. I couldn't see my life changing. What skill set did I have to offer? Stealing and fucking were all I knew. Since my parents decided to take their own lives—selfish pricks—I had to figure shit out for myself. I'd never know why they did it, but I did know what it was like to want the peace that death promised. There wasn't a cowardly bone in my body, but for some reason I couldn't go through with it. Believe me, I'd tried more than a few times, but something held me back. Control maybe? I hated the idea of not knowing what would happen next. Total darkness, could you feel that? What if hell were real? I was definitely going there if it existed. So, death wasn't for me.

"Bye, Blaize Martin." I winked and tried to hide the sadness behind my smile.

"Text me so I have your number." He waited, expectantly. As in, he wanted me to do it right then.

I blinked owlishly at him. "I'll do it on the elevator."

I knew he was watching me walk down the hallway. I could feel the heat of his eyes on my ass. But I didn't dare turn around for one last look. Blaize had penetrated my thickest layer somehow, making me feel something. At first it felt really good, but now, walking away from him and knowing I'd never see him again, sucked. It felt like I'd been punched hard in the stomach. No, I wouldn't dare sneak one last glance at Blaize Martin. I didn't want him to see what heartache looked like on my face.

Chapter 18

Anna

The week before Easter was unusually busy. I had no idea how many people had ordered corsages for their yearly visit to church. Thankfully Claire was working with me today because I had no patience and apparently my kindness button was broken, too.

As the bell above the door rang, I glanced up to see a family of four. Claire was finishing a birthday arrangement, so I had the honor of serving the royal bunch. At least they thought they were royals. All four of them looked like they had stepped out of the *Stepford Wives* movie. The man and son were identical with khakis and pastel polos, their blond hair glued in place with what I imagined were products more expensive than my rent. Mom and daughter were polar opposites, but equally perfect. Mom had shoulder length hair—I assumed she and her husband used the same bottle of color—and was wearing a green sundress with matching handbag and shoes. Her daughter, probably twelve or thirteen, was sporting shorts with so much starch they could've stood on their own. Her long blond hair was pulled into a high ponytail and fishtail-braided down her back. She was the only one who looked like she wanted to break the spell and own a personality.

"What can I help you with today?" I asked, trying to keep the sarcasm out of my voice.

"The girls need corsages for Easter," the man said, checking his fingernails.

My eyes rolled internally—I hoped—but at least I had the common sense to turn my head so they couldn't see. "Do you have a flower in mind? Or color?"

"White," the woman answered. "We always wear white on Easter." She frowned at me. Like I was an idiot that didn't know *"we"* always wear white on Easter.

"Ah, and red and green on Christmas?" I cleared my throat, realizing my mistake. I hadn't meant to say that out loud and hoped they were the type of people that laughed at comments like mine.

They weren't.

Claire was beside me, taking over before I could apologize. Not that I had planned on apologizing. I had planned on making light of the situation so they would understand I was a funny person, not a mean one.

I tried to fix it. "You seem like a family that likes to match. You know, the kids wear green and the parents wear red." My hands had a mind of their own as I spoke, growing more animated as my pitch made me sound like I hadn't yet reached puberty. "Or maybe you wear green." I pointed to the woman's green dress. "Since you like green, and the kids wear red. I could see that. I've seen families do that." Rocking back on my heels, I continued rambling. "So, white on Easter. Hats and gloves, too? What do you do on other Sundays, or do you just go on Easter and Christmas?" Clearly, my fixing had failed.

Claire elbowed me hard in the side. "Anna. Go in the back and finish de-thorning the roses." She apologized to the customers as I backed up and turned around to leave. "I'm sorry, she's overtired and under-coffeed. Now, let's see about those corsages . . ."

After the customers left, Claire found me in the back room. I must've fallen asleep on the counter as rose petals were stuck to my face when she woke me up. "What's going on? You look like you haven't slept in days and you're acting weird."

"I know, I'm sorry," I said groggily. "I didn't sleep well last night."

"Last night?" Her brows were steeply arched as she assessed me. "You look like you haven't slept in days."

"Thanks." I shot her a disgruntled glance.

"Sorry, but you have black circles under your eyes and you did fall asleep on the counter. Are you sick?"

"No."

"Have you been to the doctor?" The concern in her voice was sincere. She felt my forehead with the back of her hand.

"I have." It was a tiny white lie.

I had been to the doctor, over a year ago. He'd said I had some sort of sleep disorder and gave me a list of things to do. *"Lower your stress, no electronics before bed, try reading or light exercise thirty minutes before sleep."*

I sighed. "I'm not sick. I have a sleep disorder. It was under control for a while, but now it's happening again. It must be the added stress of a new job and relationship."

"That sucks." She shook her head and walked away.

As soon as the floral shop died down, I went home. It was my turn to stay late, but Claire "couldn't bear" to watch me yawn one more time. A quick shower sounded wonderful before slipping into my pajamas and climbing into bed. Hopefully I could sleep while the sun was still shining. I had never been much of a napper, but my body was so exhausted. Lack of sleep did crazy things to you, and I felt like I'd been hit by a Mack truck.

As I stepped into the bathroom, I squinted at the brightness. The light was unforgiving, revealing the dark circles under my eyes that Claire had kindly pointed out. I sighed at my reflection. I'd have to do better than this. Instead of a shower, I climbed into bed with my clothes on, pulled a cotton blanket over my legs, and fell into a deep, dreamless sleep.

***

Morning came but didn't bring the rejuvenation it had promised. After showering and drying my hair, I turned on the television for sound and headed to the kitchen to start coffee. A text dinged before I could get the scoop out of the grounds.

Coffee? It was Pratt.

A smile planted itself on my face and stayed there as I typed: **About to brew some.**

Make enough for me.

No, no, no. Not today. I didn't have the energy to put on makeup, brush my hair, or my teeth for that matter. Today was a day for sweats and binge watching something on Netflix.

Sorry, not—

A knock on the door interrupted me mid-text. *Shit!*

I opened the door to the most gorgeous man holding a bag out in front of him as a peace offering. "Sorry I didn't call, but I brought muffins." His puppy dog eyes wouldn't be refused as I stepped aside to let him in.

I would've appreciated the fact that he was in sweats, but of course the way they hung low on his hips did something crazy to my insides. The only thing that could possibly be worse was if he'd worn that cologne that made me weak in the knees. Then, just past the aroma of blueberry warmth, it hit me.

Nice, Pratt.

We drank our coffee and ate muffins on the couch while we watched the morning news. The nice thing about Pratt was he didn't have to converse at all times. We enjoyed comfortable silences together.

After the weather, the news began. The TV wasn't loud enough to interrupt our conversation, but something caught Pratt's attention so I turned to watch the story with him.

"A man was found brutally murdered in his apartment," said the reporter.

The screen changed, showing a petite lady with platinum hair, probably in her late forties, standing outside of the apartment complex. "I smelled smoke and called for help.

I didn't really know him, but he seemed like a decent human being. Always held the door for me. Whoever did that to him was a sick son-of-a-bleep. They said his head was bashed in and—"

I could tell the reporter wanted to roll her eyes when she interrupted the lady. Couldn't say I blamed her. Why did people go stupid when the camera was on them? But she kept a straight face. "We don't have an official report, but it looks like the fire was no accident. Back to you, Beth."

"Thank you, Amy, not an easy story to report I'm sure." The news anchor was back to business as she finished up, "Police are asking anyone who saw anything or has any information to please call the one-eight-hundred number on the screen below."

"How awful."

"I'm thinking I picked a bad time to go into psychology." Pratt pinched his brows in disgust. "A lot of sick people in the world."

We really did live in a dangerous era. Suddenly all the noise outside intensified. Taxi horns, a siren in the distance, someone playing a violin in the apartment next to mine.

"Hey." Pratt pulled me to his side. "You're shaking."

"I'm not cut out for any of this." I waved my hand toward the television. "That's why I never watch the news. I'd rather live in my fictional world where nothing bad happens."

"You're safe with me." He said it with so much conviction I almost believed him. But the truth was, I lived in a bad part of town. I wasn't safe. No one was safe.

Chapter 19

Bree

My dreams were an intense, sweet torture that night. I awoke in the middle of the night, clammy and disappointed. We had been on the beach, Blaize and me, under a gazebo of sparkly lights and candles. There was no moon, so the waves were hidden in the darkness of night, but the glorious sound of the water crashing onto the shoreline was loud and authoritative. A man was standing behind us as we held hands and announced ourselves to a small crowd of people as Mr. and Mrs. Blaize Martin. I had woken up repeating my new name, *Mrs. Blaize Martin, Mrs. Blaize Martin, Mrs. Blaize Martin.*

For some reason I couldn't stop crying. Not after a glass of water or the comedy channel. Not even when I watched a YouTube video of Jimmy Fallon impersonating several celebrities. So I did the unthinkable.

I texted him.

Hi

It was lame, I know, but the best I had. An hour passed with no response. I assumed he was pissed that I hadn't texted him from the elevator, so I thought of a reason why I couldn't have texted from the elevator. *I dropped my phone between the elevator doors, into the dark abyss.* How had I gotten it back, though? *Someone called me and I forgot to text you.* So he's not on your mind? He fucked you seven ways to Sunday and you couldn't remember him?

Sorry I didn't text. Phone died.

Still, I heard nothing. At four in the morning, I finally fell back asleep. I woke up to the buzz of my phone and slapped my hand on it so hard and fast, I knocked it off the nightstand. Scrambling to locate it, I hung off the side of the bed, fishing for the device until I had my hands wrapped around it.

A text. From Blaize.

Good to hear from you, baby.

I read it three times, and every time I read it, I heard his voice in my head as he called me *baby.* I loved it. It was sexy but caring at the same time. He had no reason to care about me, but it still sent a charge through me. And a chill. I wanted him to care about me, but at the same time I didn't. It would've been so much easier if I had succeeded in scaring him away.

Who are you defending today? Good case?

Keep it light, Bree.

I'm a bartender. Disappointed?

Seriously? I thought he was a trainer.

I'm a thief. Call it even? I didn't type that, of course.

Instead I asked: **Are you as good as Tom Cruise in** *Cocktail?*

Fuck yes.

His reply went straight to my core. I could imagine him behind the bar, a tight black T-shirt, his muscles contracting as he poured drinks and slid them across the bar to his customers. I'm sure the ladies ordered drink after drink just to watch him, lust after him. But he was mine . . . Did that just glide across my mind, smooth as a freshly frozen ice rink?

Mine. Could I do that?

I'd always taken pride in doing whatever I pleased, being in control. But if I wanted it, and I thought maybe I did, could I pull off a relationship? One man? *No.* Although I couldn't put my finger on the feelings wreaking havoc on my mind and body, I assumed it felt a lot like falling in love. Stupid, after only two nights with the dude. But it was something. Something I didn't want to let go of. Not yet.

Wanna grab lunch later? The vibration of my phone brought me back to the conversation.

I did, but didn't. I couldn't. Right? I had a pretend job to go to.

I have to work. Dinner?

Work. Stop by for a drink?

Where?

Helix on 6th ave.

Nice. I hadn't pictured him in a place like Helix. It was upscale and snooty, where I'd met Ryland—a beautiful black man with bottle green eyes from Peru—who had unknowingly bought me a pair of diamond earrings. I never went back to a place after I'd stolen so much from one person, but I hadn't heard from him or of him since that night. The chances of him coming back were slim to none.

See you tonight, Flanagan ;) I hoped he got the *Cocktail* reference.

I'll pour you my specialty, Jordan. Apparently he did. And he cast me as his leading lady.

Fuck me, what was I doing?

***

A tight black dress, classy enough for Helix, hugged my curves and made me feel worthy of stepping through the doors. The host out front might be a problem, though. He wasn't the type to give in to my flirtations and let me by. I knew I was doomed when he pursed his lips, rested a fist on his right hip, and looked me up and down like his biggest competition.

"Hi." I smiled at him, trying the friendly card. I totally sucked at friendly. "Need my I.D.?" Before he could answer, I shoved it into his hand. Having to call Blaize to come let me in wasn't an option. I'd rather he thought I'd stood him up than let him know I couldn't get past the gorgeous but flaming doorman.

He shifted his angry glare from me to the I.D. and then back up to me. "Oh," he sang, changing his tune all of a sudden. "Sugar, I've got your name written at the top here." He tapped his clipboard and grinned, showing perfectly straight teeth, so white they had a blue hue. "Go on in. Blaize is on bar two tonight." He cocked his head back over his left shoulder. "Through the lobby and on your right." He studied me without reservation before handing my I.D. back to me.

Blaize worked the bar just as I had imagined. I took my time walking over and sliding onto a stool so I could watch him. He was wearing a long-sleeved white shirt, sleeves rolled, and a dark tie. A few of his tattoos were peeking out, the tail of his snake tat spilling down and wrapping across his forearm.

He grinned when he saw me and it felt like a balloon filled with warm water opened up inside me. It took me back to one of the few good childhood memories I had, watching the Grinch grow a heart. I loved the feeling, but I hated not knowing what would come from the feeling.

"Hey." He nodded, the smile permanently painted across his beautiful face as he poured three shots for the trio of ladies in front of him. After wiping his hands on a bar towel and stepping to the right, he faced me, still grinning like he hadn't just seen me last night.

"This is nice." I pretended to look around and take in the scene, but all I could concentrate on was Blaize and the warmth circulating through me.

"It pays the bills." He shrugged. "What would you like? Anything at all, just name it."

I bit my bottom lip and leaned forward. "I don't want to get you fired." I pushed down on the countertop, testing its strength. "But I think this will hold."

He shook his head, the grin fading and his eyes locking on mine with a look that I'm sure melted every pair of panties in the room. But the look was for me, and I absorbed every ounce of it. "Holy fuck, Bree. You can't do that to me in public. This counter only hides so much."

"Sorry." I smirked. I wasn't sorry. With me, you got what you got, no take-backs. "What's your specialty? You were going to show me some Tom Cruise shit, right?"

"Yep." He nodded his head slowly, up, down, up, down, like he was stuck in bobblehead mode. Then he switched to shaking it back and forth. "No can do. Not like this." He looked down the bar and called out to the guy working alongside him. "Matt, you got this? I just need a minute." Matt answered with a nod and popped the cap off a long neck before sliding it in front of a customer.

It only took an instant for Blaize to come around the bar and lift me off the stool. He took my hand and pulled me through the room, down a dark hallway, and into a back room filled with boxes of liquor. In the back corner, he hoisted me up on a stack four boxes high, the perfect height for us to be nose to nose.

Everything happened at once, lips on lips, his palms on my waist as he pushed his body between my knees and pulled me into him. I could feel his heartbeat, his erratic inhale and exhale of breath, his heat. My pulse was in marathon mode again and my body on fire. I pressed my knees into his hips, holding onto him and the glorious things he was doing to me, just with a kiss.

He pulled back, out of breath and flashing a sweet, boyish grin. It perfectly contradicted his rough exterior. "Sorry, I had to kiss you. And the way I needed to kiss you really would've gotten me fired."

"Do it again." I reached up to cup his scruffy face in my hands and pull him closer to me. "I need more of you, Blaize."

When his lips met mine this time, I swear we became one person, melding into each other. It was overwhelming, all-consuming. I couldn't let him go if someone walked in and sprayed us with hoses.

With barely a breath left in me, I whispered, "Please, Blaize." He kissed his way across my throat and nipped at my earlobe, making me crazy with desire.

Without hesitating, Blaize pulled me to the edge of the box and held me. There was no warning, no tracing my thigh with kisses. With his fingers, he pulled my panties to the side and treated me to the most mind-blowing oral pleasure to date. There was nothing to grip, no way to hold on or breathe through it, he took everything and left behind a shaking version of me.

He gave me a few minutes to recover before unzipping his pants, donning protection, and sliding into me. "I'm not going to last long, baby. You've got me so hot, and . . . fuck." He groaned with each thrust.

My body, still riding the aftershocks, came alive again, sparks of ecstasy flicking at every nerve ending. I wasn't sure if it was the feeling of him or the sounds of his pleasure, but it was one for the books. Funny how one of the best sexual experiences I'd ever had was on a box in a back room.

After I put myself together, taming a few unruly strands of hair and letting the flush in my cheeks dissipate, we were ready for the walk of shame back to the bar. There was no hiding what had happened. I could see it in his eyes, the way he walked, even the way he held my hand as if he owned me. He definitely owned a piece of me, which was more than any other man on earth could claim, and I wasn't okay with it. The whole idea made me crazy. I wanted Blaize—that bald head, scruffy hipster beard, rough-boy tattoos, the whole package—but I was terrified at the same time. It wasn't like a virgin experiencing sex for the first time, a little scared of some pain and emotional baggage if it didn't work out. This was my life, and the way I was being pulled to him like I had no choice in the matter, petrified me.

With his hand at my waist, we strolled down the hall. But once the dim, blue light of the bar broke through the darkness, he let his arm fall back to his side. The sudden disconnection from him started a storm inside my head, making me wonder if I was alone in my feelings. After battling with the turmoil of even having a relationship with him, maybe he didn't want one with me. All of my years in the game, *I* had been the player, using men for sex and money. Now that the tables were turned, it felt terrible. Worse than terrible. The possibility that I was falling for someone scared the fucking hell out of me. The fact that it might not be mutual was nauseating. Devastating. I could handle a lot—more than most women would ever have to handle—but not that. I couldn't handle that. I had to make a move, gain the upper hand again.

"I'm going to take a rain check on that drink." I winked and flashed a devious grin that the devil himself would be impressed with. "I've been satiated . . . for now." Before he could reply, I turned on my heels and walked out of the club.

The warning sting of tears pricked the inside of my nose. *Don't cry. Don't you dare cry.*

As soon as the crisp evening air hit my skin, Blaize was beside me. "Hey, what happened?" His brows pushed together as he reached out and took my hand.

"Nothing," I said, trying to play it off. "I'm just done for the night. Ready to climb under the covers and sleep."

His head cocked to the side and I could tell he wasn't buying my lame story. "You sure you're okay? Something feels off." The concern on his face made me want to push myself into his chest and feel his strong arms around me. If I could hear his heartbeat, I could read him and see if there was anything to this thing that was happening to us. This thing that I had no name for. But my ego wouldn't allow it. *Run,* she said.

"No, I'm good." I managed a yawn and over exaggerated the action by covering my mouth. "See? Just sleepy."

"Okay, well, thanks for stopping by." He seemed unsure, stumbling over his words and an uneasy expression tugging at his brows.

"Loved it," I said, my tone flippant. I could let him go. Better yet, I could keep it casual.

Great sex + no feelings = good times for both.

Got it. Done. No problem.

My heart, however, failed algebra and decided that great sex + Blaize Martin = uncontrollable, wildly wonderful feelings. But a smart woman knew that the heart couldn't be trusted, and it just wasn't worth the risk.

Chapter 20

Anna

Fast, easy, and fated. That's how I would describe my progressing relationship with Pratt Rhodes. It seemed too good to be true, finding someone that loved most of the things I did. One Thursday night we took a cooking class together, learning to make decadent French dishes like Moules Marinières, silky truffled Pommes Purèe, and Mousse au Chocolat au Grand Marnier. On a sunny, cloudless Tuesday, he'd packed a picnic lunch and read from my favorite poetry book under a curved tree at Wagner Cove.

We did cheesy couple things like holding hands as we strolled through Chelsea Market, eating gelato. We took a carriage ride through Central Park. We hadn't made love yet, though, which worried me. But Pratt wanted to take things slow, court me like a gentleman from back in the day. He was too charming not to believe him, plus it helped seeing him out of breath, trying his damndest to hang on to control when we kissed. Overall, he *got* me, even when I didn't understand myself. However, we quickly learned the one thing he loved that I didn't: running.

Funny how the promise of a beautiful day—white cotton candy clouds gliding through the air can suddenly turn gray. I knew I hated running the first time we went. Yet here I was again, running beside Pratt through Central Park. It looked easy as I watched people resembling gazelle's, listening to their favorite music or deep in thought. I wanted to enjoy that runner's high I'd always heard about. But I couldn't get the breathing down, or the gazelle-like movement, and the only deep thought I had was how much farther did I have to endure hell? Gasping for air and gripping my side where an alien had decided to tear into me with a serrated knife, I complained, "Just what is it . . . about this . . . you enjoy?"

He inhaled through his nose, filling his lungs as if he was taking in the scent of an apple pie cooling in a nearby window. "Fresh air, working out all the poison we've been putting in our bodies, the accomplishment of running farther than I did last week. C'mon," He poked me in the side playfully. "What's not to like? It's a good way to stay fit and enjoy the outdoors."

"I can think of other ways to enjoy the outdoors." I'd meant a picnic or bicycle ride, but it sounded like I wanted sex. Which I did, so I didn't bother explaining myself. Besides, I couldn't stand up straight as I was hunched over trying to catch my breath. Cutting my eyes over, I tried to watch his face while gripping my side with my right arm.

"CrossFit," he exclaimed. "Next week I'm taking you with me. You'll love it."

Biting back a groan I said, "I've heard about your workouts—handstand pushups, rope climbs, rowing 'till you puke. No thank you. If you want to kill me, there are easier and quicker ways that don't involve me curling into the fetal position and crying."

"C'mon," he laughed. "You'll do the beginner workout." He lifted his hands in surrender. "I promise, no handstand pushups or rope climbs." He pinched some flesh on his stomach. "I have to work out more to keep up. You feed me too much and I've put on a few pounds."

It was my goal to keep the conversation going so we didn't have to start running again, but it didn't work. Pratt jogged beside me and it felt like I was sprinting to keep up with him. "Remind me to feed your more so you can't run as fast." Bent at the waist, I gripped the pain in my side that now traveled up to my shoulder. "Go on without me. I'll catch up."

Pratt was by my side in an instant, rubbing my back. "Cramp?"

I nodded, not willing to waste any of my precious breaths on words.

"Don't slouch," he said. "You need to get more air into your lungs. Slow, deep breaths. In through your nose, out through your mouth." He mimicked the words, breathing in and out dramatically.

I couldn't help laughing, despite the pain radiating through me. "Stop! You're killing me with your breathing techniques. Were you a Lamaze coach in your past life?"

"Cute." He slapped me on the rear and I yelped. Since we still hadn't been intimate, it surprised me.

Running did something to Pratt. He never stopped grinning and bouncing around like a kid hyped up on an energy drink. I loved seeing that side of him. "It's just like the commercials say . . . I have all the symptoms of a heart attack. Call an ambulance." I flashed a smile, or the best I could manage with the amount of pain I was in. Circling my shoulder, I tried to work the pain out of my arm and side. "Running works out poison? Hmph. Why does it feel like tiny gnomes are jabbing me with knifes?"

"You're not having a heart attack and gnomes aren't having a carving party." He rolled his eyes but I could see the corners of his mouth pull into a smirk. He was having fun with this. "It's a runner's cramp. Once you get used to it, they won't attack anymore."

"Used to it?" I must've looked like an owl, blinking wide eyes at his crazy suggestion. "I'm sticking with my stationary bike." I took his hand in mine and started walking, swinging our arms playfully. "I can exercise while reading a magazine or watching television."

"But where's the fresh air?" He released my hand, bent down and plucked a dainty purple flower. "I'll bet your stationary bike doesn't pass by any of these."

"True. Point for Dr. Rhodes." I made a tick mark in the air.

He twirled me around and pulled me in for a kiss. "If you won't run with me, I'll make sure you've got flowers next to your bike, sweetness."

I smiled, but the endearment didn't settle well with me. It struck a chord that I couldn't put my finger on. It wasn't degrading like sweet cheeks or hot stuff, so I wasn't sure why I hated it so much. But I did.

Hiding those feelings, I returned with, "You're too good to me, handsome."

He flashed a shy grin. Every time I offered an admiring comment, no matter the size of the accolade, he turned bashful. It was obvious he loved the words of affirmation. I think he fed off of them, standing a little taller, prouder. It paid off on my end, too. He was the most giving man I'd ever known.

"Handsome?" He smirked. "I like that. Think I'll have that monogrammed on my first doctor's coat. 'Handsome Rhodes, M.D.', yeah, I like the sound of that." He pulled me in for a quick kiss and released me before I passed out from lack of air. Each breath after a run was precious, but I couldn't think of a better way to go out than Pratt's lips against mine.

"Is this too perfect?" I pointed a finger between his chest and mine. Apparently, I had a knack for letting the things that were in my head, dip down into my mouth and spill from my lips. "I feel like something's going to happen and wreck this beautiful fairytale I'm experiencing."

Pratt wrapped an arm around my waist and pulled me to him. Even soaked with sweat, he smelled good and the close proximity to him made my body hum. "It is perfect, but it's real and nothing is going to happen."

"How can you say that with such certainty?" It was unattractive, I knew, but I couldn't keep my mouth shut. Childhood insecurities always got the best of me. Growing up in a home where everyone always left was hard on a little girl, and even harder to process as a woman in a relationship.

"Because we're in control of what happens—you and I alone." He reached up and pushed a strand of air across my forehead, tucking it behind my ear. "If we want this, we'll make it work. And I want to be with you, Anna."

I nodded slowly, my gaze locked with his. His eyes always showed me the truth. "I want it, too." Desperately. I'd already planned a life with Pratt Rhodes, and I'd do anything to make it work. *Except running.* No, if that's what it took to make him mine, I'd even figure out the running.

"I want to take you to the cabin in a couple of weeks." His hands were on my arms, holding me as if I he thought I might completely give up on exercise and lay on the sidewalk.

I swallowed around the lump forming in my throat. "In Tennessee?" I cocked my head to the side. I wanted to get away with him—consummate our relationship—anywhere was fine with me. But I wasn't ready to meet his family. "That's far."

"Not by plane. We can be there in a few hours. Can you take next Friday and Monday off? We'll make it a long weekend." He wiped a bead of sweat off of my forehead. The way he was looking at me, I could tell he was studying the bags under my eyes. I had tried to cover them with foundation, but the sweat probably betrayed my work.

Of course I could get the time off. I worked in a floral shop. "I think so. There aren't any weddings or big floral holidays in the books. Let me check with Harry when we get back, but I don't see anything standing in our way." Swallowing hard, I asked, "Will your family be there?"

"No." His glance flickered before he looked away, following a robin until it lit on a tree. He was already flushed from the run, but I swore I saw a faint blush kiss his cheeks when he turned back to me. "It'll just be the two of us."

Tennessee. I smiled to myself. Our first trip together. This was a big step. We'd finally take our relationship to the next level. My heart thundered, though, reminding me of just that. It was a big step, and we'd be so far away experiencing it. As exciting as it was, for some reason I felt equally as frightened, and I had no idea why.

Chapter 21

Bree

One week. That was all I could manage without completely losing my mind. My attempts at forgetting Blaize Martin were useless. He was all I could think about. In the shower, I imagined him there with me and how the soap suds would trail over the ridges of his muscles, muting the colors of his tattoos. With every text he sent, asking what happened, I had to shut off my feelings. Eventually, I turned off my phone.

I constantly wondered what he was doing, what he'd eaten for breakfast, how he liked his coffee. Did he drink coffee? I knew nothing about him, but suddenly felt an intense desire to be acquainted with every single detail.

I had to talk to someone and either find a way to get Blaize out of my system, off of my mind, or—as a last resort—move forward with whatever was happening with him.

On Sunday, Hailey and I met for lunch. She was the best girlfriend I had—the only one, really—but I couldn't share everything with her. I suppose everyone had friends that fit into different categories. Hailey got the PG-13 version about my relationships and never anything too personal. I created stories that she could handle. Not that she was a prude, by any means. She held her own when we were together. But I hadn't met anyone who could handle the fullness of my twisted soul.

I arrived at the bistro a few minutes late—ten—and Hailey was waiting at a table against the wall. It was a cute French restaurant that served a bowl of olives and the most amazing variety of crusty bread.

We ordered salads and Chardonnay and talked about her new pet—a kitten named Mr. Collins.

"Why Mr. Collins?" I asked.

"Maybe he has a cousin," she said in her best British accent, then giggled and looked at me sideways, waiting for me to catch on. "Gah! Seriously?" She tossed a small piece of bread at me. "*Pride and Prejudice.* Elisabeth's cousin, Mr. Collins. 'Perhaps he has a cousin?' C'mon, you're killing me."

"Never seen it." I smirked and took a sip of wine. "But it's high on the list." I lied. I'd never watch it. As we snacked on bread and olives, I told Hailey about Blaize. I needed to tell her I was falling for this amazing lover and dish about all of his wonderful qualities.

"Best lover I've ever had." I broke off another piece of bread and popped it into my mouth. "Seriously. He always makes sure I'm taken care of first. It's not even an option. One time, in a back room at the bar he works at, he lifted me onto a stack of boxes and . . ." A lady at the table next to us cleared her throat. I glanced over to see her sitting with two young girls, probably her grandchildren. My first instinct was to fill them in on life and give more detail, but I needed to talk to

Hailey and didn't have the time or patience to get kicked out. So I lowered my voice. "Well, you can fill in the blanks. It was supposed to be a quickie." Another bite of bread. "I'm not complaining, it was amazing. I'm just saying, who does that? He's so damn good." God, I was getting hot just thinking about him. Taking a sip of wine, I tried to center myself, but it was no use. I missed him fiercely.

Hailey's thick brows danced up and down. "Perhaps he has a cousin." The British accent again.

I huffed out an exasperated breath and tried to match her stupid accent, but instead sounded like a drunken Irishman.

Our salads arrived and, although I wanted to keep talking about the wonders of Blaize, it was time to change gears. Between bites of arugula and pear, I got down to the grit of the matter. "I've never had feelings for anyone before, Hailey. I don't know what to do with them or if I even want them. You know I'm not that girl."

Hailey's smile faded as she leaned forward in her seat. I could see she was finally ready to take me seriously. "Tell me more. What do you talk about? How often does he call?" She waggled her eyebrows, all seriousness gone from her expression again, and let out a giggle. "Do you sext and shit?"

Looking down, I forked a piece of arugula and swirled it around, soaking up more dressing. I couldn't look at her as I shook my head and answered, "I turned off my phone until I can figure things out." Finding the courage to glance up, I met her disapproving glare. "What?" I shrugged. "He consumes my thoughts and makes my brain fuzzy." Which I hated.

"Are you high? You can't just shut your phone off." Her eyebrows worked together to plant a mix of confusion and anger. "A guy like him won't stay on pause too long, Bree. You have to give him something. I thought you really liked him."

Do I? "I think I do, but it's scary as shit. What if I'm just riding a high and it fades, but it's too late and I break him?" I stabbed my fork into a crunchy pear and let the sugary substance dissolve in my mouth as I chewed. "I don't want to hurt him, but I know I will." I sat back in my chair, my heart begging for a reprieve from my panic. "What if I let it go too far? What if he changes and wants me to make him eggs?" My face twisted when I thought of the horror. "I can't cook. I don't like to cook. Hell, I don't like to cuddle. I'm like a dude, and I'm pretty sure he doesn't want a relationship with a dude." I was rambling but couldn't stop. The more I talked, the bigger Hailey's eyes grew.

"Whoa!" Hailey put up a hand to stop me. "You've seen him a few times and you've already plotted your life together. Settle."

"Help me," I pleaded. "You've had boyfriends. I don't even know how to play nice." And what if I did learn to play nice, have a relationship with him. What would I do for money? Fuck, not only was I not a relationship girl, but I couldn't keep a job. I tried to picture myself behind the counter of a hotel desk, greeting guests. Great, now I felt sick.

"You're doing fine. Obviously. Otherwise he wouldn't want to keep seeing you." Hailey must've noticed the terror gripping me. She took in a deep breath, letting her shoulders slump when she exhaled. "Okay, I can tell this is going to take some work. But I'm in. Here's what you're going to do . . ."

I listened to every word she said, took it in, swirled it around in my head, and plotted how I would pull it off. It sounded so easy when she said it. Falling in love, spending time with someone who made you feel amazing. Blaize was the guy. He was the one that charged my batteries. What would it hurt to give it a try?

Money would still be a problem. I'd have to find another way to get it if I wasn't going to sleep around and steal it. Or maybe he would be into an open relationship?

Doubtful.

Turning on my phone, I decided to send him a text when I saw that I had fifteen unread texts and three missed calls. Listening to his voice, reading his words, made me feel like I was on another planet surrounded by fears of the unknown. I admit, it felt good to be wanted, but the emotion that overwhelmed everything else was fear. It was just what I needed to make a final decision.

I don't want to see you anymore. Move on.

***

Three hours later I was standing in front of Blaize's door. I cursed my hands for trembling, cursed my head for playing games, cursed my heart for winning the battle. Since I hadn't seen him in a week, and I had just told him to move on, it suddenly dawned on me that he might have a woman inside.

The thought of another woman inside his apartment, doing things to him that I wanted to be doing, stewed inside my head, churning a sea of pain and nausea. In the past, I would've preferred him to move on. I would've expected it. It wouldn't have been uncommon for me to join in on a threesome, probably more into her than him. But Blaize had changed me, altered my expectations, my desires. Now I only wanted him.

As I stood in front of his door, waiting, I was fully aware of the two options I faced on the other side: elation or devastation.

Channeling some of what made me who I was, it was time. Taking a deep breath, I pounded my knuckles on the wood, trying to hide the fact that I was unsure of myself, and waited. I hadn't even considered the possibility that he wasn't home. Just before turning away, Blaize swung the door open. But something was wrong. I could see it in his eyes and posture, feel it in the air around us.

He stood before me, shirtless and in a pair of sweats. He looked disheveled and exhausted. Was he sick? With another woman? Pissed? That was it. He wasn't happy to see me. I could see it in the way his eyes narrowed, his nostrils flared, and chest puffed. I should've felt bad, knowing I was the reason he was pissed. Instead, all I could concentrate on was how sexy anger looked on him.

Pushing past him, I waited for him to shut the door.

"What're you doing here?" *Ouch.* His words stung. He didn't face me.

"I'm here to see you." He turned around and I took the opportunity to get close to him. Looping my hands around to the back of his head, I pulled myself into him. Our mouths were so close, but he wouldn't allow them to touch.

His expression mushroomed into something livid as he pulled my arms from around him and took a step back. "I don't like games, Bree."

"Neither do I." I took a deep breath and let it out. I wasn't good with apologies and intended to avoid the word at all costs. "Can we talk?"

Trying not to be obvious, I searched for any traces of another female. Following me to the living room, Blaize waited for me to take a seat on the couch before sitting adjacent in a tan leather chair. His head jerked up, urging me to get on with it.

"Shit, I'm really bad at this." I dropped my gaze to my lap. It was easier to pretend I was reading a script, not participating in real life. "I really enjoy the time we spend together. But I don't do relationships. Never have. I'll fuck it up, I can promise you that. But . . ." Pressure started to build behind my eyes and I had to restrain myself from slamming my hand onto the couch and cursing.

"So you thought it was easier to just blow me off?" His angry, non-blinking gaze sliced right through me.

Peeking through my lashes to gauge his reaction, I nodded. "Yep."

"Why are you here now?" He slammed himself back into the chair and crossed his ankle over the opposite knee.

"I made a mistake." There was so much I wanted to say, explain, but I sucked at talking. Couldn't we just agree to move on and get to the good stuff in the bedroom? "Say something."

"What do you want from me, Bree?" The sober expression on his face and the hollow tone in his voice crushed me. I hated knowing I was the cause. "Everything," I whispered. *What the fuck?* That had slipped out without warning.

His shoulders relaxed and his lips pulled up into a slow, easy grin. "Good answer." Blaize ran a hand over his chin, scratching at his beard as if contemplating his next move.

Not willing to spend another moment in misery, I stood. With a flick of a button, I opened my coat and pulled it off, slinging it onto the couch. Underneath I had worn a short black skirt, lace thigh-highs with a garter belt that kissed the hem of the skirt, and black stiletto boots. By the way Blaize trailed his gaze up my body, I knew I had his full attention. In a few steps, I made my way to him and took a seat on his lap.

I wanted to feel his lips on mine, but I paused centimeters from his face, breathing him in. "I'm scared."

"So am I," he breathed. His eyes remained closed. "But that's the best part."

Our mouths crashed together, tongues frenzied and desperate. "I missed you," he groaned.

Wrapping my legs around his waist, he cupped my ass and hoisted us up off the chair. He pressed me against the wall in the hallway near his bedroom, his body leaning in to mine until my tits were smashed against his chest.

"God, I missed you so much," I moaned, my hands possessed as they took over and tried to feel every inch of him all at once.

Blaize pulled back from the wall and carried me through to the bedroom. Tossing me onto the bed, I bounced and settled. Fuck, the way he looked at me was more than I could handle. Need burned through me as his ice blue eyes penetrated my soul. Rough and strong on the outside, he could be just as gentle.

I loved the colorful ink covering his massive arms, broad chest, hard stomach, and sides. I needed him to slam into me and make love to me at the same time. He made my head spin when he kissed me, my body come alive when he looked at me, and his touch—damn—his touch sent my world into a tailspin.

As we lay tangled together on his bed, only a sheet covering us, I felt it. Whatever it was that was happening between us was stronger than ever and refused to be denied.

"What is this?" I asked, truly curious about the attack on my body, heart, and mind.

The hard lines in his face softened as his thumb caressed my jawline. While his clear blue eyes searched my soul, he offered, "It feels a lot like falling in love to me."

His words consumed me, penetrating every pore, even the hidden parts of me that I wasn't aware of. It did feel like falling. It felt like a rush of emotions and adrenaline—beautiful, powerful, and nauseating at the same time. An ailment that forcefully infected me and I was incapable of fighting it any longer.

At twenty-two, I'd never made love before. I had thought the back room box sex was the most intense, best sex of my life, but I had been so very wrong. When Blaize carried me to his bed and worshiped every inch of my flesh, it topped the charts. When skin slid against skin, fingers intertwined, and lips united in a slow, expressive bolero, I was sure we had traveled to heaven. But when we came together, our burning gazes locked, and he whispered the three words I'd never heard before in my life, I shattered into a million pieces and felt him put every shard back together again, making me feel stronger than ever before.

Falling asleep in a man's bed was against my rules, but here I was, tangled in the crumpled khaki sheets of Blaize's bed. My left leg felt too hot, like someone had left a heating pad on. Trying not to wake him, I shimmied to the right until I was free from the weight of his heavy, hot leg. When he groaned, I stilled until he rolled onto his side, facing away from me. Spending the night was a huge step, and I wouldn't risk losing him again by fleeing, but I needed some fresh air, some time to be alone with my thoughts and consider what was happening to me. My clothes were scattered around his room and hard to find in the dark. Patting the floor, I found a shirt. It wasn't my shirt, but it would do.

As quietly as possible, I crept out of his bedroom and into the living room. His shirt swallowed my tiny frame. It smelled like him—clean and masculine and rich—so I took a moment to pull the material up to my nose and breathe him in. I noticed his wallet sitting nearby on the foyer table. I picked it up, flipped to the back, and peeled out two crisp one hundred dollar bills. I desperately needed the money and, it gave me the sense of being in control. But then I put them back.

Stepping through the glass sliders onto the small patio outside, I watched and listened to the city that never sleeps. The noise pollution was cut by three quarters at four in the morning, but there were still sounds of glass bottles rolling down the concrete, a woman laughing in the distance, and two-maybe-three drunk men singing "Let's Go Crazy" by Prince.

Before the sun peeked over the horizon, it made itself known. My eyes burned from the intrusion of light. Rubbing them, I thought about falling asleep on Blaize's muscular chest, my head rising and falling gently with each of his breaths, listening to the rhythm of his heartbeat. If what he said was right—we were falling in love—it was the most wonderful and terrifying experience I'd ever had.

Chapter 22

Anna

My nurse friend Emma from the assisted living center was getting married—wonderful! Mary and I were invited to her bridal shower with a lingerie theme—fun! Shopping for lingerie with an eighty-six year old—not so easy. All I heard were things like, *"Good Lord, how does this go? Where does this go? Is this what your generation is into? In my day . . ."*

Mary left with a post-honeymoon—post-baby if you asked me—polka dot silk pajama set. While she was paying and having it gift-wrapped, I browsed the more risqué section and found a white lace number with matching thong. I couldn't help thinking of wearing something similar this weekend with Pratt. Did he like sexy lingerie? A giggle slipped out when I thought of coming out of the bathroom in a neck-to floor flannel nightgown like they used to wear on *Little House on the Prairie.* Maybe that's what Tennessee boys preferred? *Doubtful.* I pulled a black lace camisole and short set off the rack in my size and tucked it under Emma's gift. Not that you could get much by Mary, but it was worth a shot and I didn't want to come back out to get it later.

After shopping, we lunched at a little café that offered your choice of meat and three sides. This was where I was introduced to sweet potato casserole.

"This is no vegetable," I said with my mouth full. "It's dessert," I raked my fork through as much of the brown sugar and pecan topping as possible. You would've thought I hadn't eaten in days by the way I was shoveling that stuff in.

"My mother used to make it exactly like this," Mary said. Her eyes were distant as if she were caught up in a daydream of her past. After a moment, she came back to the present, her eyes trained on me again. "There's enough butter and brown sugar in here to clog your arteries, but it's worth it, hon, don't you think?"

"So worth it." I cleaned my plate and had to force myself not to pick it up and lick what my fork couldn't get.

"How are you, sweetie?" Mary asked, worry wrinkling the skin around her soft brown eyes.

"I'm good." I offered a half smile.

She patted the top of my hand. "You're all I've got, sweets, and I'm the closest thing you've got to a mama. So cut the B.S. and talk to me."

I sighed and hid a grin. The thing I loved about Mary, you knew without a shadow of a doubt that she was on your side, had your back. But she also had a streak of meanness in her, and I believed that not only did she know when I was lying, she could hold me down and whip me like a child if I told an untruth.

With an exhale, I began, letting the truth bleed out of me. "I'm just tired. Exhausted, actually. I haven't been sleeping."

"You sick?" I couldn't tell by the way she cocked her head to the side if she was concerned about me, or worried she might catch something.

"No, just sleepy."

"Well, then, something's buggin' you. What is it?"

I lolled my head back so she couldn't see me roll my eyes. When I thought about it, I knew it would sound stupid coming out of my mouth. But she asked and I needed to talk. Besides, what possible entertainment was she getting through the assisted living gossip hotline? "I'm greedy," I confessed. "I want so much and it doesn't seem like it's ever going to happen for me."

"What do you want so badly?"

"Marriage, kids, someone that loves me as much as I love them. Happiness, contentment, a good night's sleep."

"You *are* greedy." She laughed. "I'm kidding. You want what every woman wants, kid. Of course you do, and you'll have it. I thought things were going well with your suitor?"

I stifled a giggle at her use of the word. Pratt the suitor. I was lucky to have this woman in my life. "Things are going really well between us, but . . ." I paused. She nodded for me to continue, but I couldn't form the words. This was the woman who bought our bride-to-be button down pajamas for her honeymoon.

"The sex isn't good?" she asked, a gleam of deviltry flashing in her eyes.

My eyes went wide, the air instantly congealing the liquid used to lubricate and allow me to blink. "Uh . . . no. I mean, the sex isn't *not* good, it's not bad, it's . . ." I sighed, shook my head, and searched for clarity of mind. "We haven't yet."

"Is he . . ." She waggled her hand to the left and right over the table.

"No, he's into women . . . it's just . . ." How much could I tell her at that age? That he wanted to take things slow and I was worried that he didn't want me as much as I wanted him, or should I tell her we were going away for the weekend and I was nervous about being good enough for him? Maybe both. If she were closer to my age, I'd have no problem telling her all of my fears and doubts. In fact, that's what we had always done, so why was I so nervous now? "The truth is, Mary, we haven't been together yet and that has worried me. But now he wants to take me away for a long weekend and I'm scared to death that I'll disappoint."

"That sounds perfectly normal to me, kid." Mary stirred some cream into her coffee but never looked down. She always gave me her full attention and I appreciated that. Friends like her were rare as our society became more and more selfish. "Was there a question in there?"

"I don't know. I'm just stressed about it. I guess I want to know that he wants me. Usually men are eager to get in my . . ." *Too much.* "I mean, he's different. What if . . . gah!" Rubbing frustrated hands over my face, I tried to make sense of what I was trying to convey. "It's usually so easy to talk to you."

"I'm not dead, kid." she chuckled. "I have had sex before. Don't let the age gap be a barrier for us now." She reached a hand across the table and laid it over mine. "Talk to me."

I sighed. She was right, and I needed her help. I glanced at her hand, laced with brown spots that gave her character. Her veins beveled beneath fragile skin and somehow that made me feel safe and protected. By the age and markings of her hands, I could tell she'd worked hard, loved hard, and was filled with wisdom to share with me. "I want to do this right, Mary. I think he's the one, and I don't want to screw it up like I always do."

"So don't," she said, like it was only that simple. "I know I'm an old lady and you think things have changed, but they really haven't." She lowered her voice, "Men still think with their penises and women with their heart." She leaned forward, her blue floral top bunching where she leaned against the table. She was too thin and I wished I could feed her that sweet potato casserole three times a day. Pinning me with her eyes so I would listen fully to what she was saying, she added, "And I still believe the old saying stands true today, 'Why buy the cow when you can get the milk for free?'" She pulled up one side of her mouth and her thin, gray eyebrow followed. "I say you're doing everything right. Hell, kid, make him marry you first. That's the *best* way."

Sipping my coffee, I looked down, avoiding any more eye contact. I couldn't wait for marriage. What if marriage didn't happen? I wanted Pratt too much to wait forever. I'd waited long enough and if we didn't make love soon, I'd go insane.

I had already settled it in my mind—it would happen on our trip.

***

Wednesday night Pratt stopped by to bring me food and check in. He hadn't missed the dark circles under my eyes or the way my shoulders gave away how fatigued I had become.

We sat on the couch and ate Thai out of the containers.

"I'd feel better if you saw a doctor before we left."

That was out of nowhere. "I'm fine," I said with a shrug. "A vacation is exactly what I need to relax and de-stress." I exhaled a sigh. "Besides, we leave in two days."

"Anna—"

Setting my container on the coffee table, I turned to face him. "You're a doctor. Diagnose me. What's your cure, Doctor Rhodes?" Batting my eyelashes, I tried to change the mood in the room. I preferred Playful Pratt over Moody M.D.

"First of all," he asserted. I could tell he was trying his best to divert my cute and sweet back into serious mode. "I'm studying psychology, so unless you're hearing voices I can't help you. Second, I'm your boyfriend so I shouldn't treat you. And third, I'm an intern so I'm useless to you for another year."

"You're not useless." I winked. "You bring me food." Cocking my head to the side, I flashed a grin before scooting off the couch and lying on the floor. "Come here."

I swear I saw a flash of desire in Pratt's eyes. "What're you doing?"

"Lie next to me and be really still."

Pratt was hesitant as he crawled onto the floor and laid down beside me. "What are we doing?" he asked again.

"The dude below me plays this high bass music. If you lay really still, the beat will move you. Literally."

Side by side, we lay there, our bodies still and quiet as song after song vibrated through our bodies.

"You come here often?" Pratt teased, turning his head toward me.

"Every night." My eyes locked on his.

His index finger hooked mine as we rode the next song together, never breaking eye contact. It was the most physically intense moment we'd ever shared, next to kissing.

Just before the song ended, our lips met and heat spread through my body. Torn between wanting him now or listening to Mary and waiting, I let the desire wane. The least I could do was wait a couple more days until we were at the most romantic setting, a cabin in the woods. As bad as I wanted Pratt, how memorable would a wooden floor be?

Chapter 23

Bree

Oddly enough, Blaize and I were able to act like a normal couple. We took a carriage ride through Central Park and got hot dogs from Papaya; we watched movies and talked about stupid things, like my fear of flying bugs and his obsession with weightlifting.

"At least I know if I'm ever stuck under a car, you can lift it off of me and toss it to the side." I gave his biceps a squeeze, impressed by the bulge. Being me—twisted and fucked up—I imagined him punching me. One fist to my cheek would kill me, no doubt. I had taken my share of hits, but never from a man this large. He'd probably never hit a woman in his life, but it still seeped into my thoughts.

"You know it, baby. I shoulder press Volkswagens on Tuesdays and Thursdays for just that reason." With his eyes squinted, his lips curled into the cockiest smile. I loved that smile, that sureness he possessed. I had it, too, except when I was with him. Lately, when we were together, all I thought about was pleasing him. I still held onto some control, not letting myself latch onto him like I really wanted, but on the inside, my mind knew that he owned every part of me. Well, almost.

Sitting next to him on the couch, the movie we had been watching forgotten, I snuggled into his side. "I'm sorry I can't say the words yet, but I feel them. I really do."

"I don't want you to say it until you're ready, but I hope you don't mind my overuse of the phrase. I can't help myself." He sighed into my hair, his hot breath blowing a few strands across my cheek. "You're the best thing that's happened to me, Bree. I mean that." He stroked his palm down the length of my hair and kissed the top of my head. Then, straightening as if he'd forgotten something important, he said, "Come away with me this weekend. I want you to meet my family."

He must've seen the panic on my face, or heard my heart exit my chest as it darted across the room and out the front door. "No," was all I could say. "No, no."

I stood, ready to flee. I couldn't meet his family. Now that I thought of it, we'd never talked about his family. The whole scene played out in my head. I imagined a huge Italian group of people sitting around a table with judgment in their eyes, shout-whispering things about me.

"She looks like trouble," his father would say. His mother, under her breath but loud enough for me to hear, *"Where did he pick her up? Is she a stripper?"* He surely had four little sisters—or maybe three since Leylah died—all beautiful and prep-school groomed, who would look at me with turned up noses like I brought a pungent smell in with me. No freaking way.

"Hey." Blaize took my wrist in his hand. "You don't have to meet my parents. No problem." He talked to me like I was a kitten hiding under the couch. "Let's get away, just the two of us. We can go up to Long Island, spend some time walking on the beach. Whad'ya say?"

Parents. So there were no other siblings. God, this man pissed me off, worked me over, and melted me all at the same time. The beach did sound nice, just the two of us. That I could handle. "Yeah, okay."

As I sat there, though, I realized I wouldn't be able to put him off forever. Eventually he'd want me to join his family for Thanksgiving, or Christmas. We might not last until then—probably wouldn't—and I could always break it off once I got him out of my system . . . But what if?

He needed to know who I was. All of it. It would be easier to part ways while we were barely in love, rather than wait until I couldn't bear to lose him. For me, that was now. But it had to be done. Things had to be said. For the first time in my life, I'd met someone who deserved better than me, and I loved him enough to let him go and find happiness.

All the air from my lungs pushed through pursed lips, making a loud whoosh. "I'm fucked up, Blaize. I can't meet your family . . . ever. I can't say the L word now, and maybe not ever. And if you knew the real me, you'd bolt."

Blaize didn't bother hiding his frustration as he rested his hands on top of his head, closed his eyes, and drew in a deep breath. When he opened his eyes, he pinned me with his serious, startling blues. "Do I look like a chicken shit to you, Bree?" Not able to unglue my eyes from him, I shook my head, knowing he was anything but a chicken. He closed the space between us and tucked two fingers under my chin. "Nothing scares me, and you're no more fucked up than anyone else is."

"Face it, Blaize, compared to me, you're an angel."

His eyes widened with amusement, a ridiculous smirk on his face. "I'm no angel, baby."

"I'm a sex addict." The words flew out of my mouth like birds in an open cage. Not only had someone opened the cage, but they'd propped it up with a stick and left bait just outside the door. I slapped my hand over my mouth and stood there, paralyzed. *The fuck, Bree?*

"I can tell." He smirked. "I think I'm doing a fine job keeping up."

"I'm serious." The secret was out, as much as I didn't want it to be. I might as well dig deeper, see if I could scar him while I was at it.

"Well, then, that makes me a lucky bastard." He lifted a brow and smiled. He was a bastard. "I'll just have to keep you exhausted."

"That's it?" My hands came down to slap the sides of my thighs. "Do you even know what that means?"

"You like sex more than the average woman." He shrugged an unapologetic shoulder. "Or maybe you're just honest about it." He folded his arms across his chest and stood with his legs apart.

"I'm addicted to porn, have more sex toys than Christian Grey, and I think about sex twenty-four-seven." My eyebrows peeked, waiting for him to sprint out of the room and as far away as possible from the whore in front of him. I didn't add the nugget that begged to escape my lips about having more partners than Hugh Hefner.

"Nice." He drug out the word like a stoned surfer. "When're you going to bring those toys over here?" He cocked his head to the side. "And, FYI, I'm a dude . . . I love porn."

Stubborn ass. I couldn't believe he was remaining stoic. Maybe his demons were worse than mine.

Not possible.

It should've been good enough for me, but something in me wanted to release more truths. "I stole two hundred bucks from your wallet." Well, I was fucked, so I might as well let the truth barf flow. "I've stolen a lot more from others." I searched his eyes, waiting for the shock and anger to light a fire.

I saw something flash in his eyes but he held it in. Wasn't he the slightest bit angry? "I pocketed your red panties and you're never getting them back."

Seriously? Dissatisfaction plowed through my brows. "That's all you've got? That doesn't piss me off, it turns me on." My hands rested on my hips, ready for a full blown war. He said he wasn't an angel, but what did that mean? For all I knew Blaize was a missionary in comparison. Suddenly I was angry, for no reason at all, other than the fact that I was a criminal dealing with the male version of Mother Theresa. "You come from a good family, don't you?" I spat out, my voice taught, unable to hide the annoyance. "Parents still married, four sisters who adore you. You probably take communion and go to confessional every week." My hands slapped the sides of my thighs. "God, we're not even in the same league, Blaize." My cheeks burned the more heated I became. I was in attack mode on the very man I was close to saying the L word to. There was no use fighting it—my rage controlled me—and losing him seemed the best and only option at this point.

His jaw ticked several times, his eyes full of grief when he spoke. "I'm not Catholic," he assured. "And I don't have sisters." He took a step and reached out. "Listen, Bree—"

"No, you listen!" My hands were clammy as I paced the floor, using them to express my hysterics. "This can't work." My head shook furiously as I let the facts win the battle against foolish passion. "I knew it, but I couldn't help myself. It felt too good to be with you, but the truth is I'm not a good person. I'll never be what you need, I . . ." Damn, it didn't take much to make me cry lately. Swiping the tears with the back of my hand, I turned away so he couldn't see. Crossing my arms over my chest was my way of protecting myself, putting up a shield so no one could get close. "I watched my mother sell herself to strangers my entire life." My voice had been reduced to a whisper and I wasn't sure Blaize could even hear me. At this point I wasn't sure it was about Blaize at all. This was about me and suddenly I needed to purge all that had happened, reminding myself of why I was this way. Justification for who I was. "One day, when I was thirteen, one of them spotted me. I was eating a bowl of Fruity Pebbles watching TV." I lowered my gaze to the floor, blinking away the tears. "My mother didn't even try to help me." A sob escaped my throat. "I screamed but—"

Strong arms enveloped me so tightly I could barely breathe around the weeping.

Blaize repeated, "I'm so sorry. God, I'm so sorry."

The tears stopped and I suddenly felt claustrophobic. "I'm okay." I brought my hands up between us and tried to push off his chest. "I can't breathe, Blaize. You're squeezing me."

"Sorry." He looked bewildered as he stepped back. I had no doubt this was new for him, comforting his one-night stand. Sure, he probably brought home a few crazy women, but none compared to me. I was sure of that.

"Have you seen anyone . . . talked to anyone about it?" he asked, rubbing a hand over his smoothly shaved head.

"Didn't need to," I ran my fingertips through my hair, working out a few tangles. "I'm not the first person to go through something like that. The internet is filled with cases, online help, quizzes to let you know you *are* a sex addict and your past is most likely the reason why." I huffed out a sarcastic laugh as I twisted my hair into a knot on top of my head and tucked the tail in to secure it. "Funny, isn't it? Most girls who've experienced rape become addicted to the very thing that hurt them. Oversexualization is the official term. What a fucked up world we live in."

Backing up against the arm of the couch, I perched on the edge. "Now you see why I'm not that kind of girl. I can't be with you, Blaize. I can't be with anyone. I'm a fuck 'em and chuck 'em kind of girl. Once and done." Standing up, I gathered my purse and threw up a hand. "See ya."

Blaize gripped my arm. "Your plan is flawed, babe."

I turned, leveling him with a curious glare. "How so?"

"You didn't chuck me. You came back for seconds." He chuckled. "Fifths . . . or are we up to six, seven now? I've lost count."

"The fact remains, I'm not and never will be what you want. I can't give you what you'll eventually need from me." My eyes rolled and I sighed. "Let me go do my thing and you do yours." I yanked my arm free and headed for the door.

"I drugged you the other night," he said. His arms were folded across his chest, legs spread in a defiant stance, and his expression flat.

"You what?" I ground out through clenched teeth. Surely I hadn't heard what he'd said.

"I wanted you to stay, knowing that your world wouldn't crumble if you woke up in my bed. So I crushed a sleeping pill and slipped it into your drink." He slowly stepped toward me like he was trying to diffuse a bomb.

My fingernails cut into my palms as I clenched my fists. *He drugged me?* I didn't even know how to process what he'd done. He took away my choices, my rights. "Motherfucker!" The rage boiled inside of me like an overdue volcano. "How could you do that to me?" With arms outstretched and palms splayed, I stopped Blaize from coming any closer.

"I'm sorry," he admitted. He raked a hand over his face and trailed it down his beard. "But guess what, babe," His voice was soft as if he were trying to calm the storm inside of me and there was a luminous glow of happiness in his eyes.

"There was no Cinderella moment. You didn't turn into a pumpkin. You didn't crumble."

Thinking back, I could pinpoint the night it happened. And he was wrong. I had freaked when I woke up in his bed. My whole day had been wrecked because of it.

Stalking toward him, I closed the space between us, rolled back my shoulder, and punched him in the jaw as hard as I could. He barely moved, but rubbed the spot with his fingers before his lips curled into a slow grin. My emotions raced from one end to the other, not sure what to feel. Turned on and enraged, I punched him again, in the stomach this time. He didn't flinch, so I hit him again and again.

When I was exhausted, my fists landing on his chest like the last raindrops after a storm, Blaize simply gripped my shoulders, pulled me to his body, and kissed me hard on the mouth. I pressed my lips together, refusing to let him in. With a hand to my lower back, he pulled me closer, his cast-iron erection pressing into my stomach.

"Do you feel that?" he asked, grinding into me. "After all you've told me, I'm still into you. I still want you." He rocked against me again and I whimpered. Game over. He'd won. Not something I was used to. "This is no time for Hypocritical Harriett. You've done bad things. I've done bad things. Let's do bad together."

I don't know if it was the crazed look contorting his gorgeous features, the ridiculous nickname he pegged me with, or the heat behind his eyes that worked its magic on me. But my muscles relaxed, the anger dissipating as fast as it had come in.

194

Blaize and I fought for control in a game of who was going to dominate who. He slammed me against the wall and tore my shirt, tossing the scraps to the floor. I managed to push him off of me, backing him to the couch before shoving him with all my might. He gave in, letting me straddle him and pull his shirt over his head. My mouth crashed into his as my fingers dug into his shoulders. I wanted to hurt him, fuck him into submission, break his heart, and love him at the same time. What the hell was happening?

"You fucking drugged me!" I sunk my nails into his back and raked them down his skin, hopefully drawing blood. "You're no angel. You're father hell. Fucking father hell."

Blaize wrapped his hands around my waist, lifted me off his lap, and slammed my back onto the couch cushions. He hooked his fingers in the waistband of my shorts and panties, then he jerked them down my legs. Pulling down his sweats, he hovered over me.

A gleam of deviltry flashed in his eyes. "I'm going to make sure you never fucking forget it."

Chapter 24

Anna

Early Friday morning, as I was sipping coffee and towel drying my hair, the phone rang. I was certain it was Pratt again. He'd already called to remind me to bring layers for the changing Tennessee temperatures. As I headed to answer it, I let out a groan. If we were ever going to get out of town for our weekend trip, he needed to let me get ready.

"I'm already packed and besides, I don't think I can fit one more thing in my suitcase."

My grin faded when I heard a male voice clear his throat on the other end of the line. Not Pratt.

"Miss Spencer, this is Detective Mullane. We're investigating a case and could really use your help. Do you have time to come down to the station?"

My heart skidded across my chest. Had something happened to Pratt? "Is everything okay? Has something happened to Pratt?"

"No, no, nothing's happened. Like I said, we're investigating a case in your area."

Knowing it had nothing to do with Pratt eased my fears some, but I'd never dealt with police before so I was still shaken. "I'm about to leave for a trip. Is it something we can discuss over the phone?"

"This case is very time sensitive. It'll only take a few minutes and then you can be on your way."

"What's it about?"

"We can discuss it when you get here."

He wasn't going to give an inch, and I really didn't have time to go to the station. Although I was packed and ready to go, I hadn't planned for a trip out of the apartment, and when someone said it would only take a minute, I knew that could mean hours. "Okay, if I don't have a choice," I blew out a breath. "I'll be there as soon as I can."

I had never been in trouble with the police. Maybe a speeding ticket or two, but I couldn't imagine why they wanted me to come down. I hoped it wouldn't ruin my plans with Pratt. I was really looking forward to this trip.

Before I headed out the door, I needed to let Pratt know I might be delayed. He answered on the second ring.

"Hey," I couldn't keep the nerves from shaking my voice. "It's me. I just got the strangest call from the police. They want me to come down to the station to answer some questions." I still couldn't believe they called me. I'd heard of people being selected for Jury duty, but this seemed off. Taking in a deep breath, I realized it was probably a misunderstanding and they'd laugh it off, apologizing for wasting my time. But why did it have to happen today of all days? Were the gods really plotting against me? I had been looking forward to spending the weekend with Pratt.

"What about, did they say?" He seemed distracted and I could hear the blinker ticking in the background.

"Not really. Said they were investigating a case." Twirling a strand of hair around my finger, I leaned against the kitchen counter. "But they wouldn't tell me what it was about."

"It's probably something about your building, or someone complained about the landlord." He chuckled. "I'm pulling up to your building now. I can drive you over."

"That would be great."

***

I'd never stepped inside of a police station before, so I didn't know what to expect. It was a lot less terrifying than I expected, with a few chairs in the lobby and two male officers behind a desk that reminded me of a hotel counter.

"Can I help you?" The officer on the left asked. He had a buzz cut and looked to be in his early twenties. He didn't smile or offer any comfort as I approached the desk and I wondered if they were taught not to show any emotion.

"Uh," I began, feeling like a scared child that's been called to the Principal's office. "Someone called me to answer some questions."

"Name?"

"His or mine?" I asked.

The officer gave me a look that made me feel stupid. "Who do you need to see?" I could tell he was trying not to roll his eyes. "Who called you?"

"An Officer Mullane?"

"First door on your right. I'll buzz you in. Just push on the door." The officer remained matter of fact, no expression. Didn't he know how scary it was for someone who had never been in trouble to come into a police station?

I pushed through one door only to be led to another door. When I finally reached Officer Mullane's desk, he offered Pratt and me a seat on the other side. Mullane reminded me of Matt Damon, but his eyes were a haunting blue, deep and pensive. He was a take charge kind of man, it was obvious in demeanor.

"Thank you for coming down. I just have a few questions and then you can go."

"Okay." I wrung my hands in my lap, my heart beating so hard and fast I could feel my lips vibrating. "What's this about?"

"When did you last see or talk to Stellan Fulks?"

"Stellan?" I blinked a few times and frowned. Maybe I hadn't heard him right. "I'm sorry?"

"Ma'am, do you know Stellan Fulks?"

I nodded my answer. Hearing his name shot bolts of panic through me. I couldn't imagine why they were mentioning his name.

"When's the last time you saw or talked to him?"

How did they know about my personal life, and why were they asking about Stellan now? I hadn't seen him in months. He was probably accusing me of keying his car or slashing a tire. Not my style. Though I wish I had. *Jerk.*

"Um . . ." I had to think about it, but I felt like I was under the pressure of a live TV game show. "Two, three months. At least." My forehead creased with a worrisome curiosity.

"Where did you last see him?" Mullane asked, his pen and notepad ready to record my answer.

"Uh," I looked up and to the left, searching for the answer. "We had dinner at The Cedar Plank in Newark," I began, recalling the night. "He drove me home, walked me to the door, and then he left." I folded my hands in my lap, ready for their next question. Why Stellan was doing this after months of no communication was beyond me.

I felt like I needed to add something, but felt foolish after the words left my mouth. "We didn't date long. We weren't even in love." When that last part rolled off my tongue, I would've given anything to suck it back in. I knew it looked better for me if the police believed I wasn't in love with him, but the way I announced it made it sound like I was, and I didn't want Pratt to think he was a rebound. But I had to protect myself. I wasn't built for jail time. A woman was more likely to damage a man's car if she cared about him. I did care about him—a great deal—but I wasn't capable of lashing out that way, or any way for that matter. I'm sure it would've taken a lot of anxiety away if I could've let off some steam, but it just wasn't in me. A person like me took things out on herself instead.

Mullane glanced up from his paper, judgement in his cold blue eyes. You could see the stress of the job on his face, hard lines on his forehead and surrounding his mouth. "So the last time you had any contact with him was at your door?"

"We may have talked on the phone." I sucked in a shaky breath, trying to settle down. "Can you please tell me what's going on?"

"A few more questions, ma'am." His lips curled into what I'm sure he thought was a smile. These people didn't even know me and they'd already decided I was guilty.

My frown deepened. "Why so many questions about an ex-boyfriend that I haven't talked to in ages? A man who doesn't give a damn about anyone but himself?" There it was. The anger that usually stayed bottled, ready to burn another hole inside of me in the form of a painful ulcer. Now that it was spilling out, I felt a small bit of relief. Terrible timing, though.

"Care to elaborate?" The officer asked.

"He cheated, and then posted a photo on social media, obviously for me to see." I looked at Officer Mullane and then at Pratt. I knew what they were thinking. But I didn't seek vengeance. I just walked away, like I always did. "Whatever it is he's accused me of, I didn't do it. Yes, it pissed me off that he could be so cruel. But I'm an adult and keying cars, slashing tires, or whatever else women do to their cheating boyfriends isn't my style. I'm not writing a country song." I shook my head. "I don't even like country music."

"Ma'am," Mullane cocked his head to the side, studying my face before he continued. He seemed confused but sorry at the same time. "Stellan Fulks is dead."

My hand slapped over my mouth and remained there as I processed what he'd said. Stellan . . . dead? Was this some kind of sick joke? He couldn't be dead. The words played over and over again. I shook my head and focused on a lone crumb on the table. I had the sudden desire to flick it, hard, sending it sailing into the unknown. "I—I don't understand. Are you sure?"

"Yes, ma'am, I'm sure." His features softened, He folded his hands and set them on the desk, scrubbing one thumb over the other. "I'm sorry you had to find out this way."

My head wouldn't stop shaking, as if I could will him back to life if I denied it long enough. Lifting my head, I looked at both of them, suddenly realizing they could've given me this news at the front door or over the phone. Actually, if the movies were accurate, they wouldn't have come to me at all since we weren't related or married.

My next question scared me before the words left my lips. "How did he die?"

"I can't disclose that information, ma'am." Mullane tossed a business card onto the table. "If you see, hear, or think of anything at all, give me a call." He stood and slid his chair back under the desk. "I'll let you out."

Pratt and I walked back to the car in silence. He opened the door and waited for me to climb inside. While he jogged around to the driver's side, I reached for my seatbelt and buckled it.

Pratt started the engine but didn't pull away. Concern pinched his brows. "Are you okay?" He reached across the console and took my fingers in his. "Do we need to cancel the trip?"

"No. Please, I need to get out of here."

"Who was Stellan?" he asked carefully. "Do you still care about him?"

"An ex, and no." I shook my head, studying his fingers as they rested in my hand. He had clean, trimmed fingernails. His hands weren't soft, but they were absent of callouses. "He wasn't a good person, Pratt, he cheated and rubbed it in my face. Funny thing is, she looked a lot like me, from what I could tell. Different hair color, but there was a similarity for sure." Blowing a puff of air, I smirked. "I just don't understand. I mean, I'm not a cheater, but if I were, wouldn't I cheat because I wanted variety?" With a shrug, I let the thought go. I'd never understand it, and now that he was dead, he couldn't enlighten me. "Anyway, he didn't deserve to die." I pushed my fingernail into Pratt's, watching the pink blanch before pinking up again. "I just don't know how to process it. It didn't even hurt much when we broke up, but now . . . I feel . . . I don't know . . . I mean, do I go to the funeral?"

Pratt dropped his gaze to the key dangling from the ignition. When he looked back at me, there was a softness in his eyes. "Do you want to go?"

Going to Stellan's funeral wasn't something I was prepared for. I'd never met his parents, but I had met his sister. What would I say to her? How would I introduce myself to them? Or would I? Would Pratt come with me? How would I react to seeing his lifeless body, his face covered in too much makeup, lying in a casket? "No." I nodded my head hard enough to knock something loose. "No, I don't. Is that rude?"

Pratt rubbed his thumb in circles over my knuckles. "I think it's perfectly acceptable."

Stellan was dead. And for some reason, I had little emotion about it other than the shock. Maybe I hadn't cared about him as much as I'd thought. Or maybe I cared about him so much that my mind refused to process it. Either way, all I wanted to do was push it to the back of my head and concentrate on my weekend trip with Pratt.

Giving his fingers a squeeze, I grinned. "Let's get going. I can't wait to see Tennessee."

Chapter 25

Anna

It took an hour to get from the airport to Pratt's land. We drove down a curvy country road, past beautiful green pastures dotted with cattle, and bright red barns just like the stories. On my right we passed a single wide trailer. Goats were penned on the right side and the left held more cars than occupants of the tiny home. Something about the filth—a sofa near the front entrance, broken toys, and loads of junk in the front yard—made my stomach knot. I'd witnessed poverty before, but this felt different and wasn't helping my nerves.

After we rounded a corner, the world changed. It was as if we'd entered a different city, the rows of neglected trailers and poverty a distant memory. Pratt cracked the windows, the crisp air permeating the car. A fresh fire in the distance gave me a feeling of belonging and instantly began melting away any stress I'd brought along with me. For a city girl who'd never had the desire to visit the hills, this place seemed magical. There were trees everywhere. A slight breeze blew their branches and I stared in awe at the vivid colors of their leaves—red, orange, yellow, and deep green. The few houses

I saw were painted white with wrap-around porches like I'd seen in the movies.

Thirty-five minutes later, the car slowed and turned left onto an even smaller dirt road surrounded by massive trees that must've been hundreds of years old. I couldn't see any other houses. I also noticed the lack of telephone and cable wires. Why hadn't I thought to ask if there was electricity? Or a bathroom? Good God, if I had to go outside to use the toilet . . . there *had* to be a toilet.

"Question." I held up a finger and tried to keep the worry out of my eyebrows. "Does your cabin have facilities?"

He turned, his face much too serious for my comfort level. "As in a bathroom?"

"Uh-huh."

"We have an outhouse about a half mile up the hill, but no worries," he said, his face expressionless as he kept his eyes on the road. "I keep bedpans for nighttime so you don't have to walk in the dark."

I swallowed my tongue, the whole thing, and as a result, couldn't breathe. The only solution would be not to drink. At all. The entire weekend.

His laughter reminded me to breathe, but there was no taming the wildness of my shocked eyes.

"Of course there's a restroom." His hand slammed against the steering wheel as he continued to laugh on my account. "Did you think I was taking you tent camping or something?" His eyes darted from the road to me. "You wouldn't survive it, city girl."

A few minutes later, the cabin came into view. It had to be the exact replica of a picture on the front of the Lincoln Logs box. We drove down a dirt road and stopped in front of the house. A stone path, intricately laid by hand, led to the front door. Pratt grabbed our bags from the trunk, and I carried the groceries we'd picked up on the way.

Inside was a hunter's dream. A large deer head hung over the stone fireplace and was kept company by other animals that had been preserved in their natural state—I supposed.

"Are they real?" I pointed to the raccoon standing on the hearth.

"Yes. I come from a long line of hunters. I shot that one." He pointed to the hanging deer head. "I only hunt for food, not sport." He said it like he expected me to start an animal rights speech against him. In reality, it didn't bother me at all. It made sense to hunt for food—that was the only choice of our ancestors and wasn't that what God had intended? The meat I bought at the grocery had not only been killed, but was caged and raised for death. Yes, I liked the idea of hunting. I saw Pratt in a different light then. More masculine, if that was possible. I imagined him in his hunting gear, a rifle slung over one shoulder as he trudged out with the intent to put food on the table. It was primitive and sexy.

"When did you . . .? I nodded toward the animal.

"Couple years ago." His eyes widened with what looked like pride and his mouth jerked up into a grin. "Have you ever had venison?"

"I don't think so, but I'd try it."

He took my hand and led me through the cabin. The living room and kitchen were open and the largest of all the rooms. There were also two bedrooms on that level, both with full en suite baths. A set of stairs to the right led to a loft that held a pool table, air hockey, and a large television. The master bedroom was on the left side of the house, also upstairs, but separated from the game room.

"This is the only TV?" I ran my hand along the smooth wood finish of the pool table.

"You won't miss it, I promise." He laced his fingers in mine and walked me through the back door onto a deck that ran along the length of the cabin. A hot tub sat on one end and a hanging swing on the other. There was no way up or down from there. Surrounded by colorful trees, blushing in anticipation of Jack Frost's upcoming visit, there wasn't another building in sight.

"It should be ready to go." Pratt pointed to the hot tub. "We have a crew that comes in and keeps the place up."

I glanced down at myself. "I didn't even think to bring a suit at this time of year."

He smirked. "You don't need a suit." He raked his gaze up my body, then quickly turned around to face the trees. "There's no one in a ten-mile radius."

Using the back of my hand, I tried to cool the heat in my cheeks. *Why am I still so nervous around this man?* I had no response, and thankfully Pratt didn't dare look at me before my skin returned to its original hue.

The porch swing had to be my favorite. Gently rocking, we inhaled the fresh country air, free of exhaust and food cart scent. It brought out a side of me I didn't know existed. It was like a drug, relaxing every part of me. "Breathtaking. I love it. I absolutely love it."

"You haven't seen anything yet." A broad grin took over Pratt's face, reminding me of a child at an amusement park, eager for the next ride. Again, he took my hand and rushed me back through the house.

Once I was fitted with a hat, gloves, and my coat, we trekked around back to a storage shed. Inside were five four-wheelers.

"Ever ridden one of these?" Pratt asked, patting the seat of the red one.

"Nope, but I've driven a scooter. Can't be that different . . . right?" I'd started out feeling confident about it, but the way he looked at me warily made me rethink it. "I can do it," I announced, climbing onto the blue one that was second in line. I couldn't imagine where we would go or how fast we'd drive, but it was exciting to know we had open fields to explore. The last time I'd done anything even remotely similar was when I owned a Vespa instead of a car. It took me the short distance from my apartment to work a few years ago. It seemed like a great idea at the time, low mileage, inexpensive, but I hadn't considered rainy days and driving one in the snow was out of the question.

Pratt chuckled, shaking his head at my determination. "Okay, first you have to make sure this yellow button is in the on position." He flipped it for me. "Then turn the key to the right until it starts and give it some gas here." He placed my right thumb on the throttle lever and stepped back.

I got it started right away and couldn't help dancing in my seat from excitement. But after the fifth time stalling out within fifty yards, I gave up and climbed onto the back of Pratt's.

He pulled my arms around his body. "Hang on tight."

The connection sent an involuntary thrill up my spine, and I had to fight the urge to let my hands roam across his abs, up over his chest. This was the closest our bodies had ever been, aside from the standard goodnight kiss, even though they usually led to my hands sliding up around the back of his head, fingers tangled in his hair.

It had concerned me that he hadn't tried to take me to bed yet. To date, every man I'd dated had tried by the second date at least. But Pratt exuded class, always the gentleman. Still, it worried me that maybe he didn't want me physically. Even when his body reacted, he pulled away. I didn't know what to make of that, how to process it, until he invited me to his cabin.

I had wondered if he would put our bags in separate rooms—that would've shattered any hope I had for a deeper relationship. But our bags were together in the master bedroom. This would be the weekend we would come together as a couple.

With my body pressed against his backside, feeling every contour of his back muscles, his warmth heating me from the outside in, I knew I could easily fall in love with Pratt Rhodes. As he drove us through the woods, I let my imagination run wild with ideas of being lost in the middle of nowhere, building a fire with only two sticks before nightfall snuck up, and hunting for food to eat. It was a romantic fantasy that I let myself fall into until a colorful bug with clingy legs came to rest on the sleeve of my jacket. With a blood-curdling scream, I shook my arm until the little demon flew off.

Pratt came to a stop and whipped his head around. "What? Are you okay?"

"A huge bug." My arm was still flailing in response, or maybe to make sure he didn't come back. "On my arm. I think it was poisonous."

Pratt's entire body shook with laughter and, after a few minutes, I joined him. It was settled: I wouldn't survive one night.

"You good now?" he asked.

With a smirk, I nodded, wrapped my arms a little tighter, and we took off again. A sweet smell permeated the air as we exited the woods and drove through a field. At the top of a hill, Pratt stopped and shut the engine off.

I glanced around, looking for the source of the thick, sweet scent that filled the air. It wasn't flowery, but more of a mildly sweet, savory aroma. "What's that sweet smell coming from? I don't see any flowers."

"Wheat." He pointed a finger toward a vast field on our right. "The tall grass that looks dead, that's what you smell. How about this view?" Pratt took in the whole scene, his head moving as if taking a panoramic photo.

"It's unbelievable." My head shook in awe of the scene. Layers of hills dotted with colorful trees surrounded us.

Pratt turned around in his seat and faced me. "Isn't it? This is where I would've built."

"I thought the cabin was yours."

"Mine and my brothers'. My father designed it. It was meant to be a hunting lodge for him and his buddies. We've updated it, but I'd still like to build something here."

"What would you do differently?"

"A lower level. It's hot in the summer so an underground level would stay cool. I'd put the game room down there, a bedroom and bath. On the main level, the fireplace would be front and center—wood burning but with a gas hookup for instant ignition. I'm not the best cook, but I'd like a gourmet kitchen, if I can keep the rustic feel."

I imagined myself in that kitchen, making pancakes and bacon on a lazy Saturday morning. "You've thought a lot about it."

"Yeah," Pratt flashed a bashful, boyish grin that revealed one of his dimples. "I'm a bit of a daydreamer." He rested a hand on my thigh, leaned forward, and used his other hand to brush my hair away from my forehead. Energy radiated through the air, electrifying my senses. There was something about this place that relaxed Pratt and melted the stress. I could see a change in his eyes, hear it in his voice. In that moment, I needed to feel him, be connected to him. Wrapping my arms around his waist, I rested my head against his chest and hugged him. For such a simple, informal moment, it was intimate and just what I needed.

"Thank you for sharing this with me." I squeezed him tighter. "It's beautiful and peaceful." Straightening up, I drew in a cleansing breath of the fresh, country air.

His boyish grin turned serious as he cupped my face in his hands. "I'm happy you're here."

"Me too."

He dipped his head and brought his lips to mine, a gentle kiss that deepened as I squirmed in the seat, trying to get closer. Desire pooled in my belly as he wrapped his fingers in my hair. With fresh air in my lungs, the energy all around me, and the way Pratt was kissing me with everything he had, I was fully charged.

"Anna," Pratt breathed, "you know I care about you. I want you to feel comfortable here, with me."

"I do. I'm excited to spend the weekend with you, getting to know this side of you." Gulping down my nerves, I whispered, "And taking the next step in our relationship." As hard as I tried, I couldn't maintain eye contact. Shyness took over and I studied a chunk of grass next to the four wheeler.

Pratt cupped my jaw in his palm, pulled me close, and pressed his lips to mine. Electricity, power, and softness combined.

I didn't notice the chill in the air, or the sun dipping below the tree line. If we kept kissing and I had my way, we would have each other for the first time on the back of a four wheeler.

But a moment later, Pratt pulled back, pressed his forehead against mine, and groaned. "It'll be dark soon."

The cool air nipped at my nose as we traced the path back through the woods toward the cabin. In the kitchen, we filled bowls with steaming venison stew and added thick slices of bread with a generous amount of butter. My stomach growled, eager to taste the first bite. It needed a touch of salt, but I wouldn't dare ask for any. Pratt had gone to a lot of trouble, so instead I praised him for his skills in the kitchen.

After dinner we sat by the fire with a glass of Malbec and talked. Pratt was determined to learn more about a past I would rather leave there.

"After your mother died, you said you lived with family. On your mother's side?"

"Yes." I barely recalled how we knew the Kanes. Studying a spot on the floor as if it had the answer, I gave my best guess. "My mother's cousin and her husband."

"You don't remember?" Pratt gave me a sideways look.

"I do," I lied. "It's complicated." Pratt sipped his wine, patiently waiting for me to continue. "Okay, you know how when you're a kid, you call your parent's friends Aunt and Uncle out of convenience? It may have been like that, or maybe they were cousins. I'm really not sure. As soon as I left for college, I didn't see them again. I hated being a burden on anyone."

The fire roared next to me, the smell of logs charring beneath the unrelenting licks of hot flames. It was hypnotizing to watch and took my mind off—if only for a moment—Pratt's scrutinizing gaze. So what if he didn't buy my story. I was entitled to my privacy.

"You haven't talked to them since college?" He cocked his head to the side as if he didn't believe me. Or maybe he thought I was cruel for not reaching out to someone who had been so generous. But he wasn't there. He'd never understand what it was like to live in a stranger's home, eating food you hadn't earned, and sleeping under sheets you didn't deserve to be warmed by. They weren't mean people, and maybe one day I would reach out and find a way to thank them, but I remembered feeling unwelcome, a burden, an inconvenience.

After a heavy sigh, I shook my head, never taking my eyes off the flames, and took a sip of wine. Somehow the night had turned somber and I didn't know how to undo it.

"S'more?" Pratt set his empty goblet on the hearth and stood. Thank God he was ready to move on.

"I'm still nursing this one." I lifted my glass to show him it was still three quarters full.

"Smart ass." He flashed a wide grin and stood there like he was expecting me to sharpen my wits on him in a battle of comebacks. "Do you want to wait then?"

Smart ass? "Wait for what exactly?" Was I missing something? Admittedly, it had been a long day and I wasn't at my sharpest, but usually when someone still had almost a full glass, they passed on the offer to be topped off.

"S'mores," he chuckled. "Do you want one now or later?"

"What're you talking about?" I watched his lips, making sure I heard him correctly. *S'mores?* Must've been country slang for something.

"Seriously?" He straightened and looked at me with an expression that made me feel like I was on the wrong planet. "S'mores. Chocolate and marshmallow sandwiched between a graham cracker."

I blinked at him. "Never heard of it."

"Oh boy." He shoved his hands in his pockets and rocked back on his heels. "Sit tight. I'm about to rock your taste buds."

He returned with a tray of ingredients and two roasting sticks. After loading a marshmallow on each, he handed me a stick and instructed me on how to roast the perfect marshmallow. "Nice and brown on the outside, gooey on the inside. Watch, don't let it catch fire."

After sandwiching the concoction together, I took my first bite of a s'more. Melted chocolate and marshmallow oozed from the cracker and down my chin. My eyes slid closed as I savored the treat.

"Oh my God." I moaned the words as I chewed. "So good."

"You've got a little . . ." Pratt wiped the stickiness from my chin with his thumb. His proximity, along with the encouraging warmth from the fire, reignited the spark between us.

He moved toward me slowly, studying my eyes, for permission I guessed. I'd been so fickle with him, it was understandable. Leaning in, I met him halfway and we kissed. It began slowly, a gentle nudging between two new lovers wanting more. His hands came up to cup my face and pull me into him, deepening the kiss. Remembering to take a breath, I inhaled his intoxicating scent. Something about him drew me in and lulled me into a fantastical state. The emotions and desire running through me were a dizzying mixture that had me fighting for the least bit of control. Thankfully he took the lead, as I barely had the strength to participate. God, I had never felt anything like it before.

He pulled back and looked at me with a grin that I hadn't experienced before. It was cocky and so devilish that my heart tripped over itself, tumbling into my belly. I fidgeted under his gaze, silently begging him to move faster.

He held out a hand. "Come with me." His voice was rich, like warm honey.

Somehow my wobbly legs followed him up a flight of stairs to the master bedroom. I'd glanced at his bed earlier, but hadn't thought much of it until now. With the moonlight filtering in through the windows, I could see that it was large and masculine, the frame constructed of large tree trunks, possibly from his land. I'd have to remember later to ask him if he'd built it. But I couldn't think of it at the moment, not when he kissed me like a man starved for oxygen and I was the only source of it. When his tongue slid across my bottom lip before dipping inside, my knees nearly buckled. I couldn't remember a time when a man's mouth had felt as good.

His right hand left my face and moved down my side, gently grazing over my T-shirt until it stopped at the hem. At the same time his lips moved to my neck, he lifted my shirt. That was the first time I felt the warmth of his hand on my stomach. I shuddered from the touch and he pulled back to gauge my expression. Before he had a chance to worry about what I was thinking and pull the gentleman card, I reached for his shirt and lifted it up, over his head, and tossed it aside.

We were on the same page again, in sync, and filled with the desire of a couple touching for the first time. My hands fumbled with the button of his jeans as he tried pulling my shirt over my head. Stubbornly, I held on, so he moved to my jeans. By the time we were undressed, I could hardly catch my breath. I hadn't expected the sight of him naked. Clothed he was smart, handsome, someone you'd imagine in a Ralph Lauren commercial. Undressed he gave a very different impression. He wasn't the type of man with bulging muscles, but he was fit and trim. Every bit of him was masculine and hard.

All that needed to go were my panties, and I tried to take them off myself, but he stopped me. Stepping back, he took me in. "Anna," he released my name in a husky breath. "You're the most beautiful woman I've ever seen."

If his compliment was meant to make me feel beautiful, it worked. I was sure he was lying, but I let the words fall over me and build my confidence up. Normally I would've folded my hands over my chest and tried to hide, blushing under a man's too long gaze. But he made me feel comfortable, at ease.

In one swift motion, he lifted me up and I wrapped my legs around his waist. He walked to the side of the bed and sat me down on the edge. Flashing a wicked grin, he lowered himself between my legs. I thought he was going to remove my panties, but instead he ran his lips along the inside of my leg toward my most intimate area. Instinctively, I tried to clamp my knees together, but he held me still and rubbed his thumb over my panties until I nearly lost it.

The feeling of almost being there and then the absence of his touch was overwhelming. I didn't want him to stop when he did, but I was too proud to beg him not to. With my eyes closed, I concentrated on the hammering of my heart and the chaotic rhythm of my breathing.

Trying not to sway under his touch proved to be too difficult, so I rested back on my elbows as he kissed his way across my stomach. Pratt stood and slid his hands beneath me, easing me farther back onto the bed until my head rested on a pillow. My eyes finally adjusted to the moonlit room. Through heavy lids I watched the struggle on Pratt's face. His eyes were dark pools of ink, jaw slack, and I could feel his heart beating beneath my palm. He crawled over me until we were centered and dipped his head down to my breast, softly gliding his tongue across my nipple. A moan slipped from my lips as I reached for him, gently closing my fingers around his erection.

His body stiffened and he hissed, pulling away. "I wouldn't do that or this'll be over really soon."

I was desperate to tease him the way he did me, but he pulled out of my grasp and sat back on knees. Slipping his fingers beneath the waistband of my panties, he began to pull them off of me. My hips naturally lifted as he slid the fabric off and down my legs. When he carefully maneuvered the delicate lace over my heels like an expert bomb technician, we lost the physical connection and my body ached for his touch, to feel his hands on me again.

As if he knew what I needed—I was sure he needed it, too—he placed his hand on my calf, looked up, and gave me that wicked but boyish grin that undid me further than I thought possible.

All intelligence left as the overwhelming desire took over. A voice inside screamed for him to forget about the damn condom and take me already. If I didn't have him soon, I'd die, right here on the bed.

I was glad he ignored my inner screaming voices, though, because watching him roll on a condom was enough foreplay to last a lifetime. He made it look like an art. Something that should be in books and videos. "The Art of Donning a Condom" or simply "Sexy as Hell." The guys I had been with previously—lame and I could count them on one hand—had been sloppy, trying to get the dumb thing on. It always made me giggle at first, then get frustrated that it took so long and I was no longer in the mood. One guy would repeatedly lick his bottom lip as if he were solving the most difficult math problem.

Finally, Pratt snaked his body over mine. The energy and heat between us was sharp and soft at the same time. I imagined it was what it felt like right before you were struck by lightning. The anticipation was almost too much. Lifting my hips, I made contact and my body shuddered. Whatever this man was doing to me was powerful, addicting, and terrifying. I'd make a fool of myself for sure, but I had never wanted anything or anyone this much.

At the same time he rested on his left elbow, his right hand began to trace my body. Like a magnetic force, wherever his hand moved, that part of my body lifted to meet him. I let out a shaky moan, my breathing erratic. I could feel myself losing control and somehow I was okay with it.

He took his erection in his hand and stroked the tip against my wet seam until all pride left me and I had reduced myself to begging. "Please."

"God, Anna. Ask me again," he sighed.

"Please, Pratt. I want you." And I did want him. Not just the sex that I knew would be incredible, but all of him.

Gazing straight into my eyes, he pushed into me. Everything that made up who I was changed. I couldn't understand the feelings overtaking and overwhelming my senses, and I knew in a few short hours I would be standing in the shower, sorting and overanalyzing like I always did. But for now, all I could focus on was the moment, and let the fact that I was falling in love with Pratt Rhodes sink in, realizing I'd never be the same. Thank God.

***

Warmth filled me completely before I opened my eyes. The light that filtered in through the drapes was high up on the wall. We'd slept in. Memories of the magical night we'd shared occupied me while Pratt rested peacefully beside me. The heat from his body—pressed against mine from behind—along with the memory of our lovemaking, stirred a few exhilarating feathers inside my belly once again. When I thought about the way his hands had roamed over my bare flesh, the way his hot breath had felt against my neck, and the look of amazement on his face when our bodies had finally come together, moisture pooled between my legs and I squirmed, trying to alleviate the ache.

That small movement was all it took to awaken my dormant lover. I felt the hardness of him pressing into my backside as he groaned and hugged me to him. No words were needed, none were spoken. I shifted my body, reached around, and palmed his erection, pumping it once, twice. He placed a hand on my waist, keeping me in place as he reached for another condom. Lifting my leg slightly, he guided himself in, working slowly but deliberately. He kissed a path along my throat, nibbled on my earlobe, and bit down on my shoulder when the intensity peaked. The pressure on my shoulder and feeling Pratt lose control as he breathed my name all combined to send me over the edge with him. One day I'd have the confidence to let go freely, without reservation, but today I bit into the pillow to muffle the sounds of ecstasy.

"Good morning." He kissed my shoulder and separated himself from me. "Don't move." I felt the bed shift as he climbed out and walked to the bathroom.

I couldn't have moved if I wanted to, my body still trembling from the aftershocks of our lovemaking. Flipping onto my back, I pulled the covers up to my chin and giggled. It was happening too fast, but I couldn't stop myself. As hard as I tried not to fall in love, it was how I was knitted together. I fell fast, completely, and hard, no matter if the feeling was returned or one-sided. As hard as I tried to put walls up and protect myself from heartache, I failed every single time. If my sanity wasn't on the line, it would be comical how easily I fell in love.

Looking back, it was obvious I was in love with love, not the actual person. Hindsight is twenty-twenty, right? So here I was again, spiraling down the slippery slide, my brain high on the feelings of euphoria, that tickle in my stomach as if I was on the most thrilling ride. But something was different this time. It felt right. Maybe because we had taken things slow and didn't rush into sex. If you really cared about a person—loved them—you should be able to love them without sex. That's what happened for me. I fell in love with Pratt way before we were intimate, not knowing if the sexual connection would be there. My only hope was that he was falling in love with me, too.

Pratt bounded onto the bed, bouncing me with him. He rested on his side, propping his head on a fist. "Hungry?"

I tried to give him a wicked grin, but I'm sure it came off as shy and unsure. "Fully satiated." That statement earned me a kiss and a grin so broad I wanted to do it again and again.

Chapter 26

Anna

In the middle of the night on Saturday, a spider crawled across my face. By the feel of its legs inching across my flesh, it was a big one. My arms were sleep paralyzed and it took all the force I had to lift my arm and fling my hand in the direction of my forehead where the spider had found its final resting spot. The blow to my face wasn't as forceful as planned, but did the trick of waking me and shooting my body straight up into a sitting position. Then I realized the spider had only been a dream, and my surroundings were a nightmare.

My heart was beating too fast, an irregular rhythm drumming in my chest. Scrubbing my eyes, I tried to adjust to the darkness, find something familiar, or realize I was still dreaming. The weight of the blanket across my body didn't feel right. Something was definitely off. Glancing up I noticed wooden beams on the ceiling. The bed was made from logs, the furniture, too. *Not my bed. Not my room.* I had no memory of how I'd gotten here or why I was in this room . . . in this bed. The room grew darker and the walls began to close in around me, suffocating my personal space. This wasn't the first panic attack I'd experienced, but it might've been the worst.

I couldn't breathe. Trying to fill my lungs was painful. I could only suck in enough air to keep me alive, but my chest burned with hunger for oxygen. A hand reached up and grabbed my arm, stalling the beat of my heart long enough for that painful tickle to radiate through my chest. My assailant.

"Don't touch me!" I screamed, jerking my arm loose and scooting off the bed onto the floor. Realizing I was naked, my arms crossed over my body, covering me but doing little to conceal my vulnerability. I crawled backward until I reached a wall, cowering there until I had enough strength in my legs to flee.

"Where am I?" Daring a peek, I lifted my head just enough to watch the stranger ease out of the bed. With his arm outstretched, he moved carefully toward me "Who are you? What do you want?" I cried.

He stepped closer, his arms ready to close around me. Before the stranger could answer or get his hands on me, darkness took over.

***

"Anna, can you hear me?" My body was being cradled while someone stroked my hair. It wasn't something I had experienced before, but it felt good, relaxing and comforting.

After a few minutes, I blinked my eyes open and looked up at Pratt. His eyes seemed sad. Had I done something, or said something in my sleep?

"Where am I?" I gulped.

"In the cabin . . . with me." More stroking of my hair as his eyebrows formed a perfect V on his forehead. Had I fallen? "Are you okay?"

"I think so. Why're we on the floor?" No part of my body felt sore. "What happened?"

"I'm not sure. A nightmare? You didn't know who I was. You jumped out of bed, trying to get away from me. Before I could reach you, you passed out. Anna, you were terrified, and you scared the shit out of me. Are you sure you're all right?"

The panic in his voice made me feel terrible. If there had been a trunk nearby, I would've gladly climbed inside and hid myself from his gaze. Just when things were going perfectly—all of my dreams coming true—the most humiliating moment of my life jumps in and ruins everything. I couldn't imagine anything worse, except wetting the bed.

Instinctively, my thighs clenched, checking for urine. *Nope.* I would've died on the spot.

Still, I was humiliated. A weekend getaway with Pratt—our first weekend together as lovers—was not the ideal time for one of my blackouts.

After scooting out of his arms, I hugged my knees and dropped my head. "I'm sorry," I said, my voice was so small, I barely heard the words leave my lips.

"Sorry? You didn't do anything wrong." He talked to me in a soothing tone, like one would speak to a frightened child. "I just want to make sure you're all right." Pratt stood, walked over to the bed and grabbed a blanket to wrap around me. He rubbed his hands up and down my arms, trying to warm me. "You're shivering. Let's drive into town and get you checked out."

"No." I lifted a hand. "Absolutely not." Tears pushed against the confines of my lashes, but I refused to let them drop. Why couldn't we just forget, erase the event from our perfect weekend? "I'm not cold, I'm just shaken." Picking nervously at one of the threads on the blanket, I confessed, "I have blackouts sometimes." There it was, an imperfection, not only admitted, but acted out so he could get the full effect. I readied myself for the look, the one that tried to be polite and understanding but couldn't hide the eagerness to get as far away from me as possible.

His eyes remained soft, unyielding. He rubbed my back and asked, "Blackouts? How often? Have you seen a doctor, what—"

"It's just how I'm wired," I interrupted. "My doctor has done every test imaginable." The damn thread on the blanket wouldn't break loose, so I remained focused and pulled at it. I couldn't look at Pratt anyway and didn't know if I would ever be able to again. We didn't know each other well enough to talk about embarrassing medical issues. He hadn't signed up for this, and I was sure he was thinking of a way to get out of it. I'd make it easy for him and let him off the hook. There was no point in dragging it out any further and letting my heart break more than it already had. I had no doubt it would hurt more than the past heartbreaks. Pratt was different. He was the one for me, without a doubt. And without realizing it, he was the first person I'd given my whole heart to.

Maybe love wasn't meant for me, after all. Maybe there was another path I was meant to take in this life. But what a cruel game to build me with a heart and mind that craved just that. All I'd ever wanted—since I was a little girl—was a man to love and a family to raise. Psychologists would say it was the lack of love I'd received growing up that fed such a strong desire for family—a man that loved me as deeply as I loved him.

The drive home would be tough, awkward. The thread finally broke and I twisted it between my thumb and forefinger until it was a tiny ball. Clutching the blanket tighter to my body, I tried to calm the shakes and keep my teeth from chattering as I spoke. "I'd like to pack now."

"You want me to take you home?" he asked, his voice thick with disappointment.

The room was still dark and I had no idea what time it was. I hadn't thought about how selfish it was for me to keep him up, worrying about taking me home on little sleep. Biting my bottom lip did little to calm me. My hands trembled, my breath came in and out in short bursts, and my teeth chattered as I conceded, "We can wait until morning. You must be exhausted."

Pratt stood and offered a hand to help me up. "You're still shivering. Come with me."

I gripped the blanket, pulling it tightly against me and followed him downstairs. He guided me to the sofa and covered me with another blanket before adding a few logs to the fire that had nearly extinguished. Once the fire was ablaze again, he took a seat across from me on the thick wooden coffee table. He pulled my hand into his, thumbing circles over my knuckles in no particular pattern.

"What're you thinking right now?" he asked carefully as if I would break.

"I'm embarrassed." My voice was still shaky. "And sad."

"There's no reason to be embarrassed, Anna." He leaned forward, his soft dark eyes unblinking. "Especially with me." The way he spoke almost convinced me I was overreacting. It was as if I'd dropped a glass and broken it, instead of running from him and passing out on his floor. He paused for a moment, probably waiting for me to say something, then he reached out and tucked two fingers under my chin, lifting it until I looked him in the eye. "Tell me why you're sad." The emotion I saw in his eyes surprised me. He wasn't put off by what had happened, he seemed strong, sure, and truly concerned with my feelings.

"I ruined everything." The words, that I would've liked to keep to myself, flowed freely from my mouth. "I love it here, I love being with you, and I'm so mad and sad and . . ." The only thing left inside of me was a huff of air that I blew into my shoulder to hide my swollen, tear soaked eyes.

"You didn't ruin anything." Pratt gave my fingers a squeeze. "Anna, look at me." After squeezing my eyes shut to gain an ounce of courage, I turned and looked into Pratt's kind, brown eyes. "We all have nightmares. This is so not a big deal." He cocked his head to the side and gave me a soft, sincere smile. "Stay."

It took a few beats to process his words. He wanted me to stay? Either he was drawn to the crazy—made sense considering his career choice—or he was too tired to make the drive back. I wanted to stay. I really did. I also wanted to believe him, believe *in* him. "I want to stay, I do, but . . ."

"No buts. Stay." His brows tipped up and I saw the hope in his eyes. He flashed a dimple, sealing the deal. Did he know how powerful his smile was?

"Can we pretend this didn't happen?"

"If that's what you want." He shrugged. "Although I think you're making a bigger deal than it needs to be. It's not like you streaked through the house, dancing on the tables." His eyes widened with amusement. "Of course, I wouldn't object if you wanted to."

I couldn't help but smile a little. Pratt had a way of putting me at ease. Maybe it was his tone or the way he looked at me with hopeful expectation. After a sigh, my embarrassment eased and my sadness dissolved. The perfect weekend was back on.

That night—or early morning, rather—we made love on a soft rug in front of the fire and then fell asleep there. Wrapped in a blanket, Pratt's arms snaked around my body as he held me close, I thought I heard him whisper through my semi-sleeping state the words I'd been dying to hear one man—the right man—say all my life.

"I love you."

Chapter 27

Anna

Our weekend passed too quickly, but I got to bring home the best souvenir—Pratt Rhodes. He was kind, loving, amazing, and after the weekend we'd shared, I had no doubt he was the one. Finally and certainly the one. I couldn't wait to secretly scribble *Mrs. Pratt Rhodes* and *Anna Rhodes* on a scrap piece of paper that I would then bury deep in the trash for no one to ever see.

Pratt held my suitcase as I worked the key into the lock of my apartment door. As soon as we were in, I walked straight through to the balcony to check on my flowers, calling over my shoulder, "Just set the case down. I need to check on my lovelies."

Other than needing a drink and reassurance that I loved them dearly—I talked to them, I admit. I had read somewhere that it was good for them—I saw they had made it just fine without me for four days.

When I returned to the living room, Pratt was standing with his hands in his jean pockets, a wide grin on his face. His expression was exactly how I felt inside. Giddy.

Closing the space between us, I snaked my hands behind his neck and stood on tiptoes to kiss him. "Thank you for taking me to Tennessee."

He gripped my waist and pulled me in tighter. "I had the best time. I wish it didn't have to end."

"It doesn't have to end yet. Stay for a while." *Forever.* "I can make some coffee. Are you hungry?"

I walked to the refrigerator and inspected the contents. "I have pickles." Guess I needed to stock the fridge. "You hungry for pickles?"

Pratt chuckled and called out, "Coffee's fine."

I filled the machine with water, scooped some grounds into the filter, and pressed the power button. When I finished, I padded over to Pratt and slid my arms around his waist. There was no safer, warmer place than in his arms, my head resting against his chest. He always smelled divine—fresh and clean with a hint of outdoorsman. I wasn't sure how they bottled the outdoors and made it work with Pratt's pheromones, but his scent did something to me. It was more than a turn on, more than wanting to be as close as possible to him. It drew me to him and, when I inhaled everything Pratt Rhodes, I felt alive.

"I loved this weekend. I loved spending time with you. I love you." The words flew out of my mouth without warning, straight into Pratt's white button down shirt. I did love him, that wasn't my struggle. But I had wanted to wait so I didn't sound so desperate. I thought that I'd heard him say it that night in front of the fire, but convinced myself that I had been dreaming. It was no secret that I always fell hard and fast. But it was different this time. Pratt was different, and I knew

232

without a doubt that we belonged together. I could easily envision us starting a family one day and raising them on his land in Tennessee.

Pratt's smile widened until his dimples sank deep into his cheeks. "I love you, Anna." He took my hand in his and stroked his thumb nervously over my knuckles. "I wanted to tell you this weekend, but the timing was never . . ." A ridiculous smirk twisted his mouth. "I actually whispered the words one night when you were asleep." He shook his head. "I don't know why I was too nervous to tell you again. You just do something to me." A soft chuckle left his lips, the boyish kind that let me see that bashful side of him. Something about that side of him made my love deepen. There was no question that Pratt was a strong man, fearing nothing. Something about revealing himself in such a vulnerable way made him stronger in my eyes. Irresistible, really. Reaching up, I slid my hands around the back of his head and dragged his mouth to mine. It felt different, deeper, more spark, now that we'd confessed our love.

I wanted to tell him over and over again, but chanted it inside my head instead. *I love you, Pratt Rhodes. I love you, I love you, I love you.*

I would say we made out like teenagers, but we didn't. Teens haven't experienced heartache yet, so they don't know what it's like to finally feel their heart mend and beat harder than ever before. No, we made out like adults. Adults that had waited a lifetime for each other and couldn't seem to express it any other way than connecting every part of their body that was possible with our clothes on.

After a moment of catching our breath and letting it all sink in, Pratt leaned his back against the wall, pulled me against him, and asked, "Did you really enjoy Tennessee?"

"So much," I sighed, thinking about the fresh air and simmering fall colors that lined his property. "I've always been a city girl, but there was something about it. Fresh air, the sound of crickets and owls." Several cars honked their horns in the street below. I cocked my head toward the window. "The lack of noise."

"Let's go back." He pulled back, the excitement in his voice contagious, causing me to smile. "I want you to be there for Christmas and meet everyone."

I blinked a few times as I stared into his hopeful eyes. Then something inside of me snapped off and ran for the hills, trying to drag me along. But why should I be afraid to meet Pratt's family? He was good and kind. I had no reason to suspect his family wasn't just as decent.

I gulped. I knew why I was afraid. It was always the same story. The mother would question me about everything.

"Where are you from, dear? Does your family live close? I can't believe they let you out of Christmas so easily. Are you in church?"

I would answer the twenty questions, under the scrutiny of all eyes at the large dinner table, and then the worst. All eyes on me, filled with pity.

"So you've been living alone all these years. I just can't imagine what that's been like for you. No one? Not even a cousin?"

Nope. That's why I latched onto your son so tightly. Trying to fill a void.

I'd never said that and would never, but I was sure there was some truth to it. I wanted this relationship to work. I'd never met anyone like Pratt. What if his family hated me?

"Well?" Pratt nudged my arm.

That sinking feeling, the urge to sprint out of the apartment until my legs wouldn't carry me any further grew stronger by the minute. I could feel the clingy side of me emerging at the same time. I had a decision to make and both might end with me losing Pratt.

I chose to cling. "I'm nervous."

"About meeting my family?" He raised an eyebrow and looked at me like I'd grown another nose.

I nodded, my gaze fixed on my chipped nail polish. "Yeah."

"Trust me, you have nothing to worry about. They'll love you, babe."

"Or they won't," I argued weakly. "There's always a chance they won't." My features turned stormy, considering the worst.

His optimistic smile turned into a confused frown. "Did I give you the impression that my family was perfect? Because they're not. My mom is the sweetest person on earth. She never wears makeup or dresses up. She raised three boys so she's seen and heard everything. Nothing you could do or say would ever top Matt sleep walking and peeing in her shoes in the middle of the night."

"Seriously?" My eyes widened with amusement.

"Yes." He laughed. "And that's not the worst story I can tell you." Pratt rubbed my arms as if warming me from a chill. "Then there's my dad. I love him, I do, but he's an asshole." He shoved his hands into his pockets and walked toward the window. "I'll never be the son he wanted me to be. So who gives a damn what he thinks."

Pratt focused on something outside of the window, but I knew he was struggling with a memory.

"Who did he want you to be?" I couldn't imagine anyone greater than Pratt Rhodes. Did he expect him to cure world hunger in a day or something?

"He wanted me to follow in his footsteps." He swiped his hand in the air like he was showing me an advertisement. "World renown thoracic heart surgeons, William Matthew Rhodes, senior, William Matthew Rhodes, junior, and William Pratt Rhodes."

"What about Walker? He's not even studying medicine. At least you're in the field."

Pratt shrugged dismissively. "He's the baby and since I wrecked the lineup anyway, he doesn't get the slightest bit of wrath from Dad." He shrugged a shoulder. "It's not a big deal. Really. I just get tired of it, you know? What I'm studying is important, too. Dad made his point. Continues to make his point. I just wish he'd move on to something new, like me never being able to beat him at golf." He laughed, but I knew it was a cover up. I didn't know what it was like to have a father's disapproval—or approval for that matter—so I felt ill-equipped to help him.

The only thing I could think of was agreeing to go with him for Christmas. If it would ease his time with his father, I'd take that burden. I loved Pratt with all of my heart and would endure anything for him. Besides, his mother sounded like a character from a fairytale, and I couldn't wait to meet her. Maybe it wouldn't be as bad as I was picturing.

Wrapping my arms around Pratt's waist, I offered, "I'll spend Christmas with you." Pulling back, I looked up and watched his lips tug into a smile. "I'd love nothing more than to spend the holidays with the man I love."

Chapter 28

Bree

Blaize. He had moves like no other man before him and an appetite to match. We were at Level Ten, an older but newly updated club in SoHo, when it hit me like a boulder. In the four weeks since I had met him, I hadn't been with another man.

I glanced around the room, testing my theory that I still had game. Dark hair: too stiff. Blond in the corner checking his phone: selfish lover. Stocky but fit: three minutes' tops. To top it all, most of them portrayed money. Two things became shockingly clear to me. First, and most importantly, I didn't want any other men, Blaize was it for me. Second, we were in the wrong club.

"Let's go somewhere fun." I slammed the rest of my drink and stood, smoothing my palms down the sides of my fitted green dress. If you could call it that. There was barely enough material to call it much of anything.

Claiming my territory, I slid my hand under Blaize's arm and gave his bicep a squeeze as we walked out of the club. I knew he was the best looking man in the room. Hell, it was unfair to every other man in the world how gorgeous he was. He was mine, so I did the only thing I knew to take care of him.

***

Blaize shot me a curious expression when the cab driver pulled up in front of Play, one of the most prestigious gentleman's clubs in the city. "You know this is a strip club."

"Too shy?" I teased, easing out of the cab after he paid the driver.

I'd visited Play once before, but I'd worn my red wig.

We were ushered to a table near the front stage, but I shook my head. "Something in the back." I nodded in the direction of a small table in the corner where a brunette was giving it everything she had on a small round stage. She slid up and down a pole, wrapping a leg around the metal and arching her back as she twirled. It had to be tough, working the pole like she had been, for an audience of zero. Everyone knew the front of the room was for wide-eyed bachelors and parties. The real action happened out of the spotlight.

The large man, overdressed in a three-piece suit, shrugged and took us to the table, holding my chair until I took a seat. "Your server will be by to take your drink order. Enjoy."

In a matter of seconds, a petite busty redhead in pigtails knelt beside the table—a trick they taught her to show off her ample cleavage—and asked what we would like to drink.

"Martini for me, extra dirty." I flashed her a wink and waited for Blaize to thaw from his stunned state and place his drink order.

"Same." I guess that was all he could come up with. He'd hate the drink.

Blaize refused to look at the pole dancer, keeping his gaze firmly fixed on me. He was trying to be a gentleman, but that was the last thing I wanted. I couldn't fall for him. It was too soon . . . it would always be too soon.

"She has a beautiful body," I breathed, my gaze traveling over her beautiful curves before I turned toward Blaize. "Where do you think she's from? Her skin is dark and smooth."

His eyes darted from me to her and back to me. "No idea. Hungry?" He browsed the menu, clearly uncomfortable. I almost felt sorry for him, torn between wanting to make it worse and wanting to ease his discomfort.

Our server brought our drinks and asked if we'd like anything else. Without making eye contact, Blaize ordered a couple of appetizers. I chimed in before she turned away. "I think we could use a round of shots. Patron and lime."

"You trying to get me drunk?" Blaize pulled my red velvet chair closer to his and rested a large, rough palm on my thigh.

"If that's what it takes to make you relax."

He shot me a sideways glance. "I've never been with anyone like you. Most girls would be furious if their guy looked at another woman."

Their guy? My guy? Was he implying we were an item?

This shit was getting real, and fast. I took a long sip of my drink. Now I was the one who needed to relax. "Does it make you uncomfortable to be with someone who appreciates beautiful women?"

He took a deep breath, processing my question. After a healthy pull of his martini, followed by a grimace, he shrugged. "It's every man's fantasy . . . until you're faced with it." He cocked his head to the side, studied me for a moment, and then grinned. "You're serious. This isn't a test, you're fucking serious."

I didn't say a word as he argued with himself, trying to figure the situation out.

Our shots arrived, and I lifted my glass. "To having fun. No second-guessing." I poured the liquid down my throat and sucked the juice from the lime.

Blaize lifted his glass, excitement replacing the look of concern in his eyes. "To the first woman to blow my mind."

I tried to twist his words in my head, make them sound less meaningful. *Don't do it, don't fall for him.*

The appetizers were wasted as neither of us touched a bite. I made eye contact with a slim blonde across the room in a skimpy gold dress. She strode over, introduced herself as Candy, and asked if either of us wanted a lap dance. I didn't find her attractive, but thought it would loosen Blaize up. He kept his eyes on me, a goofy grin on his face, and his hands pinned to his sides. We needed another shot.

The next lap dance was mine. Maybe if he watched, he'd see the relationship lines between us were blurred. Ava, a brunette that barely spoke English, sunk her knees into the cushion of my chair, one on each side of my hips, and rubbed her bare breasts against me. I glanced at Blaize only once to make sure he was enjoying the show we were giving him. My hands slid down the contour of her slim waist and moved around back to cup her ass. I knew better than to touch her breasts out in the open—that was against the rules—but I couldn't help myself. Her body was perfect and she'd gone well over the time allotted for a lap dance.

I watched Blaize's eyes darken as the weight of her breasts rested in my hands. Her smooth skin felt like silk beneath my fingers, and I couldn't wait to watch Blaize experience her. She smelled like they all did, mild vanilla overpowered by a floral aroma. My guess was they all shared the same lotion and cheap perfume.

"Private room?" I whispered in her ear. I was sure Blaize's credit card would cover the cost.

Ava pulled the top of her dress up and latched the hook around her neck. She slid off my lap and smiled at Blaize who looked like he was high, his eyes half-mast.

Standing, I held a hand out for Blaize, who followed without question. Up a flight of stairs and around the corner, we stepped into a room with plum walls and black velvet couches. The only light was the blue glow coming from beneath the sofas.

A waitress brought in a bottle of champagne, a bowl of strawberries, and a side of whipped cream. After setting them on a small table against the wall, she shut the door. Ava pushed the table against the door to ensure we wouldn't be interrupted again.

It wasn't my first threesome, but gauging Blaize's body language, it was his.

***

Hangover Sunday came every week as expected, but when the sun rose on this one, it was going to be a killer. I rarely puked from partying, but by three I was hugging the porcelain bowl and retching the night's variety of poisons. I could handle liquor. Mixing it with ecstasy and the cheap floral perfume of the whore Blaize and I had shared was too much.

He'd enjoyed himself and I had worked hard to make sure all of his fantasies came true. He'd said he could handle my cravings. We'd see if he really could. There was a fine line between going too far and balancing on a line that kept him coming back for more.

Chapter 29

Bree

Three days had slipped by easily. Nights were most likely spent partying and I'd tried to find a day job as soon as the cloudiness of the world's greatest hangover lifted. With zero skills that didn't involve being naked, I hadn't even known where to start.

The Comedy Cellar needed to replace two cocktail waitresses and the interview went well. Although I lied about my experience, how hard could it be to bring drinks to people? Thankfully, the manager was male, so my skill set didn't matter much. I'm pretty sure he hired my tits anyway. Excited about the life change, I sent a text to Blaize.

I got a new job. Want to celebrate?

I didn't expect to hear from him since he worked all weekend, but my phone dinged before I slipped it back into my bag.

Hey, I've missed you.

Another text came through immediately after. **Congratulations! Yes. Dinner at my place?**

Sure. What time do you get off?

It's 1 am. I'm leaving now.

One in the morning? How had it gotten so late? Nothing would be open except the pizza joint around the corner from his apartment. Greasy pizza wasn't sexy, but my stomach grumbled thinking about the thin, greasy pie and I couldn't wait to have a slice.

I'll pick up pizza and meet you there.

By the time I made it to Blaize's apartment, I was famished. The smell of melted cheese so close to me made my mouth water. One rap on the door and it swung open. Blaize snaked an arm around my waist and pulled me in, kicking the door shut with his foot.

"Damn, I've missed you." The pizza rested on my palm, high in the air like a serving tray while Blaize claimed my mouth, making me realize how much I'd also missed him. He pulled back, a smile streaked wide on his face, and then pulled me in for another kiss. "Seriously, woman," he breathed. Grabbing the pizza box, he opened it, took out a slice, and shoved most of it in his mouth. "Let me rinse off real quick. Eat, find something on TV. I'll be right back." He backed up, never taking his eyes off of me until he rounded the corner and was out of sight.

His apartment was a mess and I had trouble finding the remote, so I just enjoyed my pizza. After two slices I was full and ready to see my man. Without disappointing, he appeared, a white towel wrapped around his waist. He strolled into the room, rubbing a towel over the top of his head and flashed a grin that made me feel like the melted cheese topping the pizza. Damn, that man did things to me.

Blaize poured two double shots of Patron into red Solo cups and grabbed a couple of lime wedges. "To you and your new job." After tapping the plastic together, we tipped the cups and drained the contents, sucking the lime dry immediately afterward. "So, tell me about this job."

"I'll be serving drinks at the Comedy Cellar on Macdougal." After fishing out another slice of pizza for Blaize, I poured a little more tequila into our cups and headed to the kitchen, calling over my shoulder. "Where are the limes? Fridge, counter?"

"Counter. I'm happy for you, babe, but Macdougal street? That's not a great part of town."

I plopped down on the sofa next to him and frowned. "Seriously? You worried about me or the people who try to mess with me?"

"Can't help it," He shrugged. "I know you're tough, but you're mine." He wedged his hand under my ass and pulled me closer. Pushing me onto my back, he hovered over me, the intensity in his eyes securing me to the sofa. "And I take care of what's mine."

***

I'd never been ashamed of my body, in fact I preferred to be naked, but lying on the living room floor, post-sex, I suddenly felt bashful. "I'm cold." I lied, faking a shiver and pulled a blanket off the couch to wrap myself.

Blaize watched my every move until I was settled, the blanket pulled up under my arms and wrapped around me like a burrito. His eyes followed his fingers as they traced a path along my arm. He seemed to be deep into a daydream, a slow smile playing at his lips.

"What's on your mind?" For some reason I was nervous about what his answer might be.

"Let's get away." I didn't have to see his face to know how excited he was about the idea. Hadn't he gotten the message last time we talked about it?

Resting back on my elbows, I looked up at the ceiling, mentally tracing the firework designs. Who the hell had designs on the ceiling these days? His apartment wasn't that old. "I'm not ready," I sighed. I knew he'd be disappointed, but I just wasn't ready and I didn't know if I'd ever be ready.

"No family." He held his hands up in defense. "Just the two of us."

Turning onto my side, I faced him and the ridiculous grin on his face. No family? I could do that. Couldn't I? *Two nights away. Two nights with the same man. In a closed space.* Panic rose inside of me, building, building until my ears felt like they might pop. After a three-count inhale and measured exhale, I decided I could do it. Or at least try. *Two nights with this man.* A smile pulled at the corners of my mouth as I reached up and stroked his rough beard. This man turned my world upside down for the better. *Yeah, I can do it.*

My head tipped up slowly and then back down. It wasn't a full nod, but I think he got the message. His eyes lit up which made my smile stretch so wide my cheeks ached. "Yes, let's."

***

Five days ticked by. My new job wasn't due to start for another week, so my nights were consumed with daydreams of our trip. After packing and unpacking twice, I bought all new clothes and zipped them into the suitcase. I was determined to start fresh and this weekend was the perfect way to begin that journey. I'd never wanted to change my ways until I met Blaize. Funny, if someone had told me a few months ago that something like this would happen, I would've laughed and knocked their crazy ass on the ground. But that crazy thing people experience—some call it love, I'm not ready to call it that—really has the power to change you. It changed me—Bree, the unchangeable. Who would've thought I'd meet someone who accepted my addictions, my problems, like they were nothing. It wasn't like I was addicted to picking scabs, I was a fucking sex addict, and Blaize was certain he could handle me.

So far, he was doing a fine job keeping me satiated. I couldn't get enough of him. I wasn't sure if it was because the sex was so amazing, because he pushed my limits in every way possible, or if I was healing after telling him the truth. Whatever it was, I didn't want it to end. Of course, I knew that might wear off and I'd need a fix, but it was worth trying with him. For some reason he was worth my energy. It was going to take a lot of effort on my part, but I had to give it a shot. This weekend would be the test to see if I could stay the course.

Long Island Beach seemed the perfect place to unwind and play. Walking towards his building, rolling my small suitcase behind me, my thoughts were consumed with Blaize. His touch, the way his large palms felt on my skin, his lips and the way his scruffy beard scratched my chin and neck, and those intense blue eyes that reached into the deepest part of me and changed everything. I couldn't get enough of him.

My daydreams were cut short when I strolled up to his building and saw a few police officers standing out front. I'd always been careful about keeping my face away from security cameras when I robbed someone, but seeing the cops still pushed my guard up. The hairs on the back of my neck were standing, blood rushing to my ears to drown all sense of reason. Turning around, I found the nearest ally and leaned against the wall, trying to catch my breath.

I racked my brain, trying to remember if I'd robbed anyone from his building. *Think.* I palmed my forehead, trying to rattle a memory. I didn't think I had. Once I was certain, I pushed off the wall and took slow, measured steps toward his apartment. *Remain cool. Breathe in. Breathe out. You didn't do anything wrong.*

The three police officers outside remained busy, talking while one of them looked through a notepad. I made my way to the entrance of the building when an EMT was coming out. "Excuse me, miss," he said, steering one end of a gurney while the other pushed it through the door.

My shoulders relaxed and I exhaled the breath I hadn't realized I was holding. They weren't here for me. I stood to the side and watched the gurney pass, wondering if it was a man or woman, old or young. I would never know as the person on the gurney was enclosed in a thick, black body bag.

Not wanting to be rude, I remained outside until they lifted the stretcher into the back of the ambulance that I hadn't noticed before. No lights, no sirens—they didn't need them for the poor soul in the bag. The event almost soured my good mood, but I was too excited to share the weekend with Blaize. As I rode the elevator up to the seventh floor, my body heated with the thought of getting a quickie in before our trip.

I needed to squelch the craving before we left. Being in the car with a man who could make me wet just by looking at me, and cause goose bumps to rise with a single kiss, would be unbearable. No, I needed to have him inside of me now. My addiction was like any other—it needed to be satisfied every two or three hours or I'd get the shakes and do something stupid. It was a sickness, there were enough articles to prove it. But if you had to have a sickness, this was a fucking great one to have.

One of the wheels on my small suitcase was a little off and made a ticking noise as I walked down the hallway toward Blaize's door. With three taps from my knuckles, I planted a sexy "fuck me" grin on my lips and waited. Two more knocks and the smile faded. Fully pissed, I slammed my fist against the door. "Dude, get out of the shower already and open the door."

Nothing.

More pounding. Fucker. Leaving me out in the hall wasn't cool. I deserved more respect. Plus, I was already late, so he should've been ready. I pulled out my phone, ready to call him when the neighbor across the hall came out and just looked at me. He was an older man with salt and pepper hair that looked like it had been professionally aged for his perfectly groomed appearance. If I had to guess, I'd say he was gay and had a beautiful Shih Tzu named Oliver.

"Miss?" he asked.

"Yeah?" I looked for the dog. I knew he was in there.

"Are you looking for the man that lives there?"

I hesitated, trying not to let my anger show. So this was how Blaize was going to leave me. He didn't have the balls to tell me I was too much for him, that I was a crazy ass bitch, and that he couldn't be with someone like me. No, he was the cruel type, a coward. Instead of breaking things off, being honest, he'd set up a trip and raised my hopes for a normal life. And then the fucker up and left. No call, no text, no letter. Just gone. "I was." My face betrayed me as one brow lifted in disgust. "But I see he's not home."

"No." The man bent down just in time to catch his dog and pull him into his arms before he ran through the door. It wasn't the Shih Tzu I'd imagined, but a Yorkie was close enough to make me smirk. "He died. They took him away early this morning." He took a step toward me, dog in one hand, the other reaching out. His voice grew thick as a dark fog enveloped me. "I'm sorry, did you know him well?"

Died? My body felt like a block of stone, unable to move or breathe as the man's words attempted to break through the fog.

I felt my body slide down the wall onto the floor. *Blaize.* My heartbeat slowed until I wasn't sure it was beating at all. My breathing became shallow as I choked out the words I'd never gotten to say, "I loved him." I suffered the heaviness of something pushing me down to the depths of hell. *He was my everything.* My vision blurred as I let the darkness creep up my legs, over my knees, the thick, black cloud climbing up my thighs.

I can't . . .not yet. Not here.

As I picked myself up from the floor, the stranger offered a hand. "Can I call someone for you? A cab?"

"No, thank you." I rubbed my eyes, determined not to cry. "I've got a car waiting." That was a lie, but I needed to get out of there.

It didn't take long to hail a cab and get back to my apartment. Once inside, beneath the warmth and safety of my favorite blanket on the couch, I let the grief seep in. Tears dripped down my face as I thought about the heart-shattering loss. He had changed everything and now he was gone. Like a tornado he came into my life, plowed down my walls and disastrous way of life, and twisted it into something new and beautiful. I heard a noise in the distance that sounded like a lamb being slaughtered. Swiping my tears with the back of my hand, I realized it was me.

Blaize had died on a Friday at two-twenty-seven in the afternoon. I died the same day, time unknown.

Chapter 30

Jane

Each day Jane collected fresh blooms from the Oleander shrub. She never took enough to be noticed. Some were left to dry for tea, but most were used fresh. Pulling a saucepan from the cabinet, she added two cups of fresh flowers and one cup of water. Being careful not to inhale the steam from the boiling flowers, she used the exhaust above the stove and wore a surgical mask while working with the toxic brew.

Once the mixture was reduced to a syrup consistency, she let the mixture cool, strained the flowers, and filled six syringes. Although beautiful, the pink, delicate flowers of the Oleander plant were deadly when ingested. The two main components, oleandrin and oleandrigenin, acted as a cardiac glycoside when given in small, exact doses. A little too much caused stomach cramps and blurred vision. Concentrated and injected straight into one's system caused death.

After her first few kills, Jane had to find a way to relax her victim's muscles. Seizures were inconvenient and a hassle. One of the dying men had kicked over a lamp, sending shards of glass all over the hotel floor. The mess had delayed Jane's departure and made for a bigger clean up. Morphine was the answer, and easier to come by than she had thought. She always wore a wig and dark glasses when she met with her dealer and never told him her real name.

Lifting the vial of Morphine, she inserted each needle tip, one at a time, and pulled half a Millimeter into each syringe already filled with the toxic Oleander serum.

With six new syringes ready to go, she could begin again, fulfilling her plan. Carefully placing the syringes in a box, she slipped them into her clutch. A grin tipped the corner of her mouth as she whispered the last part of her favorite British nursery rhyme, "We all fall down."

Chapter 31

Anna

Early Sunday morning, a knock on the door woke me. Pratt's arm was draped across my back so I tried to slip out without waking him. He was exhausted from working all week to make up for taking a couple days off for our trip, so we planned on sleeping in and then spending a lazy day at the park.

Pratt lifted his head and asked, "Where are you going?" His voice was groggy with sleepiness. The knocking came again, louder this time. "It's early still, right?"

Reaching down, I ran my hand through his dark wavy locks and kissed his forehead. "I have no idea who it is, but I'll get it. Go back to sleep."

"What time is it?" He rubbed his eyes and flipped over onto his back.

"Ten." Slipping into my robe, I tied the belt and called out, "Coming." For some unknown reason, the hairs on the back of my neck stood like obedient soldiers. No telling who was on the other side of the door, but no one ever came to my door.

Looking through the peephole, I saw two uniformed police officers. The one from the station and a female officer. After unlatching the chain and unlocking both bolts, I opened the door and clutched my robe to cover any exposed skin. "Yes?"

"Miss Spencer, you remember me from the station. This is Officer Benedict. We have a subpoena to talk to you. Can you follow us down to the station?"

I clutched my robe tighter. *Subpoena?* My heart skidded chaotically in my chest. Why did they need a subpoena to talk to me? I hadn't given them any grief the last time they asked me to talk. Was I in trouble? "I don't know what more I can tell you about Stellan. I've told you everything I know."

"I understand." His lips curved up into a tight smile and then quickly dropped back down into a straight line. "This is in regards to another investigation." He rocked back onto his heels. "We'll wait out here for you to get dressed. You can either ride with us or follow us down."

Pratt was behind me, pulling a T-shirt over his head. "My car's out front. I'll drive you."

After shutting the door, I walked toward the dresser to pull out something to wear.

"What do they want now?" Pratt asked, sounding irritated. "I thought you answered their questions."

I pulled my leg through a pair of jeans. "I did. I have no idea." My voice sounded robotic, mimicking what was going on inside of my head. *Just get through it. There has to be an explanation.* Slipping a cream sweater over my head, I pulled my hair into a ponytail and ran a toothbrush over my teeth, skipping the paste since we were in a hurry. "Thanks for going with me." My brows furrowed with worry. "I'm a little nervous." The truth was, I was more than a little nervous. I knew I hadn't done anything wrong, but a lot of innocent people were rotting in prison for crimes they didn't commit. Or at least that's what the movies portrayed.

Pratt gripped my shoulders and rubbed my arms up and down like he was getting me ready for a championship boxing match. "Hey," He bent down so we were face to face. "You've got nothing to worry about. You didn't do anything wrong. They're probably just looking for mutual friendships or anything that can help them find more information. I'll be right there with you the whole time." His voice was filled with so much conviction, I almost believed him. Almost.

* * *

The last time I walked into the police station it was quiet. Today was a different story. It was loud, cold, busy, and I felt extremely uneasy. A man in handcuffs was jerked passed me by an officer to who knows where as he repeated, "I'm innocent, man. Leave me be, I didn't do nothing." Soon after he passed, I caught the pungent smell of alcohol coming from his breath and pores.

Pratt had to wait in the lobby while I was taken to a back room with a table and four chairs. Detective Benedict, the female, waved a hand for me to take a seat on the other side of the table, farthest from the door. As I took my seat, I made it clear that they were wasting their time with me. "I told you everything I know about Stellan Fulks."

Officer Benedict slid a picture across the table in front of me. "Have you ever seen this person?" Her voice didn't match her face. Dark brown hair pulled into a tight braid at the nape of her neck revealed a simple, pure beauty. But her tone was hard, her voice raspy, making me believe she was a longtime smoker.

All it took was one quick glance to be certain I'd never seen the man. "No, I haven't." The picture was of a man in a white button down, sleeves rolled up. His arms were covered in colorful tattoos. A scruffy beard made him look like a lumberjack. He wasn't the type of guy Stellan would've hung out with. Maybe he was the one who killed him? Goosebumps followed the chill that snaked across my skin.

Benedict raised one brow. "You're sure you've never seen him?" She lifted the picture off the table and handed it to me. "Take a closer look."

Holding the picture, I studied the man. His eyes were a startling blue, a stark contrast to his monstrous build and scruffy demeanor. "No," I confirmed, my head shaking back and forth. "I'm positive I've never seen him before."

"Do you know the name Blaize Martin?"

I took a moment to think, but a name like that would surely stick with you. It sounded like the name of a porn star. If I had heard his name, I would've remembered. "No, I've never heard of him."

"Take your time, really think about it. Blaize Martin." Benedict seemed to know something I didn't. She gave me a demeaning glare, one side of her mouth pulled up as if she were about to smirk.

I gave her a sideways glance, concerned that I was missing something very important. Had I not felt like I was about to throw up, I would've asked if we were on a punk reality TV show. Instead, I released a shaky breath and answered, "I don't think I'd forget a name like that."

Detective Mullane looked up from his folder and tapped his pen on the table. "Would you mind submitting a DNA sample?"

"If it would help, sure." I answered too quick. What if they were trying to set me up?

I shook my head, talking myself out of that argument. This wasn't a movie, this was real life. I could trust the law. Maybe I needed a lawyer, though? "That's the right thing to do . . . I mean, I don't have anything to hide so I shouldn't be worried about anything . . ." I couldn't hide the tremor in my voice. "Should I?"

She didn't look at me as she answered, "It's the right thing to do." Then Benedict stood and left the room.

"Sit tight," Mullane announced. "The technician will come in and get the sample. It's just a quick swab." He looked through his folder, flipping each page like it was the most interesting thing he'd ever read. I was dying to know what he was looking at. Why couldn't they tell me the whole story, what they had so far?

We sat in awkward silence, my heartbeat drumming in my ears as my nerves got the best of me.

Finally, the technician came in with his kit. He was the tallest man I'd ever seen, skinny with a thick pair of glasses and white lab coat.

"I'm just going to swab the inside of your cheek with this long Q-tip." He opened his mouth in demonstration, and I mimicked him. Crazy how a simple swabbing of your cheek could determine whether you were guilty or not. I wondered if they ever got it wrong.

"Thank you for your cooperation." Mullane gathered his paperwork, tipped his head, and offered a kind smile. "You're free to go."

Chapter 32

Anna

"Pratt?" I sobbed into the phone.

"What's wrong, sweetheart?" I could hear the concern in his voice and it instantly warmed me. "Are you all right? What happened?"

"I'm okay, I just—can you come over? I need you."

"I'll be right over. Stay put. I'm on my way." I nodded, even though he couldn't see me, and ended the call. Gripping my pillow to my chest, I laid back on the bed and watched the daylight begin to seep through the blinds. Warm tears rolled down my temples onto the sheets, but I did nothing to stop them.

Before the sun had a chance to butter the room, Pratt rushed through the door I'd left unlocked for him. "Anna?"

"In here," I called from the bedroom. As soon as I heard his voice, I regretted calling him. I should've called my nurse friend Emma instead. I wouldn't have been half as embarrassed with another female. I kept myself curled up in a ball on my bed, and pulled my lavender comforter up over my head.

Pratt sat on the bed, the weight of his body causing me to fall closer to him. He stroked my back. "Are you sick, love? What can I do?"

"No. I've done something to my hair and it looks awful." The sobs erupted again, my body shaking the mattress.

"Let me see. It can't be that bad." He began to ease the comforter down. "You'd be beautiful bald. Is that what you've done?" he said, a hint of humor in his voice. "Did you shave your head?" I knew he was trying to soothe me, but it wasn't working.

Another sob escaped as I felt the comforter slide down past my shoulders. I kept my face buried in my pillow, not daring enough to see his expression. "I didn't want you to see me like this, but . . . I didn't know who else—I didn't know who else to call."

Pratt slid his arms underneath my shoulders and hips, lifting me into his arms. I maintained fetal position, but cradled my head in his chest, wetting his white T-shirt with my tears. He rocked me gently until the sobs slowed and the hiccups ceased.

"I woke up like this." Gripping his T-shirt, I tried but failed to find the courage to lift my head. "I don't remember cutting my hair." I cried for what seemed like two lifetimes before I could speak again. Lifting my head, I looked up through soaked lashes, Pratt's face blurred through my tear-soaked eyes.

I called off the events of my morning like a grocery list, which seemed easier than reliving it through a storytelling. "I woke up, like every morning, my eyes still half closed as I walked to the bathroom to pee. I guess my brain was too tired to register anything that early, but after I started to walk back to bed, I saw it. The floor was covered in hair clippings." I pointed to the bathroom door. "I—it—God, it's everywhere. Not in a pile, just scattered everywhere. And just look at me!" My palms opened to receive my face as I buried my embarrassment and let the tears flow again. "I'm hideous."

"You're not. Let me see." Pratt pried my hands away from my face as gently as possible. "It's really not bad, babe. Not bad at all. It's . . . fun and light and . . . sexy."

I knew he was lying, but I couldn't cry any more. My head was throbbing.

"I need strong coffee . . . and a handful of Motrin," I sniveled. "Want some?"

"Coffee, yes." He smiled but it didn't reach his eyes. It was one of those smiles you gave someone when you felt bad for them because they had a fever or a sprained ankle. "Stay put, I'll bring it to you."

A few minutes later, Pratt returned with a tray. He had two mugs filled with coffee, a glass of water, and two tablets for my headache.

He set the tray on my nightstand, propped a pillow behind his back, and scooted close to me before handing me the water and medicine.

"Thank you." I offered a weak smile.

With a nod, he took the glass, returned it to the tray, and handed me a mug. I loved the first sip, the way the steam billowed off the top of the cup, and the warmth between my fingers.

"I'd like to talk about last night, if you're up to it," Pratt asked carefully like he was afraid I might break.

"I'm okay . . . now that you're here." I offered a weak smile.

"What's the last thing you remember?"

"Climbing into bed, flipping through the channels. The *Tonight Show* was on. I don't remember anything after that. Wait . . . Fallon was doing those thank you notes. I must've fallen asleep then." Or blacked out. It was happening more often lately and starting to scare me. Waking up in the tub was one thing, but how could I have cut my hair and not remembered it? And why would I have done it? Did I have to add sleepwalking to the list of oddities?

"Did you turn off the TV?" he asked, sounding like a detective wanting to get to the bottom of what happened. "Get up to go to the bathroom?"

"No, I don't think so . . . I don't remember." I twisted my hands together, wringing the stress out. "You know I have blackouts, but this is extreme." I fisted a short chunk of hair. Would I ever get used to it? No more ponytails, braids, messy buns. My neck felt like it was barely attached to my body, too light without the weight of my long hair.

"Hang on." Pratt got up and walked to the bathroom. A moment later, he returned with a pair of scissors and placed them in my hands. "Do you remember holding these? Using them . . . maybe you just wanted to trim your bangs?"

"No." My brows pinched in worry. I was mystified by the event, scared out of my wits wondering how long I was out. "I don't remember using them for anything. I don't even remember getting out of bed. What is this, Pratt?" The tears began again. "What's happening to me?" I sunk into his arms, my head throbbing harder as I cried.

"Don't worry, baby," he sighed, rubbing his palms up and down my back. "We'll figure it out.

***

Four nights passed with little sleep. Pratt spent every free moment with me, but he had a lot of work to do. Finishing up his last year of residency was mentally and physically challenging, and then add studying for his board and trying to line up his own practice after he was licensed. On top of all that, he was trying to get to the bottom of my blackouts. His team had finished up their research on drug use treatment and now were concentrating on neurological aspects of mental health. It was a subject that interested Pratt. When he talked about it, his face lit with excitement. He'd be a great psychiatrist. I would not be a great psychiatrist's wife. That was a fact no one could argue. But I needed him right now, too much to let him go. And I loved him too much to distract him with a breakup.

Chapter 33

Jane

Jane found a plump vein in the crook of the man's elbow and inserted the syringe. He was groggy, but his eyes were open, watching her. *It really shouldn't be this easy, Drew.* "Assholes always pay, but you . . ." She cocked her head to the right and smiled. "You deserve to suffer a little before you go." She injected half of the serum, recapped the needle, and gently placed it into her purse.

Jane walked around the bed, studying the young blonde. His hair was cut short and she assumed it was because he hated his tight, coarse curls. His stomach cramped immediately and Jane watched as he doubled over, clutching his belly and groaning through his drunken state. There was enough morphine in the syringe to render him useless but not completely knock him out, and just enough poison to hurt him but not kill him. With his smaller stature, and the fact that the serum hadn't taken full effect, she decided to lead him to the bathroom.

"Come, love," she said, her British accent tinged with a sweet malevolence. "Let me help you."

Almost completely dead weight, his feet shuffled against the carpet to keep up with her. Shuffle-drag-shuffle-drag. He groaned with each step, nearly pulling Jane down with him.

Getting him into the bathtub was harder than expected. The tub in his apartment wasn't as shallow as a hotel tub, so he banged his head when his ass slid off the edge. Completely dead weight now, Jane lifted one heavy leg and rotated it into the tub, then did the same with the other leg. Water would've helped her maneuver his limbs, but that wasn't part of her perfect plan.

Clammy and out of breath, Jane took a seat on the toilet lid, shoulders straight and legs crossed as if she were about to interview for a high paying job. She checked her fingernails through the disposable latex gloves and inhaled a few relaxing breaths.

"Okay, back to it then," she sang.

Dancing through Drew's apartment, Jane methodically removed the sheets, stuffed them into the washing machine, and wiped down the room with a bleach-soaked rag. She ensured not a single fingerprint or hair was left behind before returning to the bathroom where Drew lay in the empty tub, his chest rising and falling with each shallow breath.

Taking a seat on the lid of the toilet again, she looked him over, studying each feature that was too small for a man of his boasting. She recalled the way he'd treated the young brunette at the bar.

"Can I buy you a drink?" His voice had been smooth, drawing her in.

The sweet girl had been celebrating her twenty-first birthday with a few friends, having a good time until he came along. She'd accepted drink after drink, and he made sure her lemon drop martinis were strong and went down fast. After a few drinks, he'd gotten cocky, said things like, *"I usually only date perfect tens, but since it's your birthday . . ."* and *"You're a filthy little whore behind closed doors, aren't you? Think you can swallow all twelve inches of me?"*

Jane scoffed at the memory. *Twelve inches.* She looked at his tiny appendage. *A rat might mistake your penis for his mother's teet, you bloody tosser.* "I wonder what makes you think you're God's gift to women. You come on like a gentleman, treat a lady like she should be treated, and then we see the other side, don't we?" Jane removed the cap from the bottle of bleach and began to pour it over his chest. "Too bad you can't feel this. I'd like you to feel the burn."

She continued to empty the bottle, recalling the confused look on the girl's face. He'd said enough to reel her in, but then insulted her. Before she could bolt, he'd fed her another compliment.

"Men like you are a boil on the bellend." Her eyes narrowed. "You break a woman down until she doesn't know the difference between a compliment and an insult. She thinks sucking your dick is a privilege. Well, it's not, you bloody bastard." Jane snapped her finger. "God, I wish she were here to see you now. But that wouldn't go well for me, would it?"

Drew's body jerked once before he vomited on his chest. His eyes remained closed as the putrid smell erupted from his mouth again and again. Jane rushed to retrieve the syringe from her purse. She uncapped the needle, found his vein, and held his arm still as she pushed the remainder of the poison in. After a few minutes, his body lay limp and unmoving.

Immune to killing, Jane's heartbeat slowed, fully relaxed as she carefully recapped the needle and placed it back into her purse. She noticed the level of liquid bleach was at the line of his belly button. With a deep exhale, she quipped, "In just a few minutes, you'll be unable to ruin the life of another woman."

Unscrewing the cap of another bottle of bleach, Jane smiled in recollection of how the evening had ended. She'd sent the young girl away and snatched Drew up herself. A sexy outfit, the confidence of a woman who knew how to handle a man, and the British accent did it every time. She'd never lost.

With a cocky smirk, Drew had tossed the young girl aside like she had been an appetizer, then he looked at Jane like she was the main course, dessert, and after-dinner cognac. Jane smiled over gritted teeth with each of his pick-up lines until she *let* him catch her and take her to his place.

Jane let some of the bleach splash up over his face, wetting his buzz cut. "You know what the best part is?" she asked. She loved talking to them, knowing they couldn't talk back. "Watching you take your last breath. Appreciating that I'm the one that took the light from your eyes. Knowing without a doubt that I've erased one more evildoer from this world."

Jane removed the cap from the fourth bottle of bleach and poured it in. With a latex-covered hand, she gave Drew's head a shove until it submerged below the toxic liquid. Three bubbles came from his nose and no more.

"That was anticlimactic," she huffed, annoyed. Keeping her gaze fixed on Drew, she watched, hoping to see his body jerk or his eyes open in horror. She wanted her face to be the last thing he saw when he realized he was dying.

Nothing.

With a disappointed sigh, Jane stood, wiped the toilet lid and bathroom handle, then she dragged the cloth with her foot to erase any shoe prints from the floor.

She paused in living room, feeling let down from the kill. Walking back to the bathroom, she stared at Drew. He looked peaceful, quiet. Not what she had envisioned or wanted. For a brief moment, she thought about pulling him out of the tub and carving up his chest with her favorite flower, or maybe a cross. But that wasn't it. The fact that she had killed someone she hadn't slept with—or maybe it was because she killed for a stranger, a young girl—left her with a hollow feeling in her chest. It was meaningless. She wouldn't waste her artwork on him.

The way he'd treated women was wrong, no doubt, but killing him for it didn't bring her any pleasure. *You sullied everything up, Drew. Now things are soured and unbalanced.*

Jane bit her lip and stomped her foot. Since she'd walked back to the bathroom, she'd have to wipe the damn floor again. But everything had to be done in order. So she started with the bedside table, wiping the lamp, remote control, and table before moving toward the bathroom again.

She tried to sing,

"Ring-a ring o' roses,
A pocket full of —

But it wasn't right. Not for this kill. Nothing was right. She'd have to find a way to correct it, rebalance the equation again.

Backing out of Drew's apartment, she raised an eyebrow and grinned. His death was out of character for her, but she had to be pleased that she'd rid the world of his poison.

As the heavy door swung to close, she dropped the garbage bag containing the empty bottles of bleach. When she reached to grab it, the tip of her too loose glove got stuck in the door jam. Jane pulled at the glove to release it. After stretching and pulling, it finally gave way.

With an exhale of relief, she looked down at her hand. The index finger of her glove was gone.

Chapter 34

Anna

Thursday morning, the sun broke through a space between the lavender curtains I'd just put up. Eager to meet Pratt for our weekly coffee shop brew, I threw my legs over the bed, got up, and dressed. Checking my phone, I saw a text from him:

Sorry, baby, can't make it today. Work. I'll call you later.

I sent a reply before pulling my outfit off and tossing it onto the bed.

Okay. Miss you. :(

Instead of climbing back into bed, I did something crazy. Pulling on a pair of yoga pants and sliding into my tennis shoes, I went for a run. Okay, a jog. Still way more than I would normally do, but I'd gotten used to running with Pratt, being outside and getting my heart pumping. The crisp November air felt amazing on my skin, awakening my body but burning my lungs. A woman in pink running pants passed me and I tried to match her gait, hoping for a smoother run. It just wasn't in my blood to be a runner. I couldn't breathe, my muscles tightened and cramped, and my stomach warned that it would toss up whatever was left inside if I didn't stop and walk back. A few blocks were all I managed. *Wimp.*

Washing my newly short hair took some getting used to. I missed pulling it into a ponytail, and still poured too much shampoo into my palm when I washed it. After a quick shower, I sat at the kitchen table and blew the steam off my first cup of coffee. Just before the rich brew met my lips, there was a knock at the door. Sneaking in a quick sip first, I set the mug down and walked to the door. I shouldn't have been surprised at who I saw through the peephole, but I was. Every single time.

Unlocking the bolts and swinging the door open, I offered an insincere smile. "Hello again."

"Anna Spencer," officer Mullane began, "You're under arrest for the for the murder of Blaize Martin. Anything you say can and will be used in a court of law . . ." His words faded into the background as I watched his lips move.

Had he said murder? *MURDER?* It wasn't real. How could they arrest me for the murder of someone I'd never seen or heard of before? It didn't make sense.

Three things had happened this morning that were firsts for me. I'd gone for a run of my own volition, I was being handcuffed and read my Miranda Rights, and I was being accused of a crime I hadn't been capable of committing.

My wrists pinched against the metal restraints. My shoulders didn't feel right in this position, like they needed to pop or shift just an inch to feel better. My lungs burned—much worse than they had during my attempted run—trying to catch a full breath.

"Why is this happening?" I looked at one officer who offered nothing and then to the other. "Who is this Blaize Martin? Is this a prank?" I couldn't breathe. My lungs refused to allow enough oxygen in and the room was spinning. "Someone answer me. Tell me what's going on."

The officers ushered me out of my apartment, down the stairs, and into the back of the car. People on the sidewalk stopped to watch the event. I'd never been in the back of a police vehicle—or the front, for that matter—and I couldn't understand why I was in one now. "Please tell me what's going on." Gasp. "How long will this take?" I leaned forward, trying to get a better angle for my shoulders, and more oxygen into my lungs. "Did you lock the door?" Three quick shaky breaths brought on a full panic attack. "Oh my God, the coffee pot is on." I didn't recognize the voice coming from my mouth. It was high pitched and prickly. The coffee pot would shut off automatically, but still, I wanted to go home.

"We'll explain everything at the station." Both officers were cold, unfriendly. If it weren't for the radio coming alive every few seconds with people calling off codes and locations, the car ride would've been absolutely silent.

Once inside the station, I was released from the handcuffs and led to the same back room as before.

"Have a seat. Can I get you a water? Coffee?" Officer Benedict asked, much friendlier than the last time I'd met her.

"No, thank you." My hands trembled on my lap. Why was she being nice, offering coffee like we were having girl time? Why wouldn't anyone tell me what the hell was going on and why I was being set up. Were they trying to trick me into giving them information they thought I had? Why couldn't they understand that I didn't know the man? *Alibi. I surely had one.* "Why haven't you asked me where I was when that man was killed. I probably have an alibi."

"Miss Spencer, can I call you Anna?" She offered a kind smile, her head cocked to the side ever so slightly. I blinked then nodded, a new hope filling me. "Anna," Officer Benedict slid a picture across the table. It was a picture of me sleeping. "Do you recognize the person in this picture?"

"Yes, it's me." I studied the picture, wondering why she wasn't answering my question. "But I don't know who took it, and I don't recognize the room." *Shit. Did someone drug me? Is that why I'm having blackouts? It was a setup.* "Has someone been drugging me?" My voice rose along with my pulse. "Who took this picture? I don't recognize my surroundings at all." I couldn't sit still. Wiggling in my chair and fidgeting with the hem of my blouse, it was happening again. I felt like a trapped animal, scared and angry.

Both officers glanced at each other before looking back at me. "We found this picture on Blaize Martin's phone."

"What?" I screeched. The information swirled around in my head. Nonsensical information. "I don't understand." My head shook. Back and forth, back and forth, trying to make sense of what she was telling me. "How?" My voice was so small I wasn't sure anyone had heard it. Clearing my throat, I tried again. "How did my picture end up on his phone?"

"You tell us," Officer Mullane said, his tone flat. "This is you, in Blaize Martin's bed, asleep." He lifted his brows, his expression almost comical. Was he amused or were his wrinkles betraying him, giving off the wrong expressions. He couldn't possibly find my situation funny. Still, it irked me.

Slamming my hand down onto the table, I shouted, "That's impossible! I don't know this man! I'm telling you, I've never seen him before in my life." My teeth were clenched, muscles coiled tightly. I couldn't remember ever being more enraged. "I have a boyfriend. I spend most of my nights with him. Pratt Rhodes. Ask him, he'll tell you. There's no way . . . this is . . . this is insane." My voice faded with each word, the impossibility of it all.

"Witnesses have seen you with him." Benedict sat back in her chair, relaxed and sure of herself as she accused me of lying.

My back straightened. "*Who* saw me with him? And where?" These people were scaring me. I loved watching crime shows, so I knew how these things worked. They could accuse me of anything, make it look like I'd done something I hadn't, and I had a fifty-fifty shot of proving my innocence. The fear bled through and gave way to my voice. "You're scaring me. I don't understand any of this."

"Calm down, Miss Spencer." Benedict offered a calming voice like she was trying to manipulate me. "Just tell us the truth and we'll do everything we can to make it easier on you."

"I *am* telling you the truth." Tears began to pool and push against my lashes. Blinking several times to keep them at bay, I insisted, "I've never seen this man before."

Mullane leaned back in his chair as if he'd just eaten a big meal. "We have your DNA all over his apartment, on the sheets, a drinking glass."

My pulse skyrocketed and my stomach knotted. "I feel sick." Covering my mouth with the back of my hand, I mumbled through my fingers, "May I have a glass of water?"

Mullane stood and walked out of the room. Benedict encouraged me to take slow, deep breaths until he returned with the water.

After taking a sip of water, the lukewarm liquid doing little to ease my nausea, I asked, "Do I get a phone call?"

"Yes." Benedict pushed a smart phone toward me.

Staring at the digits, I tried to recall Pratt's number. Since I had him programmed in, I hadn't memorized it. "I can't remember his number." My head shook in disbelief, worry crimping my forehead.

"Who are you trying to call?" Benedict asked. "I can look it up for you." She opened the folder in front of her and flipped through the pages inside. "I have your phone records."

"Pratt Rhodes." Just when I thought she was sweet for offering to help me, she admits they have my phone records. I couldn't trust anyone.

I dialed the numbers as she called them out. He answered almost immediately. "Pratt?" I began to cry and heaved out the next sentence in a high pitched tone that would've sent dogs into a tizzy. "I've been arrested and I don't know what to do."

"Arrested?" He sounded shocked, then angry. "For what?"

I couldn't make the words form to answer him. Sobs erupted. "I don't know . . . what to do. Nothing makes . . . sense."

"I'll be right there, baby." He tried to be calm for me, but there was no mistaking the panic in his voice. "Do you have a lawyer?"

"No." I shook my head even though he couldn't see me. "I've never needed one." My shoulders slumped, knowing my situation was dire. How would I handle this? How would Pratt handle this? Would he see me in a different light? I began to shut down, the shock of it all seeping into my bones. On a whisper, I admitted, "I wouldn't even know how to find one."

"I'll take care of everything," he promised, "Don't worry, everything'll be all right. Trust me, okay?"

"Mmhmm." I answered, sinking into myself.

Ending the call, I pushed the phone back across the table like a timid child. Couldn't they see how petite and meek I was? How the hell was I supposed to kill a man the size of Blaize Martin? He was massive, strong, and looked like someone the worst criminal wouldn't dare try and tackle. It would've been comical if I wasn't so scared, my world turned upside down and shaken like a snow globe being tossed around by a ferocious bear.

Both officers held a silent conversation with each other before Mullane nodded and they stood. "We'll be right back," said Mullane.

I thought having the officers gone would ease my mind, give me a moment of reprieve. But there was nothing worse than being alone in a stark white space, the sound of silence deafening.

Chapter 35

Anna

Pratt wasn't able to sit with me in the interrogation room, but he called a lawyer. After three hours sitting in that room, Jack Morgan busted through the door and, before introducing himself, demanded, "Don't say another word without my permission."

Jack Morgan—sounded like a drink, looked like a million bucks—was apparently one of the best defense attorneys in Manhattan, according to himself.

After all introductions were made, Jack took over. "What evidence do you have?"

Mullane shoved a manila folder in his direction. "DNA match, pictures of the defendant in the victim's apartment, witnesses at his place of work who have seen Miss Spencer and the victim together."

"And this?" Jack asked.

"The victim's body as we found it," Benedict answered.

I leaned over to have a look and gasped, my hand slapping over my mouth as tears stung my eyes. Jack pushed the picture beneath the others and began to read reports.

"Who would do something like that?" I whispered. I had seen enough of the picture to know that someone had carved up his chest. It was hard to make out if it was a shape or words with all of the blood.

I watched every face, every expression in the room. Their mouths moved, eyebrows shot up, shoulders stiffened, but I remained still, unmoving like I was trapped in a cryogenic chamber. My pulse was all over the place, going from frenzied to barely beating. A clammy sweat beaded across my forehead, but I was shivering. I'd never experienced shock before, but if that's what was happening to me, I knew then that I wouldn't be able to speak until I came out of it.

They kept me in that room for another hour before placing me in a cell that smelled of old sweat and alcohol. Huddled in the corner on a metal bench, fearing all the germs that must have been surrounding me, all I had was a thin blanket and my mind to remind me of the hopelessness.

***

Four days passed all alone in a jail cell. One more and I was sure I would've lost my mind. Officer Benedict walked me down the hall into a room where my lawyer awaited. The dull white room had comfortable chairs and a pot of coffee on a side table with cream and sugar. The scent warmed me a little. Funny how you appreciate the little things so much more when they are taken away from you. I received a cup of coffee on my breakfast tray each morning, but it was served lukewarm in a Styrofoam cup and tasted like it had been sitting there for a while. Jack brought me up to speed on what was happening and what to expect next.

"Today we'll have a preliminary hearing. I'm going to do everything in my power to make sure it doesn't go to trial."

"When can I see Pratt?" I asked, my voice small and unsure. Did he ever want to see me again? "I haven't talked to him. Does he believe me?" My head sunk and I studied a hangnail. I couldn't imagine a world where he would believe I was innocent. But I was.

Jack took his bottom lip between his teeth, a look of pity on his face. "I'm sorry, you can't see him, but he's still on your side, Anna. He's working very hard to prove your innocence and I think he's onto something. A doctor by the name of Jennifer Bowman is coming by to talk to you today. We have a long road ahead, a lot of work left to do, but I feel really good about things, Anna." He reached out as if to pat my hand or offer a gentle touch, but pulled away and reached for his cup of coffee instead. "Trust me to do what I do best, okay?"

I nodded, but it was empty. I didn't trust anything anymore.

***

That afternoon, Dr. Bowman came to see me. She was a small woman with auburn hair that fell in waves just below her shoulders.

"Miss Spencer, I'm Dr. Bowman. I just have a few papers for you to fill out and then we can talk." She handed me a clipboard and pen, waiting for me to fill in the blanks. It was like a doctor's form: name, address, birth date. It asked if I had any allergies, previous surgeries, history of heart disease or mental illness in the family.

"You're left handed?" she asked, sounding intrigued.

I glanced up. "Yes." It wasn't that rare to be left handed. Once I finished with the papers, she asked me to do a couple of exercises. They were ridiculous and I didn't understand why I had to do them, but I did without questioning her.

"Last, I'll need your signature here and here. One with your left hand, one with your right. Just do the best you can."

I did as she asked. My right-handed signature looked as if a two-year old had attempted it. It was barely legible.

"Okay, let's get down to business," she began, linking her khaki-clad legs at the ankles. "With the evidence presented and some history I've gathered on you, I feel strongly about a diagnosis. I've seen it before, and have done extensive research on the condition. Anna, I think you have MPD, or Multiple Personality Disorder."

My face twisted. "Seriously?" I had no idea what she was talking about, but it didn't sound like something that fit me. "That doesn't sound right to me, but—"

"You're left handed." Dr. Bowman uncrossed her legs and leaned forward, her expression serious. I noticed how her jaw twitched before she blew out a breath. "The person that committed these murders was right handed."

Chapter 36

Anna

My lawyer wasn't able to get me out of a trial, but he was able to get me released into the care of Dr. Bowman until it began.

The psych ward wasn't the Waldorf by any means, but I appreciated a mattress that didn't feel like it was made from bricks, and a pillow that didn't give me a crick in the neck. Even though I was locked inside a room with a deputy outside my door twenty-four-seven, and still treated like a prisoner, there was a warmth to the room that concrete walls and bars couldn't offer. Still, this life wasn't for me and each day I waited for them to realize their mistake.

In the distance I heard a woman cry out. She didn't sound pained or scared, it was more of an animalistic howl that made the hair on the back of my neck stand like a prickly cactus. Would that be me soon? I imagined the day-to-day berating and medication that was offered—unlabeled, unpackaged, and in a tiny white cup—would eventually break me down and form me into the creature they thought I was. Again I was reminded of the movies and how easily doctors created crazy patients to make their jobs successful. Why me though? *Why me?*

Every day I was asked questions, put through breathing exercises, and asked about my past. I told the same story every day for a week and felt like Daniel from *Karate Kid,* wondering why the hell he was waxing all the time and never learning anything.

Two weeks passed and no progress was made. Truth was, I didn't have MPD, and if I didn't have it, Dr. Bowman couldn't use insanity to help win my case. Not that I wanted to have a disorder that proved I was nuts, but if we didn't have anything, I was going to go away for the rest of my life for a murder I didn't commit. Either way I'd lose.

After breakfast on Wednesday, Dr. Bowman sat on the edge of my bed. Her dark waves were straightened, her makeup flawless. I couldn't remember the last time I put on lipstick or felt pretty, and these light gray scrubs did nothing for my coloring. "I'd like to hypnotize you," she declared.

I shrugged my shoulders. I would've jumped through fiery hoops if it would change things. Before I agreed, I wanted to try my hand at bargaining. I had nothing to lose. "Can Pratt be there?"

"No." She shook her head and pushed a chunk of hair behind her ear. "I'm sorry."

"Why not?" I huffed, irritated. "It would be good for him, like a clinical study or something." Fisting my shirt, I pleaded, "And I would feel more comfortable if he were here." I had to see him, convince him that I wasn't guilty. How else would I know what he thought? I needed to see it in his eyes.

God, I missed his eyes, the way they lit up when he smiled, and his dimples. "I have to see him, Dr. Bowman," I whispered, not able to hide the desperation in my voice. "Please."

"I don't think it's possible for him to be present during our sessions," she sighed, "but I'll see what I can do about a visit."

At six-thirty that same evening, I heard the key sliding into the lock on my door. Dinnertime. The food wasn't amazing, but when you were counting on someone else to provide your meals, you looked forward to each one. Besides, there wasn't anything else to think about or look forward to, so a slice of ham, sweet potato mash, and a cup of chocolate pudding were the highlight of the day.

The smell of hamburger wafted through the room before I saw him. Pratt stepped through the door, holding two sacks with what I assumed were the greasiest, most delicious hamburgers and fries imaginable. Too bad I wouldn't be able to eat a bite. All I wanted to do was hold him for as long as he could be here.

Jumping off the bed, I nearly knocked him over as I leapt into his arms and wrapped my legs around his waist. "You're here!" The moment he set the bags down, my lips pressed to his, desperate and hungry as though that kiss was the only thing keeping me alive.

"I've missed you," he said between kisses. "How are you?" His tongue trapped mine in an erotic dance that had my body humming. "You look good. Are they treating you well?" He walked over to the wall, the only one that didn't have a door or window, spun me around, and rested my back against the flat surface. "It's supposed to be a really nice place." That was the first time I noticed that my walls were a light shade of pink that reminded me of sickness. It wasn't a healthy pink, but more of a white with the hint that pink once resided there before it had been drained of all its life and color. Pratt's voice broke through my scattered thoughts about paint color and the way his lips felt, his scent, and how much I missed him. "The doctors have great reputations."

"A million questions. Yes to all," I panted, gripping his shoulders, fingering his dark curls, cupping his face in my hands.

Pratt lifted me away from the wall and walked me over to the twin-sized bed. Gently, he set me down and hovered over me. The way he looked at me then, like I was the only woman in the world, made me fall even more in love with him.

"We don't have privacy here." He groaned, the heat draining from his eyes.

"I don't care. I want you. What can they do? Take a hose to us?" Reaching around to the back of his head, I pulled him down to me. "I want you, Pratt."

Foreplay was overrated when you were as tightly wound as we were. Our hands moved quickly, pulling down my scrub pants, working the button and zipper of his slacks. We didn't even bother removing our shirts or shoes. Pants around ankles, Pratt rolled on a condom and positioned himself over me. I could see every emotion he was feeling in his eyes—lust, worry, hope, fear, love. As soon as we became one, the uncertainties of my world melted away. He erased every anxiety over the upcoming trial and bonded me to this very moment in time.

Skin gliding against skin, lips locked, and tongues sliding together in a fit of passion and longing, something happened between us. I couldn't get close enough, he couldn't drive deep enough to satiate. In those moments, I realized we were two souls desperate to be bonded together forever. I had no doubt he felt it, too.

***

The only thing I remembered about my session with Dr. Bowman was the sound of her voice as she put me under. She taped the event for evidence, but there wasn't much to see.

She took me back to my childhood home and a younger version of me recalled spending time in my room with my favorite toys. I spoke about my mother, nothing out of the norm there, either. The only thing she couldn't pull out of me was her death. Apparently, I kept going back to the toys, especially a specific doll.

We repeated the same process every day for a week. Finally, there was a breakthrough. A breakthrough of epic proportion. I watched the recording in Dr. Bowman's office, sitting on the edge of my seat and chewing on my nails from the overwhelming anxiety.

"Anna, you're almost there," Dr. Bowman said in a soothing voice. "Relax and listen to the sound of my voice. I want you to go to the living room today. Tell me when you're there."

"Okay, I'm there." It was weird watching myself on the screen, my body relaxed, my voice calm—polar opposite of what I felt now.

"What do you see?"

"The television is on. It's loud."

"Okay. Who else is in the house with you?"

"No one. I'm alone." I watched my body jerk as if something had scared me. *"Wait. They're here, too."*

"Who?"

"I don't know. I've seen them before, but I don't know who they are."

"Can you ask them?"

My head shook back and forth. I glanced to the left as if someone was sitting next to me. Terror was written on my expression, my eyes wide as I moved my shoulders to the right, trying to move away from the apparition. *"No. I'm scared. They don't like me."*

"Okay, Anna, on the count of three you're going to wake up. One—two—three."

It took Dr. Bowman a long time to settle me down after that session. The camera continued recording as she tried to talk to me, ensuring that everything was okay and I was safe with her. My body shook and tears streamed down my face as I watched and listened to the tape.

"Anna, are you all right? How do you feel after watching that?"

"I don't know." My voice was thick—strangled. "It's hard to distinguish reality from fiction right now. I see myself on film, but it's like watching a movie and I feel sorry for the character. I can't believe that's me. What am I so afraid of?"

"I don't know. But if you're still up for it, I promise you we're going to find out."

Chapter 37

Jane

She was well aware of her black soul. The fact that Jane wasn't a good person wasn't lost on her. She would rather marinate in the darkness, dwelling on the pain that had led her to this place than change. Being good was easy, any stupid wench could pull it off with little to no acting skills. Being evil, however, was difficult to pull off. Jane constantly had to think, prepare, and plan. There was no room for sloppy mistakes. Everything had to be mapped out and decided before a move was made. Spontaneity lost.

Letting light permeate the darkness inside weakened her and took away her desire to hurt people. But that's who she was. A seeker of revenge. A killer. And she was good at it. A mastermind.

It was crowded and dark in her mind, but that was how she worked best. There was no room for regret. However, a fragment of regret somehow worked its way through as she recalled the one kill that changed everything.

I had to do it. The choice hadn't been hers. *If she only knew I was protecting her, maybe that would bring her back.*

Jane sat on the edge of an old wooden bench in a secluded area of Central Park, pulled off her glasses, and cleaned them with a tissue. As she watched the wind sweep the long branches of a willow tree across the ground, it reminded her of the one she was protecting. Always sweeping, mopping, cleaning up behind her and the messes she made. It didn't make sense that she wasn't appreciated for her actions, especially the last one.

Leaning back on the bench, Jane closed her eyes and remembered each detail.

The beautiful man was out, sprawled across the bed, sleeping peacefully after sipping the hangover concoction she had created especially for him. Gripping his shoulder with a gloved hand, Jane nudged him. He didn't move. More forcefully, she shook him, trying her best to arouse him. Useless, just as planned.

Postponing death was the hardest part. But everything had to go in order. Jane found the bleach on a shelf above the washing machine, filled a bucket, and began wiping down everything that might have held a fingerprint. That meant she had to be meticulous, not forgetting things like light switches, drawer pulls, and the half-empty box of condoms under the bed.

It hadn't taken much of the concoction to kill the little grey ball of hell, but it was a different story for the big, strong man in the bed. Jane had to double her usual dose to knock him out.

After wiping down the apartment, it took all of her strength to roll the Neanderthal over onto his side. Pulling the fitted sheet up, she pushed as much of the material as she could under him and rolled him to the other side so she could pull the sheets off. Once they were loaded in the washing machine, a cup of bleach and a scoop of detergent added, Jane set the machine to the hottest cycle and hit start.

Finally, she could end the life of the bastard in the other room who reeked of sex and alcohol. The tea should've killed him on the spot, but he needed an extra dose to finish him off. Climbing onto the bed, Jane pushed his legs apart, uncapped the syringe, and plunged the filled needle into his femoral artery where his groin met his thigh. If they chose to do an autopsy, they'd think the puncture wound was an ingrown hair rather than the mark of a needle. The poison was undetectable on most labs, unless they thought it necessary to do a more detailed tox screen.

It didn't take long for his breathing to slow and Jane envied the deep sleep he experienced. A sleep deep and dark enough to shut off the screaming in her head. Soon his breathing would halt and he'd have complete peace. Straddling him, she watched his chest rise and fall, concentrating on the shallow breaths coming in through his nose.

His large chest was a perfect canvas for her art—clean shaven and smooth. Jane couldn't resist. It was a stupid move, a weakness in her perfected plan. Using the tip of the needle, she carved the most beautiful Oleander flower. Blood rose to the surface of the skin where she had only scratched, and pooled more heavily where she dug deeper. It was the most stunning piece of art to date and she took time to admire it.

Thinking back on that memory, Jane debated with whether or not she would do it again or take it back and let that one live. The answer was as clear as spring water—*You do whatever you have to for family. No matter the cost.*

Chapter 38

Anna

"We're not getting what we really need from your sessions, Anna," Dr. Bowman began, unable to hide her disappointment. "I'd like to try Pentobarbital. It's a hypnotic drug that will help us go deeper, hopefully get the answers that I believe are in there."

"Of course, whatever we need to do to clear my name, but . . ." I folded my arms across my chest and added, "I want Pratt here. Get him clearance to sit in on the sessions."

Dr. Bowman sucked in her bottom lip and exhaled. "I can't make any promises, Anna. It's not how we do things here."

"It's worth a shot."

She eyed me warily, but then picked up the phone and made a call. Less than ten minutes later, she had an answer. "I got him clearance, but there will be rules and if he interferes at all—"

"He won't." A satisfied grin pulled at my lips and I couldn't shake it off. It wasn't the best scenario, but I'd take what I could get to see Pratt.

Pratt sat next to me in Dr. Bowman's office the next morning. She handed me a clipboard and asked again, "If you agree to the Pentobarbital with hypnosis, I'll need your initials here," she pointed a manicured finger, "and your signature here at the bottom."

I shifted to face Pratt, searching for his approval. "Okay, whatever it takes to prove I didn't kill those men. I know I didn't . . . I couldn't."

"Of course you didn't, babe." Pratt pulled me into his side and stroked my arms. I could see the desperation in his eyes and knew he'd help me do anything to prove my innocence. He needed this as much as I did if we were going to have a future together.

"Let's get started then." Dr. Bowman waited for me to sign the paper and take a seat in the designated chair facing the camera. She wrapped a rubber strap around my right arm, felt for a vein, and injected the medicine. Drowsiness came almost immediately.

Unsure of the time, I woke up in Pratt's arms, resting against his wet dress shirt. It felt as if only a few minutes had passed.

"What happened?" My head felt foggy. "It didn't work, did it?" I glanced up at Pratt, rubbing my right eye until my vision began to clear. His jaw ticked a few times as if he were trying to hold something back, but I didn't miss the way his eyes blinked too often and the way his brows pinched together. He had the face of a man experiencing a thousand sorrows.

"It *did* work, Anna." Dr. Bowman looked up from her notes and smiled. While Pratt seemed to be in despair, Dr. Bowman was wound up with excitement. "You were under for a full hour before I pulled you out. We got exactly what we needed." She clasped her hands together, reminding me of a mad scientist that finally got the mixture right.

"I was helpful?" My arms were too heavy to wrap them around Pratt's neck for support, they kept sliding down.

"Very." She scribbled furiously into a folder with my name on it.

"Do I have it? The MP . . ." My speech was still slurred from the medication and I couldn't think of the right order for the abbreviation. "I want to see the tape." I tried to lift my head, but it was too much of an effort.

Pratt stiffened, his chest feeling like a concrete block beneath my head. "No. It's not necessary. We have what we need." I knew he was hiding something from me. Either I had it and my life was over, or I didn't and I'd spend my days rotting in prison.

Stiffening, I slid out of Pratt's arms and found my footing. "Oh God," I gasped. "Is it true? Do I have it?" My mind reeled with the terrifying realization. "Do I have MPD?"

A slight nod from Dr. Bowman confirmed my worst fear. "Please, I want to see it." My legs trembled as I made my way to a chair and took a seat. It was too much and either the medication or the reality of my situation, or maybe the mixture of both made my stomach roil. Swallowing around the lump in my throat I managed, "I have the right to hear what I said."

"Of course." Dr. Bowman moved closer, rested a gentle hand on my shoulder, and fixed a serious gaze on Pratt. "It's her right and you know it will help her heal." She turned to me, her eyes sympathetic. "It's been a long day. Wouldn't you rather get some rest? We can look at the video tomorrow."

"No," I breathed, my eyes painfully wide. "I need to see it now." Yawning, I tried to force my eyes to stay open. The medicine must have still been in my system. I was beyond tired.

"You need to let the drug wear off," Dr. Bowman insisted. She rolled a wheelchair toward me and I held out a hand. No way was I giving up the one freedom I had left.

"I've got her," Pratt said, scooping me up.

"No, please . . ." My head bobbed like Jell-O as I tried to fight insistent sleep. "I have to know . . ." Reaching out, I gripped the door frame with the last ounce of strength I had. It slipped right out of my fingers, along with my life. They were going to give me a guilty verdict. I'd grow old in prison for something I didn't do. With my head resting against him, his strong arms cradling me, sleep took over my body before we even made it to my room.

***

I woke in time to witness the sun bring in a new day. My window overlooked a small patch of lush green grass surrounded by roses in every hue. It was a glorious site—the best thing about the place—that I would've taken time to savor had I been less nervous about the video viewing. I had slept hard until about three in the morning when I sat up in bed and realized something big had happened. The sound of the air conditioner muffled the strong beats of my heart, but I felt them. I spent most of the night hugging my knees to my chest, rocking back and forth on the bed as I cried. The pounding of my heart synched with the painful pulses of a headache. I could count always count on a grand headache when I cried that much, but so many thoughts were running through my head, so many emotions.

A commotion behind one of the bushes rattled me out of my depressing meditations, and I leaned toward the window to get a closer look. A bald, portly man that looked to be in his sixties darted from one side to the other before sprinting across the lawn. Two orderlies chased him down and restrained him. He bucked and struggled against their hold on him before going limp. I assumed they injected him with something, and I couldn't help but cringe. *I couldn't live like that. I'd rather die.*

A knock on the door preceded the lock being worked by one of the nurses. She held it open for Pratt to step through—the only person that could morph my chaotic nerves into a moment of joy.

"What're you doing here so early?" I greeted him with a kiss, trying to keep my shaking hands hidden.

"Couldn't sleep." The bags under his eyes confirmed it. "I brought breakfast." He set a bag on the rolling bedside table that carried the scent of freshly baked pastries and placed two coffees next to it.

"I don't remember much about last night." I took a seat on the bed and fidgeted with the string that hugged my ill-fitting scrubs to my waist. "Did the session work? Did I say anything helpful?"

"Yeah, it worked." A grave look washed over his face as he reached for a coffee and tried to hand it to me.

Holding up a hand, I passed on the coffee. "I can't." A wave of nausea came over me. "I have to know. What happened? You have to tell me."

Pratt wandered to the window and kept his gaze on something outside. "I think we should wait for Dr. Bowman."

"No." Fisting the velvety cream Vellux blanket on my bed for strength, I pleaded, "I want *you* to tell me. I trust you. I feel safe with you. Please, Pratt. Do I have it or not?"

Pratt turned and took two steps to face me on the bed. He knelt and took both of my hands in his, his thumbs circling my knuckles too fast, like he always did when he was nervous. "I don't even know how to say it, babe."

After a heavy blink, his eyes revealed the answer I already knew, but I still needed to hear it. Swallowing around what felt like a ball of wax lodged in my throat, I gripped the blanket tighter, preparing to hear the worst. "Just spit it out."

He squeezed his eyes shut and drew in a deep breath. When he opened his eyes, he looked at me with pity. His voice sounded foreign and distant when he said the words I knew were coming and thought I had prepared for, but hadn't. "Yes, you have MPD."

Chapter 39

Anna

Something took over inside of me. Denial? Rage? A medley of both. Pushing myself off the bed, I paced the small room. "Bullshit. How is that possible?" I picked up a cup of coffee and took a careful sip. "It's not." Some of the coffee sloshed out as I continued. "I need to see the tape. I won't believe it, her, you," I pointed the cup at Pratt, more coffee spilling out onto the floor, "until I do."

Pratt took a hesitant step toward me. "I saw the tape, babe. I wouldn't lie to you." He reached out and took the cup. His tone hushed and calm. "You can trust me." His arms enveloped me and I sunk into him, my body convulsing with sobs. "It's going to be all right, Anna," he said. "I promise, everything's going to be all right."

Hysterical and out of control, I beat my fist against his chest. "No it's not. It will never be all right. Never again." Nothing made sense anymore. For weeks we had been trying to prove that diagnosis, hoping for it—it was the only way to avoid life imprisonment—but now it also meant I was crazy. *Crazy.* I didn't feel crazy. Exhausted, confused, angry—I could go on and on about the feelings and emotions I felt, but I didn't feel crazy.

Pulling away from Pratt, pacing around the room, I started sobbing. The kind of sobbing that made my shoulders shake and my words come out choppy and barely legible. "Do they still think I killed someone?" It wasn't possible. "I couldn't harm a flea." My hands went up in the air. "I can't stand the sight of blood, for chrissakes. How could I have killed someone?" I was shouting and doing a poor job of convincing Pratt I wasn't crazy, but I couldn't stop. "Does the tape show me confessing? How did I do it? With a bouquet of roses? How can they believe it was me? How is any of this possible?" Head back and hands in the air, I announced, "Because they think I'm a nut job!"

Pratt's arms cocooned my body, trapping my arms down by my sides. I wanted to hit him, or anything. I wanted to punch something until my knuckles bled, until I felt numb. "Get away from me," I screamed. "I'm crazy! Get far away from me!"

"Shh." While holding me tightly to his body, he stroked my back, rubbing small circles meant to calm me down as he whispered again and again, "Shh, we'll fix it, baby. We'll fix it."

He couldn't fix this. How could he? Knowing he was willing to stay with me and try brought me some comfort, even though I couldn't understand why he wanted to. No one had ever stuck by me, and now that my life was in shambles, he had the perfect opportunity to run. Did he know what he was getting himself into? Did I? How many personalities were inside of me? What were they like? I couldn't wrap my head around it. It was too much to process. I could feel myself shutting down, just like I always did when things got too tough.

Hysterics turned to whimpers and whimpers settled into snivels. Pratt's shirt was soaked with my tears, "Okay," I pulled back and Pratt reluctantly loosened his grip. "Freak-out over." *For now.* I was as ready to face the harsh truth as I'd ever be. Not that I had a choice. Dr. Bowman would collect me soon to watch the tape and there was no going back from there.

"Thank you." My voice was raspy from crying. I felt somber from the sadness of truth I had to face and reality that I wasn't worthy of Pratt's company. It all made sense now, why I couldn't keep a man. I wasn't worthy. All I had ever wanted was someone to love, someone to have a family with and grow old with. Visions of holding hands with Pratt on the front porch of his cabin in Tennessee swirled through my mind and were quickly swiped away as if by the back of God's hand.

Molding myself to Pratt's frame, I hugged my arms around his waist, savoring the feeling of his warmth and safety. "Thank you for being here right now. If you could just stay until I watch the video . . ."

"You know I'll be right beside you." He pulled back, searching my eyes for something. "What's going through your mind right now, Anna?" He cocked his head to the side, waiting for my answer.

He already knew what I was thinking, but he was a good man. All he needed was my permission to let go. I'd give it to him, as hard as it would be, but I needed him today. Tomorrow he could be free.

***

Seated in Dr. Bowman's office, she readied the video. I squirmed in my seat, my nerves getting the best of me, and so anxious I was getting annoyed.

Pratt laced his fingers between mine and helped tame the shakes. "I'm right here."

"Anna." Dr. Bowman clicked a few keys on her computer, then rested her elbows on her desk and tented her fingers. "This might be very difficult to watch. If we need to stop and take a break, just say the word."

"Okay, I'm ready." Drawing in a deep breath, I try to prepare myself, but how does one really get ready for something like this? Rubbing a clammy hand down my thigh, I rested it on my knee, trying to stop my foot from bobbing. It was no use. Whatever was on that tape would be devastating. I hated watching myself on video, especially under hypnosis, and whatever Pratt saw deeply disturbed him.

Pratt gave my fingers a squeeze. I knew he was here for me and I felt safe having him close, but it didn't keep me from chewing on my lip, and my damn knee wouldn't stop jumping.

The video began as it had the last time, with Dr. Bowman talking through every step of the process. She began by injecting the medicine and used a soothing voice to help me slip into hypnosis. It seemed to take effect immediately, and she was able to put me under in no time as I drowsily followed the light of her pen and listened to her voice. A very relaxed version of me answered each of her questions.

"Tell me your name."

"Anna Spencer." My voice was low and groggy.

"Anna, can you tell me how old you are?" Dr. Bowman kept her tone calm.

"Twenty-eight."

"Do you know Pratt Rhodes?"

I nodded and smiled like a love-sick teenager.

"What can you tell me about him?"

"He's kind and thoughtful—a rare find. He opens doors and . . . he's so handsome, and fit. He's the kind of man you read about in romance novels."

My cheeks flushed and I heard Dr. Bowman chuckle in the background.

"Can you tell me about Blaize Martin?"

My head shook. "I don't know him."

"Are you sure? Think for a moment. Blaize Martin. Tall, blue eyes, thick beard, and—"

I watched my face transform. My lips pursed and my eyes pinched together as if I was angry. *"Of course I know Blaize,"* I spat. *"He was the man I loved."*

"Anna?" Dr. Bowman looked as confused as I was.

"I'm not Anna, you fool." The pitch of my voice was much lower, deeper than before. I sounded like I'd been smoking, for years.

I gripped Pratt's arm with my free hand and straightened in my seat. My eyes, painfully wide, stung with the beginning of tears. Nothing could've equipped me for what

I was witnessing. Seeing my face and voice morph into someone I didn't recognize was too much. Fear and disbelief engulfed me, threatening my sanity. Something burned inside of my chest, rising to my throat. *Don't do it.* Swallowing hard, I tried to breathe through it. A noise escaped my throat—a sob? It sounded like a wounded animal—but I slapped my hand over my mouth.

"Do we need to take a break?" Dr. Bowman asked, eyeing me suspiciously.

"No. I'm okay." I wasn't okay. I felt like I was dying inside.

"May I ask who we're speaking to?" Dr. Bowman asked.

"You may, but that doesn't mean I'm going to tell you." I laughed. *"Okay, I'll play. Only because I want that bitch to pay."*

"Who? Anna?"

"No. God, where's the liquor?" I spun around in my chair, searching the room. *"I need a shot of tequila. Patron if you've got it."*

"Who are you then?" Dr. Bowman inquired.

"Bree."

"Hi, Bree. May I ask how old you are?"

"Twenty-two." I gasped and gripped Pratt's arm like we were watching the climax of a horror flick. "What the hell?" He pulled me into his side. His lips formed a tight line and his brows pinched together. Although he'd already seen this—live—it looked as if he were suffering through it for the first time. "You can leave. I'll be okay." I wouldn't. *Please*

don't leave me. I wanted him to be the strong man he promised he would be.

"No, I'm staying right here with you." His expression remained as he watched me, sandwiching my hand between both of his.

Glancing back up at the screen, I continued to watch the scene play out. *I looked around the room. "You know I'm really going to need a stiff drink if I'm going to help you."*

Tears streamed down my cheeks but I was too preoccupied with what was happening to wipe them away. Pratt lifted an arm and wrapped it around me, but it felt too constricting so I pushed myself to the edge of the seat and leaned forward.

"I'll see what we can do." Dr. Bowman flipped through her notepad. "Are you right-handed, left-handed, or ambidextrous?"

Bree shot the doctor a disgusted glance. "I can assure you I don't have any diseases. I always play safe."

"Sorry, ambidextrous means you can use both hands to do things like writing, brushing your teeth . . ."

"Oh. None of that." She flicked her wrist in the air. "I'm right-handed."

Dr. Bowman spoke to the camera. "Anna is left-handed, twenty-eight. Bree, right-handed, twenty-two."

Bree's face twisted and her eyes squinted as she looked around the room. "Hand me a pair of glasses so I can see your eyes." Her voice—my voice—*had suddenly changed again. It raised an octave higher, was smoother, and had a proper*

British accent. "You can tell everything about a person by their eyes."

Chapter 40

Anna

"Stop the tape!" I shouted, pushing myself off the couch. My legs betrayed me, wobbling until I sat back down. Dr. Bowman clicked a button and the screen paused on my face—a stranger's face with ice cold eyes. "What . . . I don't understand. How can . . ." Resting my head in my hands, my body shook.

"I can help you understand, Anna," Dr. Bowman said. "This is a lot to take in, I know. Talk to me. What are you thinking, feeling right now?"

Lifting my head, I glanced at the screen and then shifted my angry glare at Dr. Bowman. "Different ages, a British accent. What is this? How could I possibly have an English accent, I've never even been to England." I didn't know what was going on or why, but it didn't make sense. It all seemed like a sick joke, a reality TV show gone bad. "It doesn't make sense," I growled.

Dr. Bowman offered an apologetic smile. "I know it doesn't seem like it makes sense. People with MPD often have very different alters. We're still researching how it's possible, but some have accents, some can even speak different languages. Maybe they picked up just enough on television, or studied the language in books, we don't know. They can have different birthdays, write with a different hand," she raised a hand toward the screen, "as you've witnessed." She shrugged a shoulder. "They're completely different personalities, different people altogether, if you will."

All I could do was shake my head.

"Shall we pause and pick up again after lunch, or tomorrow?" she asked.

"No. Let's get this over with." Defeat rang out in my tone and my shoulders sagged.

Dr. Bowman went back a few minutes on the video and replayed the last scene.

"Hand me a pair of glasses so I can see your eyes," *she demanded.* That British accent that still stunned me. *"You can tell everything about a person by their eyes."*

Dr. Bowman seemed startled but reached for the glasses resting on her head like a headband and handed them over. "You use glasses, Bree?"

The darkness in her eyes when she looked at the camera sent a shiver up my spine, causing goose bumps to alight on my flesh. Pratt rubbed my knee, but it didn't comfort me. Nothing could comfort me now. Sickness tried to make its way up again. An audible gulp made Pratt glance at me but I couldn't look at him.

The face on the video—my face—glanced down. When she lifted her head, glasses pushed into place, I froze. The person in the chair had the same slate eyes and dark hair as me, but her demeanor defied my belief that I could change so much.

"Don't insult me." All light was gone from her expression, her voice cold, deep, and robotic, but still tinged with the accent. *"I'm Jane. The only one who ever knows what's going on."*

I gasped aloud and both Dr. Bowman and Pratt jerked their gazes in my direction. I rolled my eyes and focused on the tape. Yes, I was fragile, ready to shatter into a million pieces. What did they expect from someone visiting the seventh level of hell? But I hated seeing the pity and fear in their eyes.

"Jane." Dr. Bowman nodded. *"Am I right to assume you're the alter in charge?"*

"Of course. Poor little Anna can't handle a hangnail. You think she could deal with what I've had to endure?"

"Tell me, Jane, do you talk with Anna and Bree regularly?"

"No, I've never spoken to Anna and I haven't talked to Bree for some time now. Foolish twat blocked me."

"Are you the oldest?" Dr. Bowman asked.

"I am." She raised an eyebrow. *"Thirty-nine, not that it's your business."* Her tone was harsh.

"Thank you for helping us, Jane. Anna's in a lot of trouble. She's being charged with murder. Are you aware of that?"

Jane snorted in disgust. "Proper English, doctor. Never end a sentence with a preposition." She smoothed her *hair back, tucking it behind both ears.* "Only an idiot would accuse Anna of pulling off the genius . . ."

"Was it you or Bree?"

"Ha!" *She attempted a laugh, but it didn't reach her eyes.* It chilled me to the bone. Instinctively I rubbed my hands up and down my arms. *"Bree can't think past her insatiable libido. She's too drunk to clean up after herself. Honestly, doc, must I spell it out?"*

"Please do, Jane. We're trying to help."

"We, as in you and Pratt Rhodes?" *She glanced to the other side of the room, and I assumed she was looking at Pratt.* A wave of protectiveness came over me and I reached for Pratt's hand. *"He thinks he's good for Anna, but he's not. She needs someone strong, who isn't blinded by the ridiculous notion of love. Men," she scoffed.*

Dr. Bowman cocked her head curiously. *"What do you think is best for Anna, Jane?"*

"To be left alone." *She crossed her legs at the ankles and sat up straighter.* "We do just fine until she falls . . . and she falls easily." *She turned to Pratt again.* "Keep that in mind, Mr. Rhodes." *She pointed a finger at the screen.* My heart ceased for a few beats. *"She falls in love easily. You may not be as special as you'd like to believe."*

"Okay, so you've been the protector," Dr. Bowman began. "What exactly did these men do that required your protection?"

"Different things. They pushed her to do things she didn't want or . . . tried to take her away."

Dr. Bowman arched an eyebrow. "Take her away from you? What would happen to you?"

"She wouldn't need me anymore and I'd fade away." Her tone matched her eyes—emotionless. *"I couldn't have Bree wreaking havoc and not be there to clean up."*

Dr. Bowman scribbled something in her notepad before asking, "If Bree is making the mess, what are you protecting Anna from exactly? Falling in love can't be that bad."

Jane glanced up at Dr. Bowman, raking her with disdain. Her body stiffened, shoulders set back in confidence. It was the first time I feared the woman on the screen, as if she were in the room and could physically harm me. *"I'm surprised you feel that way, doc. When did your husband cheat?" she asked as if she knew it was factual. "Did you catch him in the act? Was it in your bed?"*

As much as I wanted to see Dr. Bowman's reaction, I couldn't look at her and kept my eyes on the screen.

"You're very observant, Jane." Dr. Bowman chewed on her bottom lip, her gaze falling to the ground for a moment before collecting herself and concentrating on Jane again. "It's not enough to make me hate men in general, though. What happened to fill you with so much loathing?" So it was true? How could Jane have known? If this had been a movie, I would've left the theater, as creeped out as it made me feel. But this was my life. My freaking sick life.

Jane's head dropped, refusing to answer the question. Just like that, she was gone and Bree was back.

"How can they flip back and forth like that?" I hadn't meant to say anything out oud and hadn't realized I did until Dr. Bowman answered me.

"That's just how it works." She gave me a penetrating gaze. "Are you still okay to move forward?"

I nodded, keeping my eyes on the screen.

"She's too smart. You'll never get her to spill." She pulled the glasses off and held them in her lap.

"Bree?"

"Yes. It's me and I'm ready to tell you what that evil bitch did." She rocked back and forth, sliding her hands underneath her thighs. Her features were angry, but her body language revealed she was extremely upset about something.

"You know about Jane?"

"I didn't remember her at first. For the longest time I thought someone was following me. I could feel it, you know? Then it all made sense and I started remembering little things, like voices in my head."

"I see." Dr. Bowman wrote something down before returning her attention to Bree. "You said you wanted to tell me what Jane did?"

Bree spoke so softly, I found myself on the edge of my seat, leaning in to hear her words. "She killed the only man I've ever cared about." Her face softened, but her hands remained pinned beneath her. *"He was a good guy, a lot of fun. God, he could dance. Do you know how hard it is to find a guy with those kinds of moves on the floor and in the bedroom? He loved me."*

Dr. Bowman's face grew serious. She took one small step to the right, making sure the camera had full view of Bree, and asked in a low, even tone, "How did she kill him, Bree?"

Bree shook her head as if she were arguing with someone. "I am going to tell her. I really liked him and you took him away." Her eyes widened, then squinted, her eyebrows knitted together as she fought Jane for control. Watching the scene play out, she portrayed everything I imagined of someone who was crazy. *"Po-poison," she stuttered, struggling to get the words out. "Damn flo-wers."*

"How many has she killed?" Dr. Bowman's voice sounded excited, or maybe it was the sound of panic.

"All . . ." She cocked her head to the left, then the right, fighting hard to maintain control. "Of them . . . seventee—" Her head dropped abruptly, and she was silent. I wondered if she had passed out.

Turning to face Pratt, I whispered, not wanting Dr. Bowman to stop the tape. "Did she—did I pass out?"

"No." Pratt looked pale, his eyes empty. "Bree and Jane are struggling for control." It seemed he was having trouble making eye contact with me. I hadn't considered how all of this affected him, I was only concerned with myself. As sick as it made me to watch the tape, watch myself admit that I was a murd—I couldn't even let the word pass through my mind—Pratt was sitting there, holding the hand of his very ill girlfriend, the ki—killer.

Hands still tucked beneath her thighs, her head then lifted and my heart began to race. Who won? Would Jane take over and keep the mysteries hidden, or would Bree find the strength to face her and tell me what I needed to know? I suppose it was my heart's way of protecting me, letting me believe I was watching a fictional show that needed to be solved, rather than facing the reality that both of those characters were me. It was nonsensical to think I was fighting with two other versions of myself.

A somber voice spoke, and I couldn't tell if it was Bree or Jane. She kept her eyes closed. I listened for the British accent but couldn't pick it up.

"It's mother's fault. As much as I hate Jane for what she did to my Blaize, I'm glad she killed her."

My head whipped around to look at Pratt. "My mother died of a heart attack. What's she talking about?"

Dr. Bowman paused the video. "Let's take a break. We can resume after lunch."

I shook my head violently. "I can't eat." I felt sick to my stomach, anyway. "I have to know what happened to my mother."

Pratt stood and offered a hand to help me out of the chair. He looked ragged. Usually his five o'clock shadow was sexy, but today it made him look homeless and unkempt. I couldn't imagine what I looked like. My eyes burned, my mouth felt like it was stuffed with cotton, and my stomach cramped. Not from hunger, but from being so stressed and my insides convulsing trying to rid any contents inside.

"I think we could all use a break."

Chapter 41

Anna

Half an hour later, with a dose of medicine for my throbbing headache, we were seated in front of the screen, waiting to see what Bree had to say. If I hadn't been watching myself on screen—an eerie portrayal, at that—it would've made for an exciting, on-the-edge-of-your-seat movie. But it *was* me, fighting for my innocence. My mind couldn't process the fact that I had to trust someone I'd never met or spoken to, who was residing inside my own head, manipulating me at will, to free me from one prison and save me from another.

My eyes were red and sore from all the crying, but the tears still pooled and I knew as soon as the video resumed, the current would begin again. I couldn't pinpoint which emotion hit me hardest, disbelief that any of this was real. I mean, how could it be? Anger that I was in the dark while these alter egos controlled my life and did whatever they damn well pleased once they knocked me out. How did that work, anyway? It wasn't like there was a button to push that sent Anna to sleep. The whole thing confused, disgusted, and terrified me. Just then I thought about Bree with Blaize. She slept with him, which meant I slept with him. Did she use protection? And my mother—I had to stand up and run to the trash can. I hadn't eaten anything so my body heaved, but nothing came up.

Pratt was by my side, rubbing my back. He spoke over his shoulder to Dr. Bowman. "We need to call it a day. I think she's put herself through enough."

"No," I shook my head, not ready to leave the trash can. "I'm fine. Just give me a minute." Forcing myself to straighten, I pleaded with both of them, looking at Pratt first, then the doctor. "It's a lot to take, for sure, but I can do it. My stomach's just angry."

Dr. Bowman walked over with a package of saltine crackers. "This will help."

I chewed one at the pace of a gerbil and took my same seat next to Pratt. "Much better. I'm ready now."

Dr. Bowman pressed play, and Bree resumed telling us about my mother.

"Jane blames Father—thinks he should've been there to protect Anna—but Mother is to blame. She drove him away." Bree opened her eyes, but the spark I'd seen before was gone. Only hints of an accent broke through at random times, nothing like before. It was as if she had morphed into yet another alter or maybe she and Jane were still battling.

"We were poor and Mother couldn't keep a decent job. She used men for food, rent, and whatever else she thought she needed." She rolled her eyes like a teen frustrated by having to retell the tale. *"The one man that was good to Anna, Mother couldn't stand. Like she was jealous of the attention or something. Imagine that—a mother jealous of her own flesh*

and blood." She shifted in the chair, pulled her hands out, and flexed her fingers to get the blood flowing. "One night, something awful happened to Anna . . ."

Suddenly, Bree's head dropped again and she was gone. Her hand reached for the glasses in her lap, lifted them up, and slid them into place.

"Something too awful for either Bree or Anna to handle." *It was Jane again.* Goosebumps pebbled my skin as I watched the immediate transformation.

Dr. Bowman remained still when she addressed her. I could tell she was frightened by her, even though she tried to hide it. "So you were born to take the load, Jane?"

She nodded. "Mother's boyfriend raped her. She was fifteen." She had no conviction in her voice and didn't display a single emotion. "That foul creature . . ." She closed her eyes and took in a slow, deep breath that flared her nostrils. It was the first time I'd seen any emotion from her, but it was the wrong reaction. She was angry. "I can still smell him. Old sweat, cigarettes, and whiskey." Her nose crinkled ever so slightly. "Mother didn't believe her. Called her a whore and accused her of throwing herself at him. She threw us out on the street. That's when Bree and I met the first time. We thought we'd lost Anna for good. She refused to come out for close to a year."

I had no recollection of any of that happening. I remembered my mother dating someone, but he was kind and brought me candy. I glanced at Pratt, my face twisted curiously. "That never happened. I remember my mother dating a man, but he was nice. He used to bring me Twizzlers."

Pratt shrugged a shoulder and shook his head. It was obvious he didn't know what to say.

"How did you kill your mother, Jane?"

An impatient grin played at her lips. "I never said I killed her."

"But you did, didn't you?" Dr. Bowman cracked her neck to the right and then brought a hand up to rub a spot behind her head. "Bree told us that you killed your mother and several others." She flipped through her notes. "Was it seventeen or seventy?"

"You must be terrible at poker, doc." She flashed a cold smirk. "You've got nothing on me. I didn't kill anyone."

Jane's eyes closed, her head resting to the side, and she was gone.

Chapter 42

Anna

We took a day off before Dr. Bowman would use the Pentobarbital and put me under hypnosis again. Each time, I'd watch the video the next morning, taking a roller-coaster ride through hell as I watched the fight between Bree and Jane unfold. The mysteries of who they were to me and why they'd done what they did. In today's video, Jane opened up first, addressing Bree.

Jane: *"Why would you do that, Bree? You got sloppy. I've worked so hard to cover our tracks and you just had to go to the funeral and cover his body with those pink flowers. Are you that daft to not realize they would lead the investigators straight to Anna? Do you know how many times I wanted to leave my mark but didn't because I wanted to protect the two of you?"*

Bree: *"Protect us? You killed the only man I loved. And you did leave your mark, didn't you? You just had to carve up his chest. A fucking flower, Jane? That made him look like a pussy. What the fuck?"*

Jane: "Always the vulgar mouth, Bree. He didn't love you back, you know." I watched in horror as my eyes darkened, as if an evil presence had overtaken my body. *Jane straightened in the chair, looked straight at the camera, and continued explaining. "You see, I have to protect them. They can't help how they are. Bree never needed me as much as Anna until she fell for that stupid sex-crazed lumberjack. He was using her and she couldn't see it."*

My face changed again. The evil was gone, but her face looked maniacal. An insincere smile crept into the corners of her mouth. "Poor Jane can only get off by killing." The smile dropped. "Couldn't you feel what Blaize and I had?" Her fists slammed down onto her thighs. "You could've popped in, felt what I felt. Then you would've understood. Why did you take him from me, you filthy bitch?" Her shoulders began to shake as she sobbed. "Why?"

The crying stopped and just like that she was gone. And so was I. The knowledge that at least two people resided in my head, with that much control over me, took my sanity and tossed it out the window. I'd never been the type that enjoyed watching horror films. I'd plug my ears and turn my head when things go too intense. But now I was in it, living it, and I couldn't deal. Realizing I was a sex addict, a killer, and who knew what else, didn't make me stronger, it made me weak. I wanted to die and hoped someone would help me make that happen. I was useless to society, a burden to Pratt, and I have never hated anyone as much as I hated Jane and Bree—myself.

Chapter 43

Anna

My trial began twenty-one days after my arrest, and I knew it would be a long and grueling process. My defense attorney, Jack Morgan would try to prove my innocence, while the prosecuting attorney would try to convince the court that I was a heartless murderer.

Ushered into the courtroom in handcuffs and those unflattering gray scrubs, I stood behind the wooden desk with Jack. When the judge allowed, we all took a seat. My lawyer was asked to speak first. "Your honor," Jack began. His navy suit fit him perfectly, and I noticed his pants barely gave when he slid his right hand into the pocket of his slacks. He walked around to the front of the table as he continued, "MPD—multiple personality disorder—is an illness that has been around for centuries. With the plethora of research and testimonies from several doctors of psychology who've studied the disorder, I'll prove that Anna Spencer is innocent of these murder charges." He removed his hand from his pocket, locked his fingers together behind his back, and turned to the jury. "MPD is an illness where other personalities—or alter egos, if you will—take over the host body, controlling it without the knowledge of the host."

The prosecuting attorney, a man by the name of Mark Kerrier, was an intimidating creature in his late forties. He had salt and pepper hair and slate blue eyes that seemed to look straight through me, chilling me to the bone. He mocked me when he spoke to the jury and laughed at the idea of me being a host body. "What is this, a science fiction movie? Anna Spencer murdered at least seven people—"

"Objection!" Morgan was on his feet. "She's on trial for two murders."

The judge announced, "Overruled."

Kerrier continued, "Evidence will prove that Anna Spencer has committed murder. Don't let her get away with 'blaming it on the devil'." He curled his two fingers in the clichéd quote gesture above his head. "It was by her hand that men's lives have ended."

The questions went back and forth between the prosecuting and defense attorneys, addressing each person that took the stand. We broke for an hour to have lunch and then were back at it.

Jack stood, addressing the Judge. "The defense calls Emma Horton to the stand."

"What?" Reaching up, I tugged at Jacks arm. "You can't." My pleas were ignored as Emma walked up the aisle and was sworn in. Mortified, I looked down, swirling my pen in small circles on a pad of paper. Even though I heard Emma recall how kind I was and how I couldn't have hurt anyone, I knew our friendship was over. I'd never be able to look her in the face again.

I heard her voice break through the fog. "She comes to see one of my patients every week. Never stands her up. They've become really close. Mary was so lonely before Anna."

Shit, Mary. Would I ever be able to see her again? What would she think of all this? I imagined her sitting next to me, her worn out but soft hand gripping mine and assuring me, *"It's all right, kid, you're going to come out of this."* A tear snuck by without my knowledge, making its mark on the page below me.

Peeking up through my lashes, I watched Emma leave the stand. She offered a sweet smile as she walked by but I couldn't tell if it was sincere.

Jack took his place beside me and immediately began writing on his legal pad. Kerrier scooted his chair back, stood, and called his witness. "The prosecution calls Mark Scollay to the stand."

Leaning over, I asked Jack, "Who's that?"

"Manager at Helix, the bar where Blaize Martin worked."

Kerrier waited for the man to be sworn in and get comfortable behind the podium. He rested an elbow on the podium and talked to him like they were old friends. "Mr. Scollay, do you know the defendant? Have you ever seen her before?"

"Yes, I've seen her several times at the club. She and Blaize had a thing." His voice dropped when he said Blaize and I felt sorry for him. He looked like a nice enough guy, tall, clean-shaven, short brown hair with a deep side part.

"Does she look the same? I mean, same hair, eyes . . ." Kerrier rocked back on his heels. "Maybe she just looks similar to the woman you've seen."

"No," the witness shook his head. "Unless she has an identical twin, that's her."

Jack remained seated when he interrupted. "Can you point to the woman in question, Mr. Scollay?"

"Yeah." He pointed his finger at me and I cringed, dropping my gaze. "She's sitting right next to you."

"And her name, Mr. Scollay?"

He looked at Jack as if he'd been asked a trick question. "Blaize introduced her as Bree. That's what he always called her. He talked about her all the—"

Kerrier cut in. "No further questions. Thank you for your time, Mr. Scollay."

Officer Mullane was called to the stand next. A flat screen was brought into the room so he could detail each piece of evidence that affected the case. Fingerprints, DNA samples, pictures of my pink flowers on the back deck. I dropped my head and concentrated on my circle artwork again when they started showing pictures of the victim's bodies. It was all too much and made me want to jab the pen into my jugular to end the madness right then.

Something caught my attention as I was scribbling. Mullane was talking about Bree's apartment and it sounded nothing like my place. I lifted my head, the television screen demanding my full attention as I viewed rooms that I didn't recognize.

Mullane continued, "We found a few stolen items from the victim's homes. A shoebox filled with cash and jewelry. She also had several wigs . . ." His voice faded as anger brewed inside of me.

I nudged Jack with my elbow. "What's he talking about? Bree had an apartment? I had another place?" My whispers grew louder, whistling through clenched teeth. "I'm barely making ends meet . . ."

"We'll have to discuss it later." Jack looked up at the Judge, then back at me, his eyes pleading with me to be quiet. He stood suddenly. "Your Honor, a recess?"

"Granted." She knocked her gavel onto the sound block, stood, and left the room.

***

Pratt remained by my side, which astonished me, and assured me I wouldn't have to testify as it wasn't common in a murder trial. But the case was too close and my lawyer insisted it was our best option to sway the jury.

"I can't testify," I declared. "I've just learned my alter's been living the high life while I'm busting my ass for pennies at the flower shop and barely scraping by. I'm a mess." Unable to look at Pratt, I murmured, "And at this point I don't really care what happens."

"Yes, you do, babe." Pratt enveloped me in his arms but they did little to comfort me. "Hang in there, it'll all be over soon and you're going to be okay." He pulled away a fraction, lifted my chin, and said, "Trust me?"

How could I answer that? Everything I knew and trusted was false. "Of course I do."

Standing in front of the court, my legs wobbling as strangers stared at me with judgmental eyes, I placed one cuffed hand on a bible and raised the other as far as the chain would allow. The judge, a round woman with hair as black as a crow, glanced down through her reading glasses. "State your full name for the court."

"Br—" I cleared the frog in my throat. "Brianna Jane Spencer."

The prosecuting attorney questioned me first, after I was ushered to a wooden seat behind the podium.

He was cocky, a partial grin permanently fixed on his face. "Miss Spencer." He paced the floor with his hands clasped behind his back. "I think the jury would like to meet your alter egos." He turned to the jury and nodded his head as if convincing them on the spot. "Can we talk to . . ." He looked down at the notes on his desk. "Bree?"

"I—" My voice cracked and my hands trembled. "I can't make her come out."

"Okay, how about Jane? Let's talk to her." He walked to the podium where I sat, leaning in. "Hello, Jane. What would you like to say to our jurors?" He cracked a smile like this was all a big joke. He was pure evil, mocking me like that. And I was the one on trial.

Silence. Except for the sound of my heart hammering against my chest. All eyes were on me. They thought I was lying, I could tell by the way their lips turned downward. My chest heaved as I tried to take in oxygen, the shaky, shallow inhales not doing the job. Tears pushed against the constrains of my lashes but I knew I couldn't let Kerrier see my cry. Once he found the fault line in my barely-there exterior, he'd eat me alive. "I . . . I—"

"Jane, are you here with us?"

"I can't make her come out, either." I knew if they could witness Jane, the evil in her eyes, it would do well for my case. But I didn't know how to make them come out. I'd never interacted with them. If there was a code or secret handshake, I wasn't aware of it.

"C'mon. We're trying to help you, Miss Spencer." Kerrier's voice was kinder, softer, then he slammed his hand down on the podium in front of me. "Bring the murderer out!"

I flinched and cowered back in my chair, the valleys too full to hold the tears back any longer. My shoulders shook as the whole ordeal swallowed me up. There was no controlling the timing of my breakdown, it just happened. I was a blubbering mess.

"Objection!" My lawyer was on his feet. "Badgering the witness."

"Overruled," the judge droned. "Tread cautiously, counselor."

Before Kerrier could ask another question, I wanted to make it clear that I had no control over the other personalities. Sucking in a shaky breath, I tried to regain control of myself. Instead, my words came out choppy and much lower than I planned. "It . . . doesn't work like that." I was sobbing and couldn't turn it off. "I can't—"

"How does it work, then, Miss Spencer?" He turned and walked slowly toward the jury, talking to me, but addressing them. When he slid his hands into his pants pockets, his suit coat flared back like a spoiler on the back of an expensive sports car. It fit his personality. His tone was demeaning, uncaring. "You play sweet and innocent until you're bored and want to have some fun as Bree?" He looked at me with contempt. Who was this man, completely absent of humanity? "When do you bring Jane out? When a man makes you angry? Maybe he cheated. Do you think it's justified to take his life?"

"No." I shook my head until I felt my vision blur, and not from the tears. *Oh no.* I tried to shake it off. *No, no, no.* Now that I knew other people were living inside of my head, pulling my strings and making me do things I would never ever do, I was scared. Why hadn't I noticed before that my blackouts were Jane, or Bree, taking over? It was happening now, and I had no control. Kerrier's words faded into a hum that barely reached my ears, then everything went black.

Chapter 44

Anna

I woke up in my bed at the hospital. Dr. Bowman was scribbling something in a chart, while a nurse slowly released the air in a blood pressure cuff. "One-ten over seventy," she announced.

"Anna?" Dr. Bowman took a seat next to me. "How are you feeling?"

"What happened?" I sat up and scooted until my back rested against the headboard.

"You passed out," Dr. Bowman answered. "Do you feel okay now?"

"I think so." Apart from humiliation, I didn't have any aches or pains. "Did . . ." Closing my eyes, I tried to find the courage to ask the million-dollar question. I knew I needed Jane or Bree for the trial, but we were hoping the video would be enough. I didn't want everyone to witness me change. I didn't want to experience it. Now that I knew about them, would they let me in? Would I have a say? I never wanted to know what that felt like. "Did Jane or Bree come out?"

"No." She shook her head and I could see the disappointment knitting her brows.

"What about the trial? What does this mean?"

"The judge allowed a break until tomorrow morning." She crossed her left leg over her right knee and let her foot rock nervously. "Your lawyer is going to call me to the stand so I can show the tapes of your hypnosis."

Leaning my head back onto the pillow, I sighed. "Okay." I waited for Dr. Bowman to leave the room before I allowed the day to sink in. Today would go down in history as one of the worst days of my life, and tomorrow would trump it tenfold. Having to watch those tapes again, my face, body language, and accent transform into someone I barely recognized was disturbing enough, but now strangers—people who didn't even need a reason to hate me—would watch the videos, and all I would be able to do is sit there with them and watch their reactions as Bree told everyone that we killed several people. I sure as hell hoped Dr. Bowman and my lawyer, Jack, knew what they were doing.

***

The judge waited until day three to allow the tapes of my hypnosis to be shown in court. Dr. Bowman took the stand for the second time, setting up the backdrop for what the judge and jury were about to see.

"What you are about to witness is Anna Spencer under deep hypnosis," Dr. Bowman began. "Both of her alter egos will present themselves, and I have no doubt—"

The judge interrupted, "Dr. Bowman, please let the lawyers present the case to the jurors."

It was hard for me to watch the tapes again. I don't know how many times a person had to watch themselves morph into someone else for it to become less startling. Each time I watched my face change, glasses being pushed onto my nose, and the cruel things I said as Jane, it felt like a nightmare. My skin crawled and I slipped deeper into self-loathing.

Every now and then I would dare a glance at the faces in the jury section. I couldn't tell if they were shocked or appalled. Did they feel sorry for me? Or did they want me locked up for the rest of my life? I couldn't blame them for wanting a freak like me off the streets. Dr. Bowman promised she could heal me, but I didn't share her certainty.

Through the fog of my desolation, I heard Bree speaking. What little I knew about Bree appalled me. She gave her body—my body—freely to men and nothing was off limits. Slinking down in the wooden chair, I remembered how Dr. Bowman explained it all to me.

We were in her office, both sitting on the soft caramel leather sofa. "You have to understand, Anna. Most victims of rape or molestation become oversexualized, thinking sex is the answer. They believe it's the only way to receive acceptance or love."

"That's ridiculous," I scoffed. "How could something so frightening, so painful make me want to experience it again? I can't imagine anyone being degraded in such a manner and wanting to feel that over and over again."

She dropped a gentle hand to my arm and I flinched, pulling my hands into my lap. "That's why Jane came into the picture, Anna."

"To murder anyone that got close to me?"

"Maybe. It was the only way she knew to protect you." She shifted on the couch next to me and waited for me to face her. "You said to me that all you've ever wanted is a family. A man that loves you as much as you love him, someone to start a family with, to grow old with. Do you remember telling me that?"

I shrugged a shoulder. "Yes."

"That part of you wants acceptance, love. Since the crime committed against you, you've translated sex into love. Or at least, Bree has allowed you to believe that. Like I said, it's a normal response for most victims of sex crime."

"Okay, and Jane? What part of me wanted to kill all those men? My m-mother." I rubbed my eyes, determined not to start crying again.

"Jane's the part of you that hated that man for what he did to you. You wanted revenge against him for what he did, against your mother for letting it happen, for not taking your side and protecting you from the terror you faced alone. She was made entirely out of hate, protecting you from the one thing you hate the most, but want the most . . . men."

"I can't believe any of that." Flicking my wrist, I brushed her off as a poor psychologist. She knew nothing about me or the alters in my head. None of it made sense. "I would never, ever hurt anyone." My words were a small

whisper, but laced heavily with conviction. Anyone that knew me would tell you I was caring, harmless.

"Of course you wouldn't." She rested her hand on my arm again and I let it remain. "Don't you understand? That's why Jane was born. She could, she did, and because you weren't aware of her or her actions, your subconscious received the vengeance it craved so desperately, but at the same time you got to remain you. Sweet, caring, generous, Anna."

***

Tiny circles connected to form a chain on my pad of paper in front of me. During the trial I'd covered three pages in black ink with those circles. Somehow it numbed and distracted me enough to get through each day. Today, the attorneys would present their closing arguments to the jury.

Kerrier went first.

"Was Anna Spencer controlled by an alter ego when she committed murder?" He shrugged. "I don't know. I guess we can all blame our choices on someone or something else. How many times have we tried to say 'the devil made me do it' and how many times have we gotten away with that lie?" He paced in front of the jurors, stopping in front of a male that looked to be in his early thirties. "This is what Anna Spencer did. She pretended to be someone else. She gained trust, then drugged these men and killed them in their sleep. Miss Spencer used them, stole from them, and then took their lives." He took a few steps and stopped again, this time in front of an older woman with a dark brown pixie cut. "She grew the flowers that were used to poison her victims on her deck." Kerrier walked away from the jury and I thought he was finished, but he turned to face them again. "What Miss Spencer did was an act of cold, calculated murder. Don't let her get away with it."

As much as I hated the man, he was right. But I didn't want to blame it on the devil, I blamed Jane. I blamed Bree. I blamed my mother and father. Most of all, I blamed myself for not being stronger, not being able to handle the things that happened to me. The same, or worse, had happened to children and they got through it.

Jack arranged some papers on the table, took a sip of water, and stood. He talked as he walked toward the section where the jury was seated. "You've seen the tapes showing the different personalities. Jane can't see without glasses and her penmanship is illegible when she writes with her left hand, because she's right-handed. How can that be, you ask?" He scratched his chin for effect. "MPD is a serious, heavily researched disorder. It wasn't conjured up for defendants to plead insanity. Miss Spencer is just as much a victim here as the deceased."

Jack continued with his speech while I filled another page with circles. He had a lot to say, but in my opinion, Kerrier had the better closing argument. I was doomed.

Finally, the Judge turned to the jury, her elbows resting on the table as she leaned forward slightly. "People of the jury, you've got a difficult decision to make. The question is not whether or not the defendant killed Mr. Martin and Mr. Fulks. The question for you to resolve is of her state of mind. You must decide beyond any reason of doubt whether or not she acted under the influence of an alter ego. You are to base your conclusions on the evidence as presented in the trial. Closing arguments from the lawyers are not to be mistaken as evidence. You, the jurors shall determine the facts and reach a verdict, within the guidelines of the law."

The jurors were dismissed, filing out of the room into another to determine my fate. I watched their backsides as they walked, the position of their shoulders, the length and color of each head of hair, what they had chosen to wear the day they made the most crucial decision of my life. It was a visual that would be imprinted in my mind forever.

***

After two grueling weeks on trial, it took less than four hours for the jury to come out with a verdict. That meant one thing: they were all in agreement and one hundred percent certain of my guilt, or my innocence.

When the time came, everyone in the courtroom was asked to stand. Paralyzed with fear, I couldn't move. "C'mon," Jack gripped my forearm and helped me up onto shaky legs. "I've got you."

A lump formed in my throat. Not one from sadness, but one of sheer terror. Twelve people held my fate in their hands and I couldn't blame them for finding me guilty. I didn't know how I would vote had I been in their shoes. I was guilty of murder, no doubt, but should I have to pay for something I had no control over? If someone had poisoned a drink without my knowledge and I delivered the drink, was it my fault? No, it was the person with the poison. But who would they charge in this case? Jane? She was inside my head, which meant *my* body would be locked away in prison. I didn't feel guilty, but I also didn't think I deserved to be free. Someone like me shouldn't be on the streets. It was pathetic really, my cowardice. So many times I wanted to stand up and shout at the jury, telling them to find me guilty. *Don't put me back on the streets, there's no telling what my alters will do.* Then again, I wasn't cut out for prison. I wouldn't last a week.

I noticed how not one of the jurors would look in my direction. They either kept their heads down or toward the front of the courtroom the entire time. Had they been instructed to do so?

An uncomfortable silence filled the room right before the judge spoke. "Ladies and gentlemen of the jury, have you reached a verdict?"

"We have." The man that answered was tall and slender. I imagined him to be a father of four and take up the offering at his church. His voice was deep and certain.

"What say you?"

"We, the jury, find the defendant, Anna Spencer, not guilty on all charges."

Relief washed over me in a rush so fierce I felt it in my bones. My knees weakened and refused to hold me up. The edge of the chair caught me and I sank back into the seat, hoping it wasn't a dream. Someone gripped my shoulder and gave it a shake, another hand patted me on the back. Or maybe it was a slap. The room came alive with people talking, shouting. My lawyer stepped out from behind our table and, as soon as he did, Pratt was beside me, pulling me into his arms.

"Tell me what they said. I didn't hear it right, did I?" I asked, shaking and out of breath.

"Not guilty, babe," He smiled, looking victorious. "Not guilty."

A loud noise filled the courtroom, a banging that got everyone's attention and hushed the chaotic crowd.

"Order in the court," the judge commanded. "The jury has found you not guilty, Miss Spencer, but I still have to give my ruling." She adjusted her glasses and shuffled through a few papers before glancing up. I didn't hear all of what she said, but I did hear her last words. ". . . committed to therapy at Bent Creek Mental Institute under the care of Dr. Jennifer Bowman until she considers you healed and safe enough to enter the community again. But your time in the institution will be no less than two years, and I'll need all paperwork signed, of course."

Two years might have seemed like a lifetime to some, but for me it promised healing and freedom. I studied Pratt's face, joy and peace in his eyes. He was a good man—my man—but it had to end. I knew it wouldn't be easy for him, but it would be even harder for me to let him go. He would busy himself with finishing his residency and opening his own practice, while I got better. I couldn't ask him to wait for me, that was too much. And I loved him too much to ask him to put his happiness on hold. As bad as I felt using him the last few weeks and not letting him go sooner, I wouldn't have made it through the trial without him.

It was a weird sensation, receiving a non-guilty verdict, knowing I had a shot at a normal life, and feeling my heart shatter at the same time. Pratt must have seen it in my eyes, the heartache bleeding through. His smile faded as he stepped toward me and I put up a hand between us.

"I know what you're thinking. Stop it." I hated the pain I saw in his eyes and even more the fact that I put it there. "Don't do this, Anna. I love you and I'm seeing this through with you." His words laced with so much conviction, I didn't know if I could go through with it.

"And I love you. So much." I sucked in a sharp breath. "If I didn't, I'd latch onto you and never let you go." Backing up, I let the words leave my lips in a strangled whisper, "Goodbye, Pratt."

Chapter 45

Anna

~*Two years later*~

My treatments were grueling the first year at Bent Creek Institute. Jane had refused to leave my head for thirteen months. She was fierce at first, but gradually lost her fight and showed up less and less until she was finally gone. Bree exited immediately, unable to deal with the heartache of losing Blaize, and Jane's betrayal. We used the last eleven months to strengthen my body and mind so I would be able to handle the world.

Dr. Bowman signed the last document on the afternoon of November twenty-second and placed it in my chart. She made a clicking sound as she sucked in her cheek. "That's it."

I couldn't believe I was finally ready to face the world. "I'm not sure how to feel. I'm excited, really I am, but I'm nervous, too." What if Jane came back, or another alter trying to save me from something I faced in the future.

"You have nothing to be nervous about." She folded her hands and rested them on her desk, a confident smile gracing her face. "You've been healed for nearly a year now, Anna. I have no doubt you're ready. You've been ready."

Truly, I felt different, more like myself. Now that Jane and Bree were no longer in my head, the blackouts ceased and I felt alive again. A warm smile curled my lips and refused to fade. "I appreciate you so much. Everything you've done." I rose from my chair, taking the prescription she had written in case I had trouble sleeping for the next few weeks. She said that might be the case since I would be sleeping in a new space with new furniture.

My old apartment had been rented to someone else while I was at the institution, my furniture sold to the new occupant, so I had no idea what I would be stepping into. My nurse friend, Emma hadn't vanished after the trial as I imagined she would. Instead we grew closer with her monthly visits. Sometimes she would bring Mary along and we'd sit in the sun room and have tea.

My new space was only a block from the old one, but smaller, which meant I'd be living in a matchbox. Other than running a few color choices by me, Emma and Mary were in charge of furnishing my new place. They were masters at finding deals, but wouldn't tell me where the stuff came from. Mary slipped up once, so I knew the loveseat and dishes came out of a recently deceased neighbor at the assisted living center.

"I'm so happy I could help." Dr. Bowman scooted her chair back, stood, and closed the space between us. We embraced, doctor to patient, friend to friend. She really had become dear to me over the last two years, guiding me when I felt I would never escape the perpetual state of darkness. "I'll see you in three months for a checkup, but please don't hesitate to call if you need anything."

"I won't." I hugged her again, then looked around my room for the last time. It wasn't bad for an institution. My room felt more like a hotel with cherry wood furniture, cream walls, and a real lamp on the bedside table. I even had my own bathroom with a shower. Smirking, I realized it might be nicer than the apartment that awaited me. Nothing beat freedom though. Drinking freshly brewed coffee in my kitchen, in a mug that I pulled from my own cabinet. Watching TV in my pajamas all day if I wanted. The list of things I looked forward to went on and on, but one thing stood front and center above all the rest, tugging at every cell of my body.

Pratt was waiting in the lobby with a bouquet of wild flowers and a huge grin. No matter how hard I tried the first few months at Bent Creek, I couldn't shake him. He was determined to make our relationship work and my little heart, barely held together, was no match for his persistent love. In hindsight I know it was ridiculous to think I could heal without him, live without him. He's my everything and without him life doesn't matter. What I couldn't understand was why he had wasted two years of his life on me. We couldn't share more than a kiss during my treatment, so I'd never expected him to be faithful. I was surprised he hadn't fallen for someone else. Maybe he'd been too busy starting his practice to offer more of himself to anyone. I'd take that blessing.

"I'm taking you to dinner to celebrate." He lifted me off the ground, swinging me around as he hugged my body to his. An indescribable feeling swam through me—maybe the way it felt to be struck by lightning—tingling that started in my toes and tried to find an exit in each of my limbs. "Anywhere you want to go. You name the place." His warm breath fanned the side of my neck before his lips met my flesh, peppering me with kisses until he'd covered every space between my throat and forehead.

I couldn't stop giggling, feeling his excitement, feeling my own. "I'm dying for some oysters," I admitted. "The food here is crap."

His grin softened. "I know the perfect place." His lips softly brushed against mine. "Finally, I have you back in my arms." He lowered me down until my feet were firmly planted on the ground and leaned in for a kiss that stole my breath and made my head fuzzy.

Melding myself to him, not caring where we were or who was watching, I let myself get lost in the perfection that was Pratt Rhodes. His scent, the way his strong arms made me feel safe and loved, his perfect lips, and the way he loved me, pure and wholeheartedly.

Yes, I was healed. Beyond healed, really. I was the happiest woman in the world. I had to go through hell to get to this place, and wouldn't wish it on anyone, or care to repeat it. But it had gotten me to this place, with this man, and I could finally move forward with hope.

***

It was a perfect day for a picnic, not a cloud in the sky. The warm summer air of late May was a nice balance as the sun caressed my skin with its warmth. Laying back on the blanket, my arms tucked under my head, I kept my eyes closed as Pratt read aloud from *The Kite Runner*.

I dozed in and out from the sound of his smooth, relaxed voice. Heavenly. When he stopped reading, I heard the crunch of an apple and then the sound of him chewing. Propping myself up on an elbow, I rested on my side and watched him. He was gorgeous, the way the sun buttered the side of his face as he leaned against the trunk of a willow tree, his left arm crooked behind his head. Dark, unruly hair framed his features and swept across his forehead each time the wind blew.

What kind of man stuck it out with a woman like me? Two years of his already busy life wasted on the chance that I would come out of the mess I was in. A chance that I would be normal.

He knew everything—seventeen murders committed by me, or Jane, but still by my hand—and yet he still hoped, trusted, waited for me. Starting with my father, all the men in my life had left me. Pratt did not. He was a different breed. The good kind. My kind. *Mine.*

Pratt opened his eyes and glanced my way, a slow, easy smile pulling at his lips. "I thought you were asleep."

"I think I might've dozed a few times." A lazy sigh escaped my lips as I sat up and stretched. "What a perfect, beautiful day."

Pratt pushed off the tree and joined me on the navy and white plaid blanket, then he pulled a bottle of chardonnay from the picnic basket. "Ready for a glass?"

"Yes, please."

We both sipped the cool, crisp wine, watching the breeze dance through the branches of the willow tree, and a pair of robins flit around from branch to branch.

"You know I've been so busy with the new practice," he began, disappointment creasing his forehead. "I'm sorry I haven't been able to spend as much time with you as I'd like, planning special nights—"

I rested my hand on top of his. "You're more than I've ever dreamed of, Pratt Rhodes, and I'm so proud of you. Don't you dare apologize for taking the time to build your career."

"I—" He struggled for words like something was eating him. My heart began to race, wondering if he was going to ask for a break, now that he knew I was okay and could handle the change. It made sense, and I should've prepared myself for it, but things were going so well between us. He cleared his throat and I braced myself for the worst. "I just wanted to do this differently. But I don't think it can wait." He drained the last bit of his wine and I followed, knowing I'd need it to get through this. "Truth is, I don't like you living in that tiny apartment by yourself. It's not safe."

Relaxing my shoulders, I exhaled a sigh of relief. I was wrong. This wasn't a breakup, he was going to ask me to move in with him. Dropping my head to the side, I smiled, knowing what my answer would be. Of course I'd love to move in with him. I'd finally have the chance to take care of him for once, instead of the other way around. Dinner would be ready when he came home, but first he'd greet me with a kiss. Afterwards, we'd cuddle up on the couch with a glass of wine and he'd tell me what he could about his day without breaking that patient-doctor confidentiality. I wouldn't have to pack a bag when I spent the night, and he wouldn't have to leave my place at the crack of dawn to get ready for work. There wasn't enough hot water in my apartment for him to shower and leave for work, anyway.

Pratt huffed out a bashful sigh. "Let me start again." He lifted his glass to his lips and tipped it up, not remembering he'd already drank it, and set it back down. I'd never seen him that shy and out of sorts. Pulling my hands into his, he rubbed his thumbs over my knuckles. "I love you, Anna. I want to fall asleep with you in my arms each night and wake up with you by my side every morning."

"Yes." My head bobbed with excitement.

"Yes?" He chuckled. "I haven't even asked yet."

"It makes sense," I insisted. "I'm either at your place or you're at mine every night. We haven't slept apart since I got out six months ago. Wouldn't it be easier if we moved in together?"

"Babe . . ." Pratt smirked as if I had said something amusing. "You're absolutely right. You've got me." He raised his hands in surrender. "I do want you to move in with me." He smiled deeply, his dimples making an appearance. It reminded me of the first time we met and I noticed how he smiled with his whole face, the motion crinkling the corners of his eyes. His mouth relaxed, dimples retreating, but the sparkle in his eyes remained. He gripped my hands in his again, giving them a squeeze. "As my wife. Anna Spencer, marry me."

My body tensed, numbness creeping up my body until it reached my brain. Nothing made sense. Everything around me blurred but I didn't feel dizzy. Goosebumps pebbled my flesh, but it was warm outside. Then everything made sense. The setting—beneath a willow tree with Belvedere Castle in the backdrop. Wine and a picnic basket filled with our favorites—caviar and blini, brie with roasted pears, melon wrapped in prosciutto.

Pratt continued, "I should've planned something more romantic, I know, but my head was spinning trying to think of something over-the-top that would wow you and I failed." He looked at me sweetly, his nose crinkling with disappointment. "The only thing that kept playing in my mind was the first time we came here. You asked if Belvedere Castle was open to the public and mentioned it would be the perfect spot for an engagement or small wedding."

"You heard that?" Blinking several times did nothing to contain the tears. "I remember that day. I was mumbling to myself." I shook my head, embarrassed. "I never meant for you to hear that. Back then, all I dreamed of was marriage and kids." Oh how my life had changed.

"Not now?" Pratt cocked his head to the side, a frown pulling at his beautiful lips. "What changed?"

"You." Swiping a tear with my thumb, I shook my head. "You changed everything." Pratt's eyebrows knitted together in worry, the joy now removed from his features, and I added quickly, "No, not in a bad way." I reached up and tried to erase the defeat from his lips. "Marriage and a family is all I used to think about, all I wanted. It didn't matter who fulfilled that dream, I just wanted it. Then you came along." New tears stung my eyes and pooled at the lashes. "No one has ever treated me the way you do. I've never had anyone stay when things got bad, and boy, did they get bad." My voice was thick with emotion, recalling where I was two years ago.

I sighed before I continued. "Of all the people that had a reason to run, you did . . . but you didn't. I'll never understand it, but I'll always be in awe of you for it. I love you, Pratt Rhodes, and that's enough for me." Closing my eyes, I smiled and drew in a satisfied breath. He was enough. Anything after that was an extra cherry on top, but I was fully satiated just having him in my life.

"How could I ever leave you?" His face beamed, the love in his eyes evident and overflowing. "You've enraptured me." He reached up and cupped my face in his hands, his dark eyes locked on mine, claiming me. "I'm in love with every part of you and can't imagine life without you in it." Leaning in so his lips grazed my ear, his voice low and gravelly, he asked, "So you won't marry me?" There was a playfulness in his tone, barely, but it was there.

"I never said that," I breathed, my eyes painfully wide. "Of course I'll marry you. I just wanted to make sure you—" Before I could finish, my body was swept up into Pratt's arms. He pulled me down on top of him, my face cradled in his hands.

"So that's a yes?" A toothy grin exposed those sexy dimples again, and his brown eyes conveyed so much love I could feel its warmth radiating through me. He covered my mouth with his in a deep, satisfying kiss.

Tears dropped down but I was unable to stifle the giggles that erupted out of pure joy. "Yes, absolutely, without a doubt, yes!" Covering his face in kisses, we both laughed and rolled until he was on top, then me again. I couldn't help my roaming hands, feeling every inch of what was all mine. Lifting my hips, I reached between us and stroked his growing erection through his khaki shorts.

Pratt groaned, a deep throaty sound that sent a rush of excitement to my belly. I loved that I could elicit those noises from him. "No one's around. Whad'ya say we consummate this engagement?"

"No way," I breathed. "We can't." Popping my head up, I looked to the left and right. He was right, we had the place to ourselves, but anyone could round the corner at any moment, which made me nervous. But when Pratt worked the place behind my ear with his mouth and pressed his fingers against my clit, stroking my inhibitions away. I was all in.

A whimper on an exhale was the permission he needed. Flipping me over, the world tilted, the blue sky as my backdrop as Pratt peeled my shirt off. He squeezed one breast as he pulled the other one free from my bra and sucked in a tender nipple. Gripping the picnic blanket, I arched my back, giving him more, needing more. Everything he did felt amazing, each nerve ending alive and greedy. It was as if a switch was flipped the moment we were engaged, opening the door to more sensations and allowing more feelings to be experienced. Maybe because I felt safer than ever before. Or perhaps having him in my life fixed everything. I was healed, but a constant gnawing in the back of my mind had kept me fearful and unsure these last six months. Not so much with Pratt. He was more than a stitch, holding me together while I healed. With him by my side, I was whole.

Pratt kissed and sucked my nipples while I lifted his shirt over his head. He seemed to have a one-track mind as he worked me over, not pausing to help me get his arms out of the shirt. With his black T-shirt over the back of his head, arms still through the sleeves, he unclasped my bra, slid it off my shoulders, and tossed it aside.

I unbuttoned his shorts and slid the zipper down. Reaching inside his boxers, I found my prize, circled my fingers around him, and began slowly stroking. He mimicked my movements, his fingers dipping into my panties and stroking my sensitive bud, causing me to cry out. The closer he brought me to the edge, the harder I gripped him.

Pratt paused, his muscles stiffening. "Fuck, I forgot the ring." He lifted his head, lust swimming in his dark eyes. "I have it."

I could tell he was about to pull away from me, dig in a pocket for the ring, and interrupt the most heated moment of my life.

"After," I panted. "I want you. Don't make me wait. I need you right now."

Pratt rocked back onto his knees and, with more aggression than I'd ever seen in him, he jerked my shorts and panties down. Pulling his shorts down just enough to free himself, he was back on top of me, positioning himself between my legs. The fact that we were outdoors like wild animals, our surroundings natural yet extremely taboo had me so turned on I could barely breathe.

Pratt rocked forward with one fluid motion, joining us and stealing the last bit of breath in my body.

Pratt was gentle, fusing our mouths together in a passionate kiss as he made love to me. Pulling back, his face inches from mine, he whispered, "You feel so good." His eyes slid shut as a deep moan rumbled from his chest. "So fucking good."

The sound of his moan released some savage side of me, needing more, wanting to get closer to him. "Harder," I begged. "I need—" There was no doubt a piece of Bree still resided inside of me, but I couldn't risk Pratt finding out. The sexual hunger was good for both of us, he couldn't argue that, but this was no time to ring a warning bell. Besides, I was healed and had everything under control.

Pratt obliged without me having to finish that thought, slamming into me so hard my back slid across the blanket and onto the grass. The harder he pistoned in and out, the better it felt.

I whimpered with each thrust, urging him on. "Yes, *oh God,* yes."

Fingers digging into the ground, his body slamming into mine, my back inching across the cool grass, the world shattered, a thousand prisms shimmering around me. Waves of pleasure shot through me. It was too intense to make a sound. All I could do was hold on, unearthing grass and dirt into my palms. Just as my body began to settle, Pratt increased the pace with his impending orgasm and another wave rolled through me. His whispered curse words mixed with the most beautiful compliments caressed my ear, and my arms came up to grip his shoulders as we rode the last aftershock together.

"Holy mother of all things amazing and . . . damn-fuck," I sang, letting my arms fall back behind my head.

Pratt chuckled. "I don't think I've ever heard you curse."

"I've never needed to." Giggling, I added, "I'm not very good at it."

"Agreed, but you're cute." With a sly smile, he dropped his head and kissed me softly.

"How far did we travel?" Lifting my head, I tried to find the blanket.

Pratt pushed himself up, stood, and zipped his shorts while I shimmied my own back up. "A nice little piece. How's your back? Did I hurt you?" He turned me around before I could walk the few steps to get my shirt and bra.

"Not at all." I pressed my body into his as he wrapped his arms around me. "That was incredible." I felt complete, like my past and all that I'd been through had melted away because of him.

After dressing, Pratt pulled out the ring he'd forgotten to include in the proposal. It was his grandmother's—a princess cut diamond with a baguette on each side—and fit my finger perfectly. When the sun hit it just right, prisms danced along my hand.

My eyes widened in disbelief at the beauty, and the gesture. I had learned just recently about his relationship with his grandmother and how devastated he was when she passed.

The fact that he gave me her ring—something so precious—astounded me.

Reaching up, I cupped his face in my hands, pulling my gaze from the ring to look into his eyes. "I don't deserve you, Pratt Rhodes." It was meant to be loving and playful, but apparently that's not how he took it.

"That's bullshit." Deep lines of tension pulled the joy from his eyes and I immediately regretted my words. Not that I didn't believe them, but because I didn't like to see sorrow weighing him down like that. Pratt knew a lot about my healing process, but I'd also hidden quite a bit from him. It wasn't over, I had a long road ahead building confidence, trusting myself again, trusting others. "You were made just for me, Anna. We fit, we're good together." He shook his head and it seemed he was searching for what to say or maybe how to say it. "I know it's only been six months, but you must know by now that I'm in. One hundred percent." I lowered my head, but two warm fingers slid under my chin and lifted my gaze. "You're mine and I'm yours. I will take care of you, just as I know you'll take care of me. We deserve this, babe. Let it sink in and believe it. You deserve to be happy . . . *we* deserve to be happy."

His words had the power to pull tears from my eyes. "I know, you're right." Pratt caught a tear as it rolled down my cheek and wiped it away. "I'm not used to happiness," I admitted. "But I want it. I want you." Wrapping my arms around his waist, I anchored my body to his. "I love you so much."

The joy back in his voice, Pratt said, "I love you more."

Our engagement hadn't been traditional, which went along with the whole picture of us. We weren't your average couple, we weren't normal people, and I was A-Okay with that.

Chapter 46

Anna

We were married on the terrace of Belvedere Castle in late June, surrounded by white gardenias and the most beautiful cream-colored roses that had streaks of peach veining through the inner buds. Harry, my old boss from the flower shop, had graciously donated them, but didn't attend the wedding. I wore a simple raw silk dress that I'd found at a small vintage shop in Chelsea. It hugged my curves and flared faintly at the ankles.

Our ceremony was simple and sweet, with only a few people in attendance. Emma and her new husband were there. They were kind enough to bring Mary, who made sure I had something borrowed and something blue for the big day. She didn't look well, but tried her best to hide it from me. I made a mental reminder to check in on her after the honeymoon. Pratt's parents flew in, but his brothers were unable to get away. I was kind of glad we kept it small and informal. Knowing that everyone was aware of my case and had probably read about it or heard news stories that exaggerated every detail was enough to make me crumble under the pressure. Add to that the excitement and nerves of marrying my best friend, the man that I was crazy in love with, and I was a hot mess. No, it was not a good day to meet his entire family.

Pratt couldn't take more than a week off from work as he didn't have anyone else working with him in his new practice. In his profession, you couldn't schedule depression and suicidal tendencies or ask the patients to put their thoughts and feelings on hold until you returned.

One of his colleagues took any emergency calls while we were gone, but they weren't his patients so he was doing Pratt a huge favor. *"My wedding gift to you. Enjoy yourselves,"* he'd said. So we spent a week on Sanibel Island, enjoying the emerald water. We sailed, watching dolphins play and show off next to the boat, dined on oysters Romanoff and Yukatan shrimp. Every night we stood on the shore, watching the sun melt into the sea, clapping when it disappeared and hoping to catch a glimpse of that famous green flash. It felt like a dream, and I feared I would eventually wake up in a prison cell. I had been so close to that reality that it still terrorized me.

We made love every morning and fell asleep tangled in heavenly bliss each night. We weren't trying to start a family, but we'd agreed to do nothing to prevent it. We had waited long enough to be happy, and decided not to step in front of fate's plans for us. I couldn't help praying that I was carrying his child.

Standing on the beach, watching the sun rise on our last day of the trip, I allowed a quick thought of a little boy with dark, unruly curls running through the house with a cape tied around his neck, shouting, "Here I come to save the day!" Or maybe we'd have a little girl, same dark curls and brown eyes so big and curious she took your breath. I imagined brushing her hair and telling her stories about princesses and talking unicorns. I wanted it so badly. But did I deserve it? What if I was like my own mother? Taking Pratt's hand, I decided not to ruin our last moments on Sanibel worrying about things I had no control over. Instead I watched a beautiful brown pelican dive into the water and fill his mouth with small fish. Sanibel was magical—exotic wildlife, colorful shells in every shape and size right there on the sand, and absent of anything touristy.

I couldn't wait to bring our kids to this place one day.

***

We returned home late Tuesday evening to several messages from Pratt's answering service.

"Babe, why don't you handle those calls while I unpack?" I massaged his shoulders for a moment while he listened to the first message. "I'll make some tea."

After our bags were unpacked, everything put away, I put a pot of water on to boil and looked around the apartment. It was a lovely space to call home. Floor to ceiling windows in the living room overlooked the city, one of the walls hosted two bookshelves filled with books of every genre, including a few of my favorite collections of poems. The kitchen was a dream compared to anything I'd ever known and I couldn't wait to prepare meals for my new husband. Pratt wasn't gifted in the decorating department, so I practically had a clean slate to add some personal touches to our home. Leaning against the kitchen counter, I glanced at my new husband—one hand holding the phone, the other buried in his dark curls as he concentrated on his task. I finally had everything I'd ever wanted.

While the kettle was warming our water for tea, I went to the bathroom. My heart sank when mother nature decided it wasn't time to be pregnant. Since Pratt was busy with work, I let myself sob quietly for a few minutes and then splashed cool water on my face and laid a wet washcloth on the back of my neck. Even when the timing was wrong and you didn't expect to start a family right away, it still hurt once you'd let your mind wander to the possibility. I should've been grateful to have more time with my new husband without the overshadowing of morning sickness and bloating. But it hurt. I'd appreciate it later, when the cramps subsided and my emotions weren't all over the place.

The kettle whistled, pulling me out of the dark haze I'd let myself slump into. Rushing to the kitchen, I turned off the stove, moved the kettle off the heat, and added a few scoops of tea petals to the pot. Counting down three minutes, I poured the brew over a strainer and filled one cup. Suddenly all I wanted was a good night's sleep.

Pratt was finishing up with a patient over the phone when I entered the room, so I set his cup in front of him and kissed him on the top of his head. Then, as I walked down the hall toward the bedroom, a sweet little British tune that I couldn't ever remember singing before, spilled from my lips:

ELEANOR GREEN

"Ring-a ring o' roses,
A pocket full of posies,
A-tishoo! A-tishoo!
We all fall down."

~The End~

Be the first to know when Eleanor Green has a new release, by signing up for her newsletter.

Newsletter signup: http://bit.ly/1kPrTZ8

I take your privacy seriously and will only contact you will important news like release dates, cover reveals, and exclusive giveaways for subscribers.

ABOUT THE AUTHOR

Eleanor Green writes New Adult and Contemporary Romance swirled with mystery.

She currently lives just outside of Nashville, Tennessee with her husband and two children.

CONTACT ELEANOR

Email: contact@authoreleanorgreen.com

Website: http://authoreleanorgreen.com

Facebook: https://www.facebook.com/AuthorEGreen

Twitter: https://twitter.com/AuthorEGreen

OTHER BOOKS BY ELEANOR GREEN

Torn

Wait for Me

Stay with Me

Hot for the Holidays